Death & the Visiting Firemen

Death & the Visiting Firemen

H. R. F. KEATING

PUBLISHED FOR THE CRIME CLUB BY

DOUBLEDAY & COMPANY, INC.

GARDEN CITY, NEW YORK

1973

All of the characters in this book
are fictitious, and any resemblance
to actual persons, living or dead,
is purely coincidental.

First Edition

ISBN: 0-385-05876-4
Library of Congress Catalog Card Number 73-83596
Copyright © 1959 by H. R. F. Keating
All Rights Reserved
Printed in the United States of America

Death & the Visiting Firemen

ONE

"Well," said the young man who looked like an actor, "what do you think of the boss? Pretty shady, eh?"

The actor, if such an actor could be an actor, was handsome. Regular features, dark curly hair, a long face well set off by the absurd high white collar. And with something unmistakable about him.

"Tell me," said Smithers, "where were you?"

A faint flush on the smooth cheek.

"I was at Harrow actually."

Smithers patted a little nod of acknowledgement at him. A kind little nod. He had won.

That was why no Darlborough boy could touch him. Never mind the baldness, the stoop, the tired gait, the easily imitable flick of the hand at the ever present layer of chalk on his waistcoat, the old clothes.

Now the whole party sat in silence, greyly waiting. Jerked into activity at an hour only bearable approached from long wakefulness.

At last the actor, too young to know he was defeated, laid a long delicate green-gloved hand on the little black rail behind Smithers.

"All the same," he said, "he isn't quite the thing, is he?"

He looked pointedly at the enormous mass of the man sitting above them. The heavy figure strained and stretched at the seams of the bold yellow coat. Above the caped collar, one, two, three, the sharp horizontal lines of the folds in the flesh. The skin mottled.

"I do not wish to be unfriendly when we are to see so much of each other in the next few days," Smithers said, "but I really cannot discuss my host with a fellow guest in these terms."

"Guest?"

The young man laughed. With a trickle of hysteria.

An intrusion of something private on what was still a public occasion, however odd. Each one of the party reacted.

First. The girl sitting opposite the actor. The mass of unvarying blonde hair, the emphatic figure, the slash of deep red lipstick.

"It's so horrid, so early. Nobody wants to talk to me." She looked at the actor: somebody.

Second. Sharing the seat with her, but at the other end of it, the very other end, the man of sixty with the eager glance which years of sudden doubts had failed to repress. With a shy smile, quickly effaced, then replaced.

"It's years since I was up so early. This is what they call between the white and the rose. So I believe."

Third. On the far side of the actor from Smithers. Altogether unconscious that the first hard streaks of day exposed the crows' feet and the wrinkles, the woman asserting her claim still to be in the thirties. Never quite over into the trough of forty. And earning her right: with elan.

"It's wonderful to see it all. The new day. I like it. Only where's the sun? Oughtn't there to be some sun?"

Now Smithers.

"No, we get the day first, that's the white. Then later comes the sun, the rose."

"Oh, I see. I wondered what it meant. But I thought it was one of those things that everybody else understands."

"But tell me," Smithers said, "don't I know you? Aren't you Daisy Miller, of the old Drury Lane days? My name's Smithers."

"Old days it is, I'm afraid, Mr Smithers, but they were good old days all the same."

"It certainly seems a long time since 'Only A Rose' and we seem to have come a long way."

Smithers looked at the ugly dockside. At their vehicle, beautiful and completely incongruous. He looked at his fellow passengers.

"You don't want to start thinking, dear," said Daisy Miller. "Not these days. Too many things happen which no amount of thinking can alter. And after all, this is exciting too, in its way."

Scarcely a move of the head from Smithers, but a bow.

He turned and leaned over towards the man with the quick shy smile.

"There didn't seem to be time for introductions," he said. "My name is Smithers. I teach history at Darlborough."

"I'm Fremitt."

Again the quick deprecatory grin.

"I'm in fire prevention."

"You must be the president," said Smithers. "Our host told me you would be here."

"Well, yes, I am president. But only this year, of course."

"All this"—Smithers gestured—"must be a heavy responsibility."

"It is. It is."

The jump of assent. Then the curb: a request for a minute written in the proper form, due consideration, the safer course.

Smithers allowed Fremitt his silence and leant back again on the precarious seat.

A faint sunlight came through the mists. Nobody moved, nobody spoke. Then abruptly above them the fat man jerked himself round and looked down.

"Where the devil is the major?" he said. "I told him to meet us at four. It's nearly five now and there's no sign of him."

"I don't see why he's allowed to be late when you made me get up," said the girl.

And at the hint of the shared bed, too plainly hinted, the actor glinted anger. Before the control clamped.

"I told you last night," said the fat man.

With distaste.

"I told you last night, the boat's due already. We've got to be there. That's what you don't understand. You've got to do things the right way. Every time. It's the secret of success. It's simple enough, but they won't do it. And they come unstuck."

"If the boat's due, why hasn't it come?" said the girl. "I can't see any bloody boat."

"I don't know why it hasn't come. Someone's made a mistake. It'll lose them money in the end, always does. And now leave me alone. I'm going to have a nap."

The girl flounced round.

"Richard."

Her voice a coo, but importunate.

"Yes?"

The actor acknowledged no debt. No overt debt.

"Richie, talk to me."

"There isn't a great deal to talk about at this time of the morning."

"But, Richie——"

With a lunge the fat man stood up and swung round. The crazy vehicle shook. Hands instinctively clutched the slight rails.

He leant down over the girl, slowly clenching his right fist.

Below him the girl's face was upturned. Fear, and something else.

"What did you call him?" the fat man said.

"Call him?"

"Yes, you stupid creature. What name was that? I thought you told me he was called Charles."

"Charles?"

"Yes. Charles. Charles. Your brother Charles. What's his full name? Not Charles Kett, I suppose."

"My brother?"

Her laugh was forced. But a touch of defiance in her bearing, a sign of a game being played, and perhaps won.

"Oh, Charles couldn't come. He got flu. There wasn't time to tell you last night."

The game almost certainly won.

"Everything was so rushed," she went on. "This isn't Charles. This is a—— This is just a friend. It's Richard Wemyss. Surely you know Richie?"

"No."

The heavy face completely blank.

"How silly. I thought you did. Well, this is him. Richie. Richard Wemyss, the actor, Richie this is Mr George Hamyadis."

"I haven't ever seen him in anything."

"Well, he's had rather bad luck. Haven't you Richie? He ought to have been in the West End only he was let down. He's done films though, those advertising ones."

"I see. And you brought him along instead of your brother."

"Yes. Yes, that's it. That's exactly what I did. Charles got flu ever so suddenly. So I thought of Richard. Wasn't I clever?"

"I suppose you promised him money? My money."

"Naturally, he can't afford to do it for love."

"Not for love?"

A pounce. And a smile stamped on the heavily jowled face.

"No," the girl answered. "Not for love."

On the black rail Wemyss's green-gloved hand clenched tightly.

"All right then. Not for love. For money."

A shake of the enormous frame.

"I'm sorry for all this," he said. "But I can't stand anyone altering my arrangements. I don't make them for fun."

He turned and slumped in his seat. Below him eyes sought boots. Footwear became an absorbing interest, a spotted flycatcher out of season, a page of an illuminated psalter, a chart of shallows.

The mists parting. The sun hinting at warmth. A long silence for minds quietly to flex again.

Now. From behind the distant banks of mist, still too thick to allow anything to be seen, the long sobbing note of a ship's foghorn.

Again the fat man got up.

"Where the hell has the major got to?" he asked. "The boat will be here at any moment. What's happened to him?"

No answer. The fat man looked at the party, up and down, one by one.

"Kristen," he said, playing the patience game, "you look about as old fashioned as a jet bomber. Can't you do something about it?"

"I can't help looking up to date. You like it all right as a rule."

"Listen. I shaved my beard off because I didn't think it looked right with these clothes. I've had that beard ever since I left home for America. Thirty or forty years. But if the thing was to be done right it had to go. So it went. Don't you realise this is something big? Look at Daisy, there's nothing wrong with her."

"She finds it easy," the girl said. "But I'm just what they call contemporary. I can't help it."

Daisy Miller. More than this needed to hurt.

"I always say it's a pity none of you young things get much chance of costume work, there's nothing like it for teaching you how to act."

"Oh, I can act all right. But I'm damned if I can look like an old fashioned picture book. Can you imagine it: Kristen Kett as Little Miss Muffet? You'll just have to take plain sex and like it."

"I'll grant you that," said the fat man.

Out of the mist the huge bulk of the liner. Tugs weaving in front of her. Ducks in a pond chasing crusts.

"Mr Dagg," said the boss.

Not a word all the long morning wait. The silent figure of the driver, reins on knees, whip held upright and unmoving, an eye only for the four matched greys below him, with their occasional snorts in the chill morning air and stamps on the stones of the quay.

"Mr Dagg, we'll move off as soon as she ties up. We can't wait for the major all day. I spoke to the ship on the radio telephone yesterday. Most of them should be up by now and waiting to see us."

"Ay, ay, Air Marshal."

A cockney voice. Independence, eccentricity, the world seen through self-made spectacles.

Past the mist curtain the liner presented itself quickly. Its decks well lined with people.

"And is every one of them a fireman?" asked Daisy Miller.

"Not exactly a fireman, if I may say so."

Fremitt, quickly pedantic, as quickly polite. He flickered the shy smile towards her, was silent, saw more was needed.

"They are in point of fact," he said, "members of the American Institute for the Investigation of Incendiarism—er—Incorporated. That is what we should call, perhaps, fire prevention officers. Of various standings, and many, I believe, with their wives."

"You must think me awfully silly," said Daisy. "And now I realise that you must be the one I've heard about, the President of the British Institution for the Investigation of Incorporation. But I haven't got it right."

"As a matter of fact we call ourselves the Fire Prevention Society. But it comes to the same thing, almost exactly."

"And much easier to remember."

From Fremitt a blush, come and gone.

"No sign of the major?"

The hammering voice from above them on the box seat next to the driver.

"All right. I'll have a word with him later. We'll go forward now, Mr Dagg, if you please. Look your best everybody. Remember this is for most of them their first glimpse of the real Britain."

Smithers's face a blank. Held blank.

More orders.

"Forward on to the open space. Then stop and blow that horn thing. Off we go."

"Generally called the yard-o-tin, Air Marshal."

Now an advance.

With a creaking lunge the long-preserved stage coach, the High Flyer, moves off behind the matched greys. Hands clutch for the slight rail bright in fresh black paint. And relax again when the motion shows itself as lolloping, easy, confident.

From Richard Wemyss: the tall green hat raised in a gesture of greeting. But five-eighths of an inch too high.

From Daisy Miller: gay frothy bonnet inclined for homage. Not twelve degrees: not ten. The exact eleven.

From Kristen Kett: an appraising stare. Greedy.

From Smithers: a half shrug.

From Fremitt: a wave stopped, begun again, stopped.

Above on the box. From Joe Dagg: a reverie of skill. From the boss, from George Hamyadis, night club impresario, travel agent, business man, business unspecified: impassivity, the poker player.

Then the horn call.

Cheers from the crowd at the side of the liner. Three imitations from excited members of the Institute for the Investigation of Incendiarism. Two very inaccurate, one passable.

And a long anti-climax. Occasional efforts to renew the cheering from the liner. Richard Wemyss raised his hat slightly once.

"Why can't they let down the gangplanks?" said Hamyadis. "They're behind schedule. It won't get them anywhere."

"Shall I give them another one, Air Marshal?" said Dagg.

"Why does he keep calling him Air Marshal?" Wemyss asked.

Loudly, but not too loud. A barndoor cock, with discretion.

"Perhaps he was one in his native country," said Daisy Miller.

Not with belief, with optimism.

"And where is his native country?" Wemyss said. The hot pursuit of easy game.

"Richie," said Kristen Kett. "And I did so want you two to like each other."

The insistence on the exact untruth.

"Is there such a country as the Levant?" asked Daisy.

"The Levant is more of a geographical term than a country, if you'll forgive an old schoolmaster," said Smithers.

"Oh, I see. Like trade winds."

Then nothing. The fizz slowly declining to the single bubble wavering its way to the surface.

Full daylight. Aboard the ship conference delegates appearing and reappearing. Complete lack of purposeful activity. The sun already warm. The horses in front of the coach restive. Their sharp smell pervasively present to all the passengers. And time passing.

"Ah, there you all are."

From the range of muddled buildings behind them an unexpected voice. They turned. Coming towards the coach a man in the late sixties, tall, upright, thin; straggling indeterminate grey moustache and hair; bright blue eyes beneath heavy eyebrows; dressed in the early nineteenth century costume they were all wearing; carrying a Gladstone bag.

"Why weren't you here on time, major?" said Hamyadis.

"Awfully sorry, my dear chap, thought I could get a better connection, found my Bradshaw was out of date. Hope I haven't been a nuisance."

But before the excuse a pause. A moment to quell anger.

The major walked rapidly towards them. Then stopped.

For two and a quarter seconds the man a waxwork. Time enough for an uneasiness. Something not as expected.

"But, good heavens," the major said looking up at Hamyadis, "you've shaved off your beard."

"Some of us are prepared to go to a hell of a lot of trouble for this business," said Hamyadis.

From the major no reply. No soft answer turning away wrath. Instead complete indecision. A problem from the blue being wrenched into focus. Then at last:

"Well, as I say, I hope I haven't been a nuisance. Late on parade. Doesn't do—I know it doesn't do. But always doing it. Semper eadem."

He stopped beside the coach.

"May I introduce myself? Major J. G. Mortenson, Indian Army retired. Like to amuse myself with coaches when I get the chance. Down here as what you might call an expert, hired expert. Anything I can tell anybody, nothing gives me greater pleasure."

Smithers took on himself the reply.

"I'm sure we're all very pleased to know you, major. We sadly lack information. Let me introduce you to our party as far as I am able. I suppose you know none of us. Let me see now. Miss Miller, Miss Daisy Miller, the musical comedy singer, you must know her by repute."

Quickly to his hat went the major's hand, the stiff sharp, military salute. From Daisy the open smile with the hint of nostalgia.

"Miss Kett, Miss Kristen Kett. In her sphere doubtless as distinguished, or as likely to be. A film actress."

Again the salute. Received with a smile. A claim stated.

"Then there's Mr Fremitt, Mr John Fremitt, I believe, president of the Fire Prevention Society. He is here to extend an official British welcome to our American guests."

Fremitt's sunlight gleam smile. The major's inclination of the head.

"And lastly, Mr Wemyss, Mr Richard Wemyss, also of the acting profession."

To the major's hinted bow a correct nod.

"Our host of course you know."

"Yes. And old Joe Dagg and I have met on a good many occasions of this sort over the years. Believe me, when he holds the ribbons you're in good hands."

Above them on the box Joe Dagg without turning gave a twirl of the long whip held upright still and said:

"Morning, colonel."

"You mustn't take old Joe's way with the ranks too seriously. I was never near a colonelcy. In fact only became a major on the point of retiring. Joe has his own way of going about things."

"I can see your aid is going to be invaluable," said Smithers.

For Wemyss the quick look of reminder from the fourth form repertoire.

"And myself. I mustn't forget. I'm Smithers. I teach history at Darlborough."

"Then I know what you are doing here. I've read and reread the section on coaching in your *History of Travel,* sir. Only wish I could afford all fourteen volumes. I don't suppose you've much need of my services."

"Don't be too sure of that, major. Do you know, this is the first time I've actually ridden in a coach? I'm afraid my knowledge, such as it is, is sadly bookish. It was that that tempted me to accept this offer."

A tinge of regret.

"Now you are here you'd better get aboard, major," Hamyadis said. "We must do something to liven things up."

The major put a foot on one of the spokes of the rear wheels and heaved himself up resignedly.

"Mr Dagg," said Hamyadis, "give them a hoot on that horn and then drive about a bit. Put on a show."

"Right you are, Air Marshal."

But no more response.

Once again the long shining horn raised in the air and the simple music. A long call then a little tune.

"Not generally done to play tunes," the major explained—the quiet commentary voice—"but in the circumstances perfectly justified. Usually the horn is kept as a signalling device only. There are calls to indicate to traffic ahead every possible happening of the road."

Now the liner's side once more an amphitheatre. A quiet word to the horses from Joe Dagg. The coach moved forward. They took a wide sweep round the open space between the dockside and the quay buildings. The passengers played their parts, as actors, as sportsmen, as willing but ignorant.

With an exception. In mid-phrase Major Mortenson's commentary ceased. Total abstraction. But too much was happening. On the second circuit they gathered speed. When the horses changed from a walk to a trot the major jerked to and told them. They went on to a canter. From the liner applause. More people at the rails. A buzz of excitement.

Wemyss leant forward and spoke loudly above the clatter of the horses' hooves, the creaking of the coach, the jingle of harness, the grating of iron-rimmed wheels on the stones of the quay.

"He's lucky, the boss. If they got bored with the whole idea on the boat they might have gone up to London by train. And he's got a pack of motor coaches waiting for them to follow our journey in. He'd have lost a lot of money."

No answer. None to make.

And faster went the coach, with tighter turns. A sense of exhilaration. The major, eyes gleaming, everything else forgotten, commentary staccato.

Now, in the centre of the circus ring still at speed, tight short circles. With the sense of tipping in every part of the fragile vehicle.

"Perfectly safe," said the major. "But damned exciting, eh? Currite, currite eques nocti."

The others held hard to the slender black-painted rail and nodded. With as little movement of the head as possible.

Only above them Hamyadis stood up and turned easily to watch the ship all the time.

"Gangplanks going down at last," he said. "Finish up now, Mr Dagg. Give them a curtain though. Make a show of it, make a show of it all the time."

"Right you are, Admiral."

From the tight turns larger sweeps and increasing speed. When they were pounding along at the stretch the coach jerked round to face the black wall of the liner's side. And at it.

A blur of wild cheers.

The ship looming high, high over them.

And at last the merciful squeal of locked wheels. The horses fighting against the momentum of the vehicle. Rearing forefeet.

A final stop with a bare yard separating the animals from the deep gap between the quay's edge and the ship's side.

As the noise of the wild halt dimmed, the sound of running feet from the direction of the gangways.

The first of the delegates. Shouts, yells, cheers, hats flung high. Laughter. Success.

On the coach, hands sweaty at the palm released from their hold. Smiles of relief. Hamyadis sat down quietly. The horses breathed heavily. Joe Dagg turned round on the box and winked at the major. The wink returned. Round them the gathering crowd.

Invested with a broad smile the major said to Daisy Miller:

"This as exciting as the first night of 'Only A Rose'?"

"I've never been so——"

She stopped. A tangle in the stream's smooth flow.

"I know this sounds silly. But do any of you believe that sometimes people have premonitions about things?"

"I see something's worrying you," the major said. "Just the effect of physical excitement. Well known thing in its way."

"Oh, no. This was something quite different."

A simple statement.

"You see, I ought to have been excited just now. Anything like that usually makes me tingle all over. But instead all the time I felt a stronger and stronger sense of warning."

She shrugged. An effort.

"I suppose," she said, "it's much too late anyhow to change all the plans."

TWO

"Good morning, gentlemen, the name is Schlemberger. Foster P. Schlemberger, president of the American Institution for the Investigation of Incendiarism Incorporated."

The voice stridently America of America, no lazy Southern charm, no Bostonian distinction. The straight whisky rye, the hamburger, the bulbous automobile.

And the man's appearance when they had picked him out of the crowd of his compatriots backed the voice. Wide-brimmed hat, rimless glasses, multi-coloured tie, cream-coloured suit generously cut, white and brown shoes.

Foster P. Schlemberger threw away a half-smoked cigar. The time was 6.37 a.m.

"Mr Schlemberger, may I extend the heartiest of welcomes to Britain to you and all your fellow delegates," said Hamyadis.

Not the bowing merchant of the markets; no servile handsoaping; no fawning; no cringing. Nothing that could be pinned down. From the American a long look of appraisal. A meaning look. Then:

"Delighted. Delighted. But am I speaking to——"

The glance down at a small plastic 'public man's memory aid' in the hand.

"—to—er Mr John Fremitt, president of the British Fire Prevention Society."

Curiously emphatic.

"No, my name is Hamyadis. I've had some correspondence with you."

"Oh, yeah, yeah. I remember the name. Though my secretary handled all the details."

"This is Mr Fremitt."

Fremitt leapt up from his seat, hurried to the side of the coach, leant over, considered turning and climbing down, leant over again. Foster P. Schlemberger shook him by the hand. For a long time.

"On behalf of the Fire Prevention Society, er—welcome," said Fremitt.

"On behalf of the Institution for the Investigation of Incendiarism Incorporated"—unabashed the syllables—"I am happy to accept your most kind welcome," Schlemberger said.

"Perhaps I should introduce these other ladies and gentlemen," said Fremitt.

But conversation had become impossible. The interchange of welcomes had spread a prairie fire of cheers among the delegates. Noise, noise pure and simple.

Hamyadis jumped down from the box, heavily but without care. He took Schlemberger by the elbow and piloted him round to where a light ladder could be fixed to the side of the coach. With a jerk he took it from its place and hung it for Schlemberger to climb. As soon as he was on board Hamyadis swung his heavy bulk in one massive heave up on to a wheel and into the box.

"Get clear of all this," he said.

Joe Dagg sounded the horn.

"That's the 'Clear the Way'," said the major.

Its effect was to thicken the crowd to suffocation point.

But by shouting and waving and using the horses as a wedge a path was cleared and the coach began to move. When they got to the dock gates the spectators had strung out enough for talk to be possible without faces being thrust within inches of each other. Loudspeakers began to hector the ship's passengers to their motor coaches.

Fremitt performed introductions. They stopped and there was a shuffling of places. Hamyadis told Kristen Kett to sit inside the coach. She climbed down the narrow iron ladder with pantomime squeaks of fear.

The obedience routine: the sex mouse.

"And I'll be all alone in here," she said. Her head poked inside the coach. A wiggle of the hips.

Wemyss leapt over the side of the vehicle. Misjudged the height, landed awkwardly, recovered.

"Not all alone," he said.

He handed her in. Triumphant gallantry.

Hamyadis talking evenly to Schlemberger.

As soon as the door had closed Kristen poked her head out of the window.

"It's too hot in here," she said. "And it smells musty."

"No laudator temporis acti there," said the major. "Did you know, Mr Schlemberger, that the inside seats used to be for first-class passengers? They paid a good deal more and had the privilege of sitting still when the others had to get down to go up hills. On the old stage coaches, which came before the mail coaches, there weren't even proper seats on the roof. The passengers who clung there had to help push when it came to a hill."

"Very interesting. Very interesting."

Schlemberger looked pleased. A sum disbursed, profits beginning to come in.

"And what's next on the schedule?" he asked.

"We go to Winchester, stopping at an inn on the way for a real old coaching breakfast," said Hamyadis. "I've had a couple of marquees put up for the rest of the party. There'll be bacon and eggs, devilled kidneys, kippers, porridge, everything. Ending up with a stirrup cup before we go on."

"You understand we've had to take certain liberties," said the major.

Rancour avoided, but with effort.

"I guess I daren't take such liberties with my stomach," Schlemberger said. "Was there chilled tomato juice in those days?"

No sign of irony in the dead-pan voice.

"I've seen to all that," said Hamyadis. "Coca-cola stirrup cup too if you want it."

He spoke quickly. A stage direction.

The coach moved off again. Schlemberger an incongruous twentieth-century figure among the dressed-up party. The party incongruously dressed up.

Schlemberger looked round.

"So this is old England?" he said. "My first visit."

"There I have the advantage of you," said Fremitt. "I've paid two brief visits to your delightful and exciting country. Just on business, you understand. The last was only for a few days because of dollar restrictions. But I was over there before the war for a month. A firm in Chicago asked me to come to advise them on development."

"Guess the boot's pretty well on the other foot now," said Schlemberger. A statement.

"I've never had the luck to cross the Atlantic," Smithers said. "We schoolmasters are expected to keep our advice for the young."

"And nobody's ever crossed the road, much less an ocean, for my advice," said the major. "Been the same all my life."

From Daisy Miller no contribution. Smithers turned to her.

"Were you ever over there?" he asked.

"No," she said. "Or, that's to say only once, a long time ago. We took a show to Broadway but it never caught on. I scarcely remember it."

"You two didn't meet over there?" Smithers asked Fremitt and Schlemberger.

"No, I've never visited Chicago in my life," Schlemberger said. "We held our congress there one year, but I had to be in Reno for my second divorce. I certainly wish the two hadn't fallen together."

"I think in many ways I must have lived a rather isolated life during my Chicago visit," Fremitt said quickly. "When I returned people kept asking me about the gangsters but I saw nothing of them."

"Used to think of marrying, of course, when I was a young fellow," said the major. "Vivamus, mea Lesbia, atque amemus."

A silence.

"Is England much as you expected?" Smithers said to Schlemberger.

"Guess not."

Schlemberger was silent for as long as it took the clopping horses to go thirty yards.

"Guess I expected it to be a mite more . . . Well, more kind of feudal," he said.

They passed through the suburbs of Southampton. Schoolchildren stared and waved. Girls giggled. Middle-aged men pretended not to see them.

"Feudal?" asked Smithers.

"I might as well come straight out with it," said Schlemberger. "I wasn't a hundred per cent in favour of holding the congress over here." The smooth fall of conversational cards on the green baize. And suddenly a joker. "In fact if it hadn't been for domestic reasons I might have quit the presidency when the vote went against me. Back in Kansas we hold strong views about British policy, particularly your colonial policy."

"Now that's an interesting thing," the major said.

Breaths held. A heavy siege gun rumbles into action. For battle? As a toy? As both?

"I happen to have been in the Indian Army myself, so naturally it's a subject that interests me."

"Well, sir, I don't want to say anything that might be offensive. Not right at the start of what I hope will be a long and valuable friendship. So with your permission I'll just change the subject."

Pent breath released. Uneasy smiles.

"I would like to say," Schlemberger went on after a pause, "that during the ten days of the congress any of you ladies and gentlemen are welcome to attend any of our lectures or our sightseeing tours. Just say the word."

"I'm sure that's very handsome of you," said Smithers.

"Excuse me," said the major, "but I'd like to have this matter of colonial policy out."

Tension. And exasperation.

"I can take hard words as well as the next man," he went on. "And I hold no brief for a great deal that's been done in the colonies."

"Just as you like, major," said Schlemberger.

The horse lifts its head scenting battle. A gleam in the eye of the wary wrestler.

"Let me tell you a little story," said the major. "Just listen to me and then give me your honest opinion."

"Major."

From above them on the box the almost forgotten voice of Hamyadis. A new element.

"Major, I suggest you tell Mr Schlemberger and the others something about the coach and its history."

Bland. The order given.

"We've a good many hours to while away yet," said the major. "We've got on to a very interesting subject."

A contract broken. Unexpectedly, wantonly.

"But I want Mr Schlemberger to know the history of the coach."

A rebellious child taken by the shoulders, turned round.

"Mr Schlemberger," said the major, "you can see there's a bit of a dis- agreement between Mr Hamyadis and—or rather between my employer and myself. I leave you to decide. Would you like to hear about the coach straight away or would you like to hear an old soldier's tale about a little town on the North-West Frontier called Anamapur."

The coach gave an unexpected lurch.

"Steady on, guv," came Joe Dagg's voice. Soothing.

"All right, you'd better tell your tale, major," said Hamyadis. "Otherwise we'll get no peace."

He humped forward on his seat above them.

"Well now," the major leant back, expansive, the storyteller. "This is a tale with a moral. For you Mr Schlemberger the question to keep in mind is: who was oppressed and who was the oppressor? It happened about the turn of the century. In the district of Anamapur there were only two things which counted: the wealth of the town and the rapacity of the tribesmen who surrounded it. All through the history of India the situation had oc- curred time and again. The town would build up its wealth, the tribes- men would sack it. Until the British Army put a garrison there. Only a handful of men, but enough. For once the town grew wealthy and remained unsacked."

"Very admirable, but——" said Schlemberger.

"No, let me finish. One day the secret of the town's defences was sold to the tribesmen, by an Anglo-Indian trader, a man with the very English name of Brown."

The name an epithet. Into the past historic the present definite.

"It was a matter of knowing just exactly where one single sentry from the little garrison was posted. A silent death for him, poor chap, and that was that. But the ones who died in the fighting were luckiest. The town was sacked, and there were no survivors, not one."

Schlemberger leapt in. Cat on to mouse.

"Very instructive, major, very instructive, no doubt. But you must forgive a suspicious old hick who's been smelling out fire insurance rackets all of forty years if he asks one little question."

"Come," said Smithers quickly, "an allegory is an allegory. We mustn't expect every detail to be absolutely water-tight. You ought to have simplified it a bit, major. Then you wouldn't have had to account for the story existing in such detail when everybody is supposed to have been killed."

"I hadn't meant to go into details," the major said, "but as a matter of fact there was one survivor from the garrison. Left for dead but still with a spark of life in him. I—I heard the story from his own lips."

"Now then, major," said Hamyadis without turning round. "We would like to hear about the coach."

The child humoured.

And suddenly they were no longer a knot of people on a raft in the wide sea. With a hoot and yells down on them swooped motor coach after motor coach. The visiting firemen.

"I guess I ought to get myself some of this fancy dress," said Schlemberger.

"Waiting for you at the inn," Hamyadis said. "We're nearly there. That's why the coaches are passing us."

Schlemberger insisted on changing into costume before they ate the breakfast. But his concession to Olde England went no further. He drank tomato juice.

When they had all taken their places, Joe Dagg said to Hamyadis:

"Well, Air Marshal, think it's time we saw something of this youngster who's going to give such a shock to the highwayman?"

"Certainly, if you like. He's a boy you can rely on to do the right thing at the right time. And that's something I'm prepared to pay for," said Hamyadis.

Dagg got up and left the room.

"Highwayman," said Schlemberger.

Not a question. Not a statement. Scarcely a feeler. A doubt.

"Highwaymen have always been thought of as pretty dangerous fellows," said the major.

Quick to exploit an opening. The alert soldier.

"They were? That is—are?" said Schlemberger.

"You probably find it difficult to believe that such a small country as this could have lonely roads," said the major. "But let me assure you you'll see some pretty lonely places between here and London. Places where anything might happen. Experentia docet."

"Experience teaches?" said Schlemberger. "Used to be the motto of my old High School. Pretty sound motto at that."

A fox in city streets, still cunning, still wary.

"Miss Miller," said the major. "You've done a good deal of travelling about in the course of your profession. Did you ever encounter a highwayman?"

"A highwayman? As a matter of fact I never did. But then I always say I'm a lucky person."

An understanding established. An opening quickly and easily taken up.

"Guess I ought to have brought a gun," said Schlemberger.

A plea. A request, with timidity, for the comfort of laughter.

"Do you carry a gun?" asked Kristen Kett.

The child. The illicit toffee.

"George carries one too," she added. "Don't you, Georgie? He keeps it under his pillow. It's got one of those silencers."

A boast.

"You're a silly little fool," said Hamyadis.

An admission.

From the others a rustle of protest.

Then an interruption. Eagerly accepted relief.

Joe Dagg came back into the room his hand resting on the shoulder of a boy of about eight.

"Here he is, Air Marshal," Joe said. "My Peter. One young lad ready and willing to deal with any highwaymen encountered."

"This is a bit of a surprise I've been keeping for you," said Hamyadis. "I thought it might amuse your fellow delegates, Mr Schlemberger, if we staged a little hold-up. We're going to have a highwayman ride out of a clump of trees somewhere on the route tomorrow and hold up the coach. He'll take money from the men and a kiss from the ladies, and then as he escapes this youngster will shoot him down."

"Guess that'll be very amusing," said Schlemberger.

He grinned. A touch of ruefulness.

A warmth. Something shared.

"Yes," said Kristen Kett, "and Richie is going to be the highwayman. He rides very well. Don't you Richie? Much better than old Charles."

A caress. In public. And responded to.

"We haven't decided who the highwayman will be yet," Hamyadis went on as if she had not spoken. "I'll let you know."

He got up from the table with his meal unfinished.

"I don't think we had better delay the start of the coach too long," said Fremitt. "No doubt there is a programme to be adhered to."

The others finished their food quickly. Richard Wemyss sat over a last cup of coffee for three minutes unconvincingly.

"Pardon me," said Schlemberger as they stood beside the coach waiting to mount, "could I try the effect of travelling inside?"

He looked down at his costume.

"I shall give myself the pleasure of accompanying you," said Fremitt. "Then we can talk shop without inflicting ourselves on the others."

The rest of the party climbed on to the roof seats, Kristen preening. Wemyss quick to sit beside her, to sit close. Peter Dagg scrambled up and sat between his father and Hamyadis. Another horn call. Conference delegates rushing from the breakfast marquees. Cheers, waves, shouts. The clop of the horses' hooves and the hot smell of the road.

They lunched on the way. Hamyadis had planned a sightseeing tour of Winchester for the delegates and wanted them to arrive in the early afternoon. Without relief horses their pace was necessarily slow.

But there were no gritty sandwiches, no tepid drinks tasting of the thermos.

They sat in their places on the coach, in the shade of a huge oak, its leaves paper thin from the long summer. Out of two large hampers Hamyadis produced a full scale cold meal. Lobster, duck, champagne.

Gleaming plates, sparkling glasses.

The warmth of a summer sun from a cloudless sky. Idle conversation.

"I guess this is more the way I kind of thought of England," said Schlemberger.

Hamyadis refilled his glass.

"You must remember," Smithers said, "all this is only made possible because we are a big enough industrial nation to warrant a visit from your conference."

"Remember it, but try to forget it," said Daisy, finishing her champagne. Smithers leaned towards her and said quietly:

"You've managed to forget your premonition of this morning I hope?"

"No," she said, "I haven't. Something like that only happens to me once in twenty years, and I can't forget it. But there's nothing I can do about it, so I don't intend to spoil the party."

"You have had similar feelings before, then?" Smithers asked.

"Yes," she answered. "And they did bring trouble. The last time I had a turn like this morning was over my husband."

"I certainly respect such intimations," Smithers said. "We must hope though that this once you're mistaken."

"I'm sure I hope so," she answered.

"Come," said the major, "you're looking too thoughtful for a fine day like this. Let me fill your glass."

"I won't have any more wine, thank you," she said. "I'd disgrace us all by falling asleep."

"Mr Hamyadis," the major called up to the box, "does the commissariat run to pani?"

Smithers noticed his hands grasping the cloth of his coat as if ready to rip two holes in it.

"Pani," said Daisy Miller as she took the iced water Hamyadis had passed down. "You can't expect us to understand you if you don't cure yourself of all this Latin, major."

"Hindustani this time, I'm afraid," the major said. "You can't stop an old dog's tricks, you know."

A slow relaxation.

"Hindustani," said Daisy, "isn't that extraordinary."

Pleased by a simple fact. But at the back of the eyes a reservation.

A start again. The uneventful road.

Near the outskirts of Winchester Joe Dagg turned round in his seat and said:

"Like to take the ribbons, colonel?"

"Very decent of you," said the major.

He stood up promptly. A rare chance. A trace of hastiness.

"Here, Pete, hold these a minute while we change places," said Joe Dagg thrusting the reins into his son's hands.

The boy said nothing, but gathered the reins for his thirty seconds driving with minute care. He sat crouching forward looking at the horses, absorbed in the concentration of imitation. Joe Dagg swung backwards off the box and to the roof of the coach itself. The major swung forward the same way though less adroitly. He took the reins from Peter and settled himself in the driving seat.

With deliberation, slowly as if giving a demonstration. Minor adjustments occupied him.

"You'll see a bit of driving now," Joe Dagg said. "The major's a rare one with the ribbons. He'll give you the trimmings."

He stood up again and looked back over his shoulder at the major.

"All set, colonel?"

"Set fair," said the major.

The pace quickened a little. They reached the outskirts of the city. Again they were overtaken by the cavalcade of motor coaches, hats waving from them at every angle. Frenzied centipedes. People on the pavements cheered as they went by. Richard Wemyss played to them.

Joe Dagg stood up again and turned round.

"You remember the turn into the pub, colonel?" he said.

A hint of solicitude. The mother bird watching the nearly grown fledgling outfly her.

"Sharp as can be," said the major over his shoulder. "I had a good look at it the other day. I'll take her right in."

"You mind my paint then, colonel," said Joe.

The major appeared not to hear, except that the pace quickened a little.

"That's the pub on the corner," Joe said, still standing and facing the way they were going.

Hamyadis turned round.

"It's one of the really old coaching inns," he said. "It's got everything. A courtyard in the middle, old stables. The lot."

As they got close to the building they could see the archway entrance was right on the street. A sharp turn would be needed to get the horses and the coach in.

The major gave a little shout. The pace quickened once again.

"Steady does it, colonel," said Joe Dagg quietly.

"Now," shouted the major.

There was a squeal of iron rims scraping and protesting on the road surface. The coach swayed.

The passengers clutched at the rails. Schlemberger poked his head out of the window, and whipped it back in again.

The leading horses entered the archway.

"Easy, easy," Joe Dagg shouted. With all the force of his lungs.

The coach lurched into the direction of the turn. The major flung his whole weight the other way to balance it.

A splintering, slow and deliberate.

The vehicle pitched forward and with a scraping crash hit the wall of the archway.

THREE

The horses gave a high pitched neigh and kicked their forelegs in a flurry of hooves and flashing horseshoes.

"The stupid fool," shouted Hamyadis.

He jerked to his feet crouching beneath the low roof of the archway. Then with a bound forward like a racing swimmer he leapt to the ground beside the horses. Their wild legs all around his head.

"Come down, you damn' brutes."

Without hesitation he stepped forward and caught hold of the rein linking the two leaders. He leant his full weight on it.

The plunging horses lowered their heads.

"Be still, damn' and blast you," said Hamyadis.

A curse.

And the horses obeyed.

No one was hurt. Even the horses in spite of the noise they had made and the whirl of flying hooves did themselves no harm. Joe Dagg inspected the coach and said the damage could be repaired by the morning.

"You want to keep an eye on that near side leader, Joe," said the major. "She's not reliable."

"I'll keep a tight hand on her, captain," said Joe.

All the party heard the rank given. A boy sent to the bottom of the class.

"It isn't right," said Kristen Kett. "I don't feel very well."

But beneath her make-up her cheeks looked pale.

"Richie," she said, "could you take me in?"

"Certainly," said Richard Wemyss.

He flicked angrily at the coating of distemper from the wall that was smeared across one side of his coat. Taking Kristen's arm he walked her solicitously into the inn.

"Now I really begin to get some idea of what the old coaching days were like," said Smithers.

"I always suspected I wouldn't have altogether liked them," Fremitt said.

"There's not only these little accidents, but exposure to the weather. A journey in those days must have meant taking a terrible risk."

"Dad," Peter Dagg said, "you did tell the major not to go so fast, didn't you?"

No one answered him. But Hamyadis said:

"Before dinner this evening I would be glad if you could all spare me twenty minutes or so. I want to get the details of this hold-up tomorrow fixed. Shall we say seven forty-five? By the coach?"

An impersonal announcement. With an addition: in direct speech.

"Major, you'd better be there ten minutes early."

As the blue and gold-faced clock above the inn stables struck a quarter to eight Smithers, still in coaching costume, came to the door leading to the courtyard. He flicked at chalk-dust as on a green-black academic gown. No boys rose to their feet.

Standing on the other side of the cobbled courtyard near the coach were Hamyadis and the major. Fremitt joined Smithers from a corridor where he had been looking intently at a fly-blown calendar two years out of date.

He smiled shyly.

"You're very punctual," he said. "I make it exactly seven forty-five."

He pulled a half-hunter from his costume waistcoat.

"I'm used to appearing exactly on time," Smithers said. "One minute early and you catch your form letting off high spirits, and one minute late and they've gone too far."

"And I generally find I arrive for an appointment two minutes early."

A moment of doubt. The quick smile.

"Or actually two and a half. It seems rather exact, I suppose."

Fremitt glanced at his hands. Self-examination.

"It's all a question of habit," said Smithers. "Yours is no more exact than mine."

The necessary answer.

Fremitt looked at him sharply. An assessment.

"Yes," he said, "though your habit seems contrived not to lead you into embarrassing circumstances."

A pause. In the eager eyes a moment of questioning, and the realisation that it was too late.

"A thing my habit has just done for me," Fremitt said, weighing the words.

Smithers turned and looked at the major and Hamyadis.

"I'm afraid it could only be described as a dressing-down," said Fremitt. "Or at least so it appeared to me."

"Unpleasant," Smithers said. "But it's our agreed time. Shall we join them?"

"I tell you frankly," said Fremitt. "I do so with reluctance. Or at best some hesitation."

"Your position is stronger than mine," Smithers said as they crossed the yard. "You are on duty: I came here for pleasure."

Fremitt appeared to stand straighter.

Through the archway from the street Schlemberger walked in talking to Joe Dagg. Peter skipped along half sideways beside them waiting to thrust a twig into the crackle of the conversation.

"Is that so?" Schlemberger was saying. "Why, in the States divorce is looked upon as an essential prerequisite of the pursuit of happiness."

"I'm not criticising it, wing commander," Dagg said. "You asked and I told you."

A paragraph completed.

"Dad," said Peter, the twig in at last, "what's an ex?"

"An ex, boy? What have you got into that head of yours now?"

"I guess Junior there's referring to a recent remark of mine," said Schlemberger.

A question answered, a point cleared up.

"Now then, lad," said Joe Dagg.

"But, Dad, what is an ex?"

"Back in the States we believe in answering that sort of question entirely frankly," said Schlemberger.

"Are you going to tell me then, sir?" asked Peter.

"You tell him," said his father.

"Well," said Schlemberger.

A drawn-out syllable. A hesitation. Choosing of words.

"Guess you could put it that I've had two wives, and now all I've got is two heavy bills for alimony."

"Dad never had any wives," said Peter.

"Now then, that's something we don't talk about," said Joe.

A boulder flung into a breach as turbid, mud-yellow water seethes through. Then something better.

"All ready and correct, Admiral," Joe said, stepping smartly up to Hamyadis.

From the inn door came Kristen Kett, leaning heavily on the arm of Richard Wemyss. From the archway, Daisy Miller.

"I don't know what time it is," she said, "but I'm going to apologise for being late. It's generally safest. I went down the road to put a letter in the box and got talking to the postman who was just collecting the mail. Such a chatty old dear."

"Georgie," said Kristen, leaving Richard's arm, "you won't want your little girl, will you? She knows all about this."

Perhaps a test.

"You'll stay," said Hamyadis.

"But Georgie . . . Georgie, I don't feel very well."

No answer.

Kristen walked away. But not too far. Wemyss walked after her, but not too fast.

"Well, let's start," said Hamyadis. "Would you be so good as to take your places on the coach? I've had it propped up so there'll be no danger as a result of that piece of abominable carelessness this afternoon."

For a little nobody moved.

The insult applied to them all.

Then the major said to Daisy:

"Will you allow me to hand you up?"

"It'll be a pleasure, major," she said. "Rehearsals are like cold swims: all right once you've begun."

Everybody moved towards the coach.

"Not that I've ever been so silly as to have a cold swim," said Daisy.

With some ceremony, perhaps prolonged deliberately, they took their seats, only Hamyadis and Richard Wemyss remaining below.

Left behind. Isolated. Two men: antagonists.

"Get up, Wemyss," said Hamyadis.

"I understood I was to take the part of the highwayman."

"The plan has been changed."

"But it's in my contract. I'm not sure I would have come except on the understanding I was to play that part. I'm certain I wouldn't have done."

"What contract?" said Hamyadis.

The iron finger crushes the shell.

"Well, of course, not exactly a contract. But I came to a definite understanding with Miss Kett acting on your behalf that I was to have the part."

"Get up."

"But I could sue you for this."

"You can try, but it won't do you any good. Now get up and stop arguing."

"Very well," said Wemyss. "But under protest. I feel I've been let down. From now on . . ."

He climbed the iron ladder up on to the roof of the coach.

The shell ground to powder.

Kristen Kett gave him a wan smile and said to Hamyadis:

"That's all very well, Georgie, but who is going to play the highwayman?"

"Never mind," said Hamyadis.

"But I've a right to know. I can't play with just anyone."

"Major," said Hamyadis, "have you got the pistols?"

"Georgie, I've got a right to know. After all, whoever it is is going to kiss me."

"Major, the pistols."

"I'm frightfully sorry, old boy. Fact is I forgot to bring them down. Mea culpa."

"Go and get them."

The major dropped off the side of the coach without a word. Heavily.

As he turned to go towards the inn Hamyadis said:

"I'm very sorry, Mr Schlemberger, that this—gentleman's incompetence should put you out twice in one day. I think I can promise you it won't happen again."

"That's of no consequence," said Schlemberger. "I'm very happy right where I am just now."

Hamyadis walked away impatiently. Schlemberger said in a low voice to Smithers who sat next to him:

"Very embarrassing situation. I'm just a mite surprised the major takes it so coolly."

"I think it fair to say that he's awkwardly placed," said Smithers. "It's not a subject one can refer to easily, but the life of a man on retired pay in this country nowadays is in many ways very difficult."

A polite warning.

"I get you," said Schlemberger. "I can see as far as the next man. Money troubles. I guess they're one hell of a lot worse than love troubles. And I've had both. I'll right out now and tell you something. The way I have to pay alimony I don't have a cent in the bank, ever. I wake up nights and think about it. If I got sick, or had to quit for any reason, I'd be finished. You know what I'd do? I'd go straight out and walk under an automobile."

He sat staring ahead. A bleak future.

"Mind you," he added, "the major's position may not be a hundred per cent the fault of your inflationary tendencies."

He looked at Smithers. Elementary shrewdness.

"I was talking to him this afternoon," he went on. "We got on to the subject of the way a guy amuses himself on what he called 'a spot of furlough'. He told me one of his stories. About someone he called 'a brother officer'. Something to do with a gambling club in London for officers back from India and all those places. This 'brother officer' went there and lost all he'd saved over the years."

"Such places exist, or existed, I suppose," said Smithers.

"Major Mortenson seemed pretty bitter about this one," Schlemberger said. "And do you know something?"

Smithers said nothing.

"I reckon the guy's his own brother officer," Schlemberger said.

"Georgie," Kristen called.

"Well, what is it now?" said Hamyadis turning towards the coach again.

"Georgie, I do think you might tell me who the highwayman's going to be."

"Why?"

"I want to know."

A demand. Suddenly all or nothing.

The others on the coach moving to disassociate themselves. Fremitt glanced round as if seeking a subject for conversation, decided that conversation would not help, took off his hat and began to examine the braiding.

Hamyadis strolled towards the coach until he stood directly beneath Kristen. He looked up at her.

"You would like to know?" he asked.

Demureness. A demure bison.

"Now, tell me," he said, "what right have you got to know about the decisions I happen to take? Let's hear all about it."

"I told you before," Kristen said, "if I'm going to play opposite someone, I have to know who it's going to be. And besides we're friends. You've always told me everything up to now."

"Ah, I see," said Hamyadis.

He softly brought his hands together.

"Friends. But isn't that nice? And I thought we weren't quite friends any longer. And now I find all those hard words have been taken back, all those unkind thoughts."

"But—— But I didn't."

Smithers put out a hand on to the coach rail as if he might be going to pull himself to his feet.

Kristen turned in her seat, leant over, staring directly down at Hamyadis.

"All right," she said, "I'll take the hard words back. I'll take them all back. We'll start again. You tell me this little thing and I—I'll forget everything."

"How charming, how perfectly charming. All that bit about snatching the gun from under my pillow and—what was it?—'shooting my face full of holes'. All forgotten. How delightful."

"I didn't mean it, you know I didn't," Kristen said.

She sat up straight again, turned for an instant to look at the others, saw glances averted, turned away.

"Georgie," she said. Urgently, quietly. "Just tell me."

"Tell you what?"

A sob, choked back.

"I just want to know who's going to be the highwayman. That's all."

"Then you must just wait your turn."

Calculated.

"But—but you said. Listen, Georgie Hamyadis, I know enough about you to blast you to hell."

"I don't think so. And, Kristen, aren't you forgetting: we are not alone."

Kristen turned back to her seat.

"I'm sorry," she said to no one in particular.

The sulky schoolgirl.

Wemyss, next to her, got up, went to the side of the coach and leant down, white-faced.

"I'd like a word with you," he said quietly to Hamyadis.

"Certainly," Hamyadis said, "though I generally prefer to discuss finance rather more in private."

"I don't want your money," Wemyss said.

Still all too easily heard.

"Then what do you want?"

"I want some respect shown to Miss Kett."

"Indeed. Now what exactly is your claim to be her defender? We might as well have the whole unsavoury business out, now we've gone so far. I take it you're what is called 'interested' in the lady?"

"What my relations with her are is nothing to do with it. It's just a matter of—of common decency."

"Except that I've been given to understand nothing of the sort," Hamyadis said. "Nothing to do with common decency at all."

"I won't be insulted," Wemyss said.

"And, if I choose to insult you, what will you do about it?"

"I—I'll get even with you. I warn you. You may think you can treat me like dirt. But there comes a time. I've got a certain amount of control, but after just so much it goes. And then I don't hold myself responsible. It's been pointed out to you already that you're not immortal. . . . Watch out, that's all."

Back to the dignified pose.

And the major came out of the hotel into the calm sunlight and trotted across towards them holding a box of pistols.

"Thank you, major," said Hamyadis.

The voice calm as the sunlight.

Without a word the major handed the box to him.

"One will be quite enough," Hamyadis said. "You'd better put the other in a safe place in case you contrive to mislay this one."

The major took back the box with one of the pair of pistols in it.

Without another look at him Hamyadis said:

"Now this pistol must be hidden somewhere for the highwayman not to see it and little Peter to be able to snatch it up and fire as the highwayman turns to ride off."

"There might be a secret compartment in the coach," the major said. "They sometimes had them to hide valuables in."

"Valuables like important letters?" said Hamyadis.

"I dare say they were often used for that, too," said the major. "I could find the place for you this evening. Or perhaps Joe knows where it is."

"I never found it, if it's there, colonel," said Joe.

"I could look about straight away," said the major moving towards the coach.

"There's no need, major," said Hamyadis. "You told me the other day such places existed. I spent two or three minutes just now finding it. It wouldn't be suitable to hide a pistol in. Would it, Christine?"

"I don't know," Kristen said.

Hamyadis smiled.

"We'll just put this pistol under the seat, I think," he said. "Here, Peter, put it where you're sitting."

He handed up the pistol and Peter poked it under the seat.

"Is it loaded, sir?" he asked.

"There's a little powder in it," said the major. "But the barrel is blocked. Mind you, if you wanted to put it back into use it wouldn't be difficult. The block is only a little lead. You could melt it out with a cigarette lighter. Nothing easier."

"Is it really real then?" said the boy.

"It certainly is," the major said. "The pair is from my own collection. They're by Durs Egg."

Peter laughed.

"Very famous early nineteenth century maker of pistols, my boy," Major Mortenson said. "This pair are small weapons specially made for coach passengers to carry in their pockets for protection against highwaymen. They're as fine a pair as you'll see, though I say it myself."

"When you've finished, major," said Hamyadis.

"Oh, yes, of course. Sorry, got carried away. Arma virumque, you know."

"Very good then," said Hamyadis. "Now when the highwayman comes up to the coach, keep your seats. Here are some purses to hand over. There'll be kisses for the women. Then as the rider turns, the boy fires. Quite simple. We'll do it now."

From the pockets of the bold yellow coaching coat he took a handful of small bags tightly knotted with long leather strings. They clinked as he reached up and distributed them.

"Is it proper money?" said Daisy. "I played with someone once who made out they couldn't get the feel of the part unless they were given real money in a purse."

"You stage people," said the major. "Wonderful sensibility."

"He was sensible in a way all right," Daisy said. "At the end of the run he pocketed the purse."

"I think I won't tell you whether the money is real or not," said Hamyadis.

He laughed. The cat suddenly gets to the cream.

"Now," he said. "You are on a stagecoach making your way along a lonely road, like on the downs over there. You look about. No one in sight. You are happy."

He turned and walked rapidly along the side of the inn yard and disappeared behind a stable door.

"He's up to something," Kristen said. "I hope . . ."

"People always think that actors in a scene like this do nothing but mutter 'Rhubarb'," Daisy said. "But what always happens to me is that I get a terrible feeling I want to gossip about anybody a bit downstage."

"You've known our damn' shady friend a good many years, haven't you?" said Wemyss.

A wild blow.

"Poor George," Daisy said. "He looked so pleased with himself just now.

You're quite right, Kristen. He's going to do something he thinks is clever."

Fremitt leant over towards Smithers and said in a low voice:

"He certainly is an odd man in many ways. Or perhaps you don't think so? He seems to take liberties, if that isn't too strong a word."

Before Smithers could reply the door of the stable burst open.

Hamyadis came out mounted on a huge black horse. The yellow coat and hat had been replaced by an enveloping black cloak and a thin black mask. The heavily jowled face, the powerful shoulders still unmistakable.

With an expert movement of his knees he urged the horse forward.

"Stand and deliver," he shouted.

"Pretty good," said Schlemberger.

He grinned and put his hands up.

Smithers, then Fremitt, followed suit.

Daisy said:

"I don't think I am going to be kissed, not now. I'll do a rather big faint. Somebody will catch me, won't they?"

"Adsum," said the major.

"I hope that means 'Yes'," Daisy said.

She lowered herself towards the major's arms.

Hamyadis urged the big horse nearer the coach.

"Your money or your lives."

A shower of purses. Adroitly caught.

Wemyss threw his last. Hard and high.

Hamyadis heaved the horse back by main strength, flung his arm up with surprising quickness, caught the purse at his finger tips, and with a swing of his immense bulk regained his seat.

"Well," said Kristen, "you certainly can ride."

"But not so well as your Richard," Hamyadis said.

The bait grabbed.

"I don't expect Richie's half so good," said Kristen.

"I was riding long before he was born, so it's not so unlikely. There was no other way of getting about in that part of the world when I was a young man."

"Isn't that romantic?" Kristen said.

"You know I can never feel quite the same about a bicycle as I can about a horse," said Daisy.

"Well," said Kristen, "I'm ready for my part of the hold-up."

She sat forward holding her face out to be kissed.

Hamyadis urged his horse nearer the coach again. He took Kristen's bonneted head in both his hands and kissed her. With savagery.

"Now," he said. "Are you ready, Peter?"

The boy nodded. Too excited to speak. Bright-eyed.

"Ho, ho, you're in for it now, Admiral," said Joe Dagg. "The sheriff of Dead Man's Gulch is going to drill you through."

"You mustn't mix up your history, Joe," said the major. "Otherwise we'll have the highwayman drawing his automatic and turning into a gangster."

"Oh, he couldn't do that," Kristen said, "he only has it with him at night."

"When you've quite finished discussing my personal affairs," Hamyadis said.

He looked intently at Kristen. Eyes behind the narrow mask hard.

"I forgot," she said.

Petulance.

A sudden smile on the heavy mouth under the mask. The eyes harder.

"Poor Kris," he said. "You'd be glad to see the end of me, wouldn't you? And now, ladies and gentlemen, I thank you for your purses."

He wheeled his horse under him, and started off. Peter snatched the pistol from under his seat, waved it towards him and jerked at the trigger. There was a satisfying bang. Hamyadis threw up his hands and slipped heavily from the saddle.

He fell with a thump on the hard cobblestones of the yard, and lay still.

The performance was excellent.

FOUR

Tableau vivant. Time passed while the whole party on top of the coach sat and stared at the inert figure, face down halfway across the inn court-yard. Even the horse after a moment's alarm dropped its head and cropped at a tuft of grass growing between the cobbles. Only the hands of the sta-ble clock seemed to move, gold across blue.

They moved a perceptible distance. Forty-five seconds passed between the time the gross figure of Hamyadis slid to the ground and the moment Daisy Miller spoke.

"Poor George," she said, "you ought to have arranged for some extras to enter with a hurdle and carry you off. Like they do in those Shake-speare productions when you have to pretend the stage hasn't got a curtain."

There was no response.

"He's hurt," said Smithers.

"He didn't utter a sound," said Schlemberger.

Unwilling to pay out without proof of loss.

"You don't think he's—— Perhaps he's dead," said Kristen Kett.

She sat up straighter, looked about. Emergence from the dark.

"What a horrible thing," said Smithers forcefully.

A declaration. A setting up of the norm.

He scrambled quickly, awkwardly down, and went hurriedly across towards the stone still figure.

Nature morte.

But Smithers's jog trot, shambling, inefficient, undignified, was not quick enough. The torpid summer air moved to a wind on his cheek as Kristen Kett, her costume draperies fanning out, rushed past him. Beneath the long clothes the tanned legs pounding.

She reached Hamyadis long before Smithers, flung herself to the ground and with a wrench heaved over the massive body.

Which laughed. Which gave a long gurgling, luxuriant laugh.

And when Hamyadis had finished, still lying on his back his arms flopped out beside him, he mimicked coarsely Kristen's voice:

"You don't think he's—— Perhaps he's dead."

Kristen stood up. Her face totally without colour, the make-up standing out like coloured countries on a map.

"No such luck, eh?" Hamyadis said.

Kristen turned away.

"I don't feel very well," she said.

Hamyadis leapt to his feet, put an arm briefly round her waist and said: "Don't be a silly little fool."

He walked over to the coach.

"Don't suppose I fooled you, Mr Schlemberger. A little trick I learnt all of forty years ago. I couldn't resist seeing if I could still do it, for fun instead of in earnest."

"Guess I had my suspicions," said Schlemberger.

"I must see if I can do it a little better tomorrow," Hamyadis said. "We mustn't disappoint our audience. Everybody must be ready to play their part. Mr Dagg, I want no remarks about sheriffs. In fact you had better keep silent."

"All right, Air Marshal, I know I'm ignorant. I'm so ignorant they wanted to take me round the schools as a horrible example. I'm not like my boy here: I haven't had education with no expense spared. But I can keep my mouth shut when called upon."

"There was one thing," Fremitt said. "It seemed to me that the pistol produced quite a large explosion. Is it really safe with so much powder in it?"

"Safe as houses," the major said. "All that I've done is to convert the weapon into a child's toy pistol. It fires what amounts to a cap."

"I'm glad to hear it," Fremitt said. "It looked to me as if there was some danger of the hand getting scorched."

"Not a bit," said Major Mortenson. "But I'll put a little less powder in for tomorrow if you like. Let me have the pistol, Peter. I won't load it till the morning in case it gets damp, but I don't want it left in the coach all night. It's too precious to me for that."

"Peter," said Hamyadis, "put the gun back under the seat."

The boy hesitated, looked from Hamyadis to the major.

The major stood up abruptly. The coach rocked.

"I prefer to keep the pistol myself," he said. "It's a valuable piece."

"You can charge expenses, major," said Hamyadis. "But that gun stays on the coach tonight. I don't want it forgotten again."

"But the coach house is unlocked," the major said. "Anybody could come in and take it. There are plenty of people about with precious little sense of meum and tuum."

"Put the pistol under your seat, Peter," said Hamyadis.

The elaborate pretence of weariness. The enjoyment of power.

"Very well," Major Mortenson said. "I'll allow it to stay there, but under protest."

"If there's nothing else to fix up," Schlemberger said. "I guess if you'll pardon me, everybody, I'll go and discuss the conference arrangements with my committee."

He climbed down the iron ladder on the coach side and walked away, purposefully.

"Thank you very much for your assistance," said Hamyadis. "Thank you, everybody. I think it should go all right tomorrow. I won't be on the coach at all. And I'm keeping it secret just when the highwayman is going to appear. It will aid the illusion."

He went back into the inn. A heavy tom cat, walking alone.

The others dismounted, talking a little about the weather and the sights of Winchester. Not about the rehearsal. John Fremitt did not contribute to the conversation. He sat still until all the others had got down and would have stayed longer had Smithers not looked up and asked him if he was coming.

"Oh, yes," he said with a start. "I'm sorry, my dear fellow. I was— That is I was thinking."

"There is a good deal to think about," said Smithers as they walked across the cobbled yard.

Fremitt made no reply.

At breakfast next day it was Joe Dagg who warned them that the time of departure had been fixed for ten o'clock. It was he who collected Hamyadis's three big cases, each with his initials stamped in large letters, from where they were piled in the hall, slightly in everyone's way.

And Joe saw that the whole party was safely installed before, surrounded once again by demonstrating conference delegates, they set off in bright sunshine, with three horn calls, with a clatter of hooves, to the sound of cheers.

"Well, Joe," said the major when the horses had settled down to a steady trot and the outskirts of Winchester were slipping quietly by, "I see you're in charge of us this morning."

"Don't know anything about anybody being in charge, colonel," said

Joe. "All I know is that the boss gave me my orders before that silly rehearsal business yesterday. Start out at ten, he says, and follow the route."

"I suppose it was a bit silly, his little trick," Daisy said. "But I couldn't help admiring him for it. You know, I've known him for years and years and I'd no idea he could ride a horse. Let alone do it so well. Kristen, were you in the secret? Was it a put up job between you?"

"The hell it was," said Kristen. "He never tells me anything he doesn't want to. I tell you I haven't seen hair or hide of him from the time he left us last night. Not that I wanted to, only he might have just popped in all the same."

"Don't you really know when this famous hold-up's going to happen?" asked Daisy.

"No, I don't," Kristen said, "I wish it wasn't going to be today though, I don't feel up to it."

"Does anybody know about the hold-up?" the major asked. "I certainly don't. Of course he discussed the general idea with me, but I thought it was to take place later in the journey."

"That's what Kristen told me in the first place," Richard Wemyss said. "I thought it was to happen much nearer London, where the press and everyone could see it. I think the whole thing's been bungled."

"That's where you're wrong," said Joe from the driver's seat. "He told me. It was going to be on Friday on the telly. But they couldn't do it. So it's going to be filmed. The film car's picking us up in an hour or so."

"Then the hold-up shouldn't be long," said the major.

Wemyss took off his hat and brushed it with the sleeve of his coat.

"Wrong again," said Joe. "They're following all day if need be. The boss said it was the only way to make it really exciting. He thinks of these things. You've got to hand it to him for that."

"So it might happen at any time," said Schlemberger. "What about my boys then? They'd surely like to see me at the wrong end of a pistol."

"They're following us today," said Joe. "All the way until the hold-up."

"I didn't know we were going to be televised," Fremitt said. "I'm not sure that I've considered all the implications. Doesn't anybody really know when it's going to take place? I should like at least the opportunity of not being present. Smithers, were you consulted?"

"Only in the most general terms," Smithers answered. "I submitted a memorandum on the sort of thing that happened when a highwayman stopped a coach. But I heard nothing about the actual particulars. This television business comes as much of a shock to me as to you."

"I hope you're not going to spoil it all," said Wemyss. "It may be something like a bad smell to you, but it's important to me. And to Daisy and Kristen. That's what we made the journey for. Isn't it, Kris?"

"I don't know about Daisy, but I had my own reasons for coming."

An irrelevance. Meant if anything to tease.

"I suppose," said Smithers, "that having undertaken the trip one ought to go through with everything involved. Though I must say I take it badly that Hamyadis didn't give me full particulars."

"Well, thank you very much," said Wemyss.

He smiled. With charm. For almost the first time on the trip.

"But all the same," he added, "I think you must be beginning to see my point about our absent friend. A bit much, eh?"

"I will admit," said Smithers, "that there has been an atmosphere about this whole trip that I didn't expect."

"I'm glad you've noticed it at last," said Wemyss. "I was beginning to think there was something wrong with me. Of course, I came to it as a complete outsider. I hadn't met our friend until the evening before we started and I only saw him for a few moments then. But right from the start it looked odd to me. What about you, sir?" He turned to Schlemberger. "You're as much of a newcomer to it all as I am. Did you notice anything odd?"

"It certainly hasn't quite gone as I'd have expected," said Schlemberger. "I feel a mite responsible."

"My dear fellow," said Fremitt, "if anybody should feel responsible, and I really don't think that they should, then it must be myself. After all I am your official host."

The shy smile.

"That's pretty big of you," said Schlemberger. "But it's just not so. I fixed all the arrangements. My organisation picked Hamyadis Tours on my say-so, I've got to admit that."

He sat back. A penitent freed.

"Dad," said Peter Dagg sitting next to his father on the box, "what does it mean the trip having an atmosphere? The old coach does smell a bit inside, but it's all right when you get used to it."

"I don't know what it means any more than you do, son," said Joe. "I never noticed any atmosphere."

"But we did," said Wemyss.

"Perhaps it was the cause of your premonition," the major said to Daisy. "I feel concerned."

"No," she answered, "the premonition was something quite different. I thought it had all come true when I spoke to George lying there on the cobbles and he didn't answer. I was almost glad. I thought, 'Well, at least it's nothing worse'. I never somehow expected George to die a quiet death, not in all the years I've known him."

"You've known him a long time, have you?" said Wemyss.

A pounce.

"No," Daisy said. "I haven't. Or did I say I had? I'll tell you how it was. I met him first years and years ago. And we've always been very pally when we bump into each other, you know how it is in the profession. But if you're asking whether I know him really: the answer is I don't. I certainly don't."

"But you must know quite a bit about him," said Wemyss.

"No, I don't."

Firmness. A lesson.

"I've heard quite a bit about him, but that's not the same thing."

"But——" Wemyss began.

"Tell me, Miss Miller," Smithers interrupted.

"Miss Miller," said Daisy. "You ought to call me by my christian name. You're a friend."

An acknowledgement.

"Well, then, Daisy. I was going to ask you if you were worried about your premonition still. But perhaps you'd rather not speak of it."

"Oh, no, dear. I want to talk about it all the time. It's the only way. Otherwise I wouldn't leave it at just wishing I would go home: I'd suddenly pack my bags and go right in the middle of the night."

"But if you're worried, you ought to do just that, dear lady," said the major.

"I don't know about that," Daisy said. "But anyhow I can't go, so there it is."

"But if you're worried I could certainly persuade Hamyadis to release you from any contract," said the major.

I could easily kill a giant.

"No."

From Daisy a pistol shot.

"Don't be so silly, major," she added quickly. "I don't want to break a contract. I never have in all the years I've been on the stage."

"People are always saying that," Kristen broke in. "I think it's silly. If you don't treat 'em rough they treat you rough."

"You be careful, dear," Daisy said. "You can break too many. I ought to know. When I was a young thing I used to walk out of show after show."

"Pardon me," said Schlemberger.

The alert owl.

"Pardon me, didn't I understand you to say you had never broken a contract? I'm purely a suspicious old hick."

"That's exactly what I did say," Daisy replied. "When you get to my age it's what you do say. It helps to spread the trouper tradition."

"And I thought the fire business was tricky," said Schlemberger.

"I expect it is, dear," said Daisy, "in its own way. But there's no denying it the profession does look very like a jungle on the days when you're feeling a bit low. I dare say it does on the days you're feeling good too. Only then you're one of the wild beasts and happy about it."

"Talking of wild beasts," said Smithers. "Would I be right in thinking that one of them has just begun to stalk us?"

They all turned round. About fifty yards behind them running quietly along the broad sweep of the main road there was a small smartly painted lorry, on it pointing at them the lenses of a film camera.

"And aren't those the coaches coming after?" said Wemyss.

"So we can expect the hold-up at any moment, I suppose," Fremitt said.

"I feel quite excited already," Daisy said. "George was quite right. Not knowing when does give it a bit of real excitement."

"We've a tidy way to go yet today," said Joe Dagg. "You may have to wait."

"Do you know the road ahead, major?" asked Schlemberger. "Can you tell us what would be a likely point for this attack to take place?"

"I was just trying to think," said the major. "Of course, we're on an old Roman road from here nearly to Basingstoke and it doesn't pass through many places. They mostly lie off it a bit to one side or the other. So there will be plenty of opportunities."

"And did you tell all this to Hamyadis?" Schlemberger said.

With excitement.

"Yes, I did," said the major. "But, mind you, that was a fortnight or so ago. We went over the whole route together then. I doubt if he'd remember it all."

"That's where you're wrong," Kristen said. "He was talking about it to me yesterday. He knew everything about it."

"He certainly is a remarkable man in many ways," said Schlemberger.

"I'm glad somebody thinks so," said Kristen. "But then you've no cause to be jealous, have you, Mr Schlemberger?"

She turned and looked up into Richard Wemyss's face. Coquetry.

"Don't you flatter yourself, my girl," said Wemyss.

A sudden flush of anger.

"I only go by what I hear," Kristen said.

"Well then," said Wemyss, "you can hear this."

The colour mounting in his cheeks. A reversal resented.

"I know quite well why you insisted on me coming on this trip with you. But I came because it suited me, and for no other reason. Don't let's have any misunderstandings about that."

He spoke quietly, leaning towards her, but with too much force for all that he said not to be clearly heard by everybody. Even Joe Dagg sitting above them. He turned round in his seat and said:

"You go in and win, captain. You go in and show her you're one better than a stinking rich old dago."

Wemyss suddenly white. The nostrils rigid.

"You don't want to be shy, captain," Joe went on.

A plough tears cheerfully at spider strands, at mouse work.

"I think you completely misunderstand the situation," said Wemyss.

"'Course I do, captain," Joe said. "If I saw the vicar's wife kissing the cowman behind the milking sheds I'd misunderstand the situation. That's what I was born for. But I can't help opening my big mouth. And what I say is: when there's a chance of putting a wog in his place it ought to be did, and quick."

"I'm beginning to wish this wretched highwayman business would start," Smithers said quietly to Fremitt.

Richard Wemyss stood up and faced Joe, swaying slightly to the rhythm of the coach.

"I think I must ask you to mind your own business," he said.

"Well," said Joe, "it is our business you know. We none of us like to see young love going astray."

"I notice nobody else associates themselves with your remarks," Wemyss said.

"Oh, well, perhaps they don't not in so many words. But I'm sure—— Oh, never mind."

A sudden wrinkle in the smooth balloon.

"I'll say no more. Only that if I spoke out of turn, it was because I've more reason to than most."

He put his arm round the shoulders of his son and the coach jogged on in silence.

But not for long.

"It's a curious thing," said Schlemberger, "but neither of my exs ever thought to marry again. You never can tell with a woman. As soon as my second left me she and my first got together about the alimony and they've been together about it ever since. The whole business of marriage is entirely beyond my comprehension."

Some salt for an open wound.

"Well, you know, Mr Schlemberger," Smithers said, "we over here are apt to feel that the idea of marriage is beyond the comprehension of America as a whole."

A bull grasped by the horns converted into a discussion group, neatly sitting round.

"Oh, come now," said Daisy, "you won't often find me defending America, dear. But you mustn't think it's only Reno, you know. Even in the profession there are lots and lots of nice people never thinking of divorce or anything, just happily quarrelling on from year to year like everybody else."

Then Schlemberger: something in agreement.

And the major: a doubt.

Smithers next: an admission of hastiness.

Now even Wemyss: some contribution a little off the point.

And Kristen: a contradiction.

Amounting in all to a conversation, a quiet conversation, a veneer of normality.

And before and behind them the road slowly clopped away. Cars passed with faces craned to watch. Horses in a field galloped as far as they could racing the team in the traces. At a discreet distance the film lorry kept its camera trained, behind it the coaches of the delegates, emitting a cheer at anything like an incident. Above, the sun from a cloudless sky. Only the faintest of breezes from the motion of the coach to relieve the heat. The acrid smell of the horses. Drowsiness. The conversation trickling away to warm silence. The pace varying with the road, slowing almost to a stop up an incline, briskening for a slope down.

At the bottom of a long gentle hill with the hooves now clacketing out sharply with a stir of exhilaration suddenly from Joe Dagg ever alert:

"Whoa, whoa."

The abrupt change in the rhythm. Startled glances.

Squarely in the middle of the white road ahead the black figure, unbudging. Dressed in black from head to foot, astride the black horse, black masked: Hamyadis.

"Stand and deliver."

The coach came to a final halt. From behind, the squeal of car brakes as the film van slewed aside to get the best view and the delegates' coaches fanned on to the verge. But aboard the coach nobody had attention to spare for the noise from behind, only for the now silent figure ahead.

Hamyadis sat without moving watching the highwayman's prey, a pistol held unwaveringly trained on them.

"He's only doing it for the film people," said Wemyss.

Without relaxation.

No one else spoke.

At last Hamyadis urged his horse forward and slowly approached the coach. Even the spectators behind were now silent.

When he was right up to the side of the coach Hamyadis spoke for the second time.

"Your money or your lives."

With authentic brutality.

No one answered.

"Do we throw the purses now? Is this being broadcast? Ought I to speak?" asked Fremitt in a whisper.

Smithers pulled his dummy purse from the deep pocket of his caped coat and offered it to Hamyadis, who took it, tossed it in the air, slipped it away and said:

"Thank you, sir. And the next one."

All the others held out their prepared purses. Hamyadis took Schlemberger's and Fremitt's and put them quickly into his pocket.

He then sat for a moment silent.

The major dropped his outstretched arm and put his purse on the seat beside him. In an instant Hamyadis had reached forward and with a vicious jerk whipped it up.

"You must pay like the rest," he said.

"But—but—— Dammit, it's only a game. What does it matter? Cui bono?" said the major.

"Come," said Hamyadis, "you know as well as I do that the purses contain real sovereigns."

"But my dear fellow, I just got tired of holding it out. I swear——"

"All right, all right, major. We'll say no more about it."

Hamyadis kneed his horse violently a yard or so along the coach until he was within a few inches of Richard Wemyss.

"And you needn't think I wasn't watching you," he said. "You know, I find it hard to decide whether it's worse to try and slip a couple of coins out of a purse or to forget about the whole thing."

"I don't know what you mean," said Wemyss.

"No? Then let's say the highwayman asks you to put an extra—we'll call it an extra—sovereign into the purse before you hand it over."

"Are you accusing me of stealing?" Wemyss said.

His blotchy face.

"You heard my request," said Hamyadis.

"Now look here——" Wemyss began.

But Hamyadis cut him short by flicking the purse from his hand.

"We'll discuss this afterwards," he said.

He tossed the purse up into the air and let it fall into his palm. Then suddenly he gave a twist of his wrist which sent the leather purse strings whistling through the air and into Wemyss's face.

They left a pair of angry red lines.

Wemyss leapt up.

"I'd sit down if I were you," said Hamyadis without moving.

Wemyss looked at him. There was time to draw two deep breaths. Then he sat down.

"I shan't forget," he said. "I may be even with you sooner than you think."

"My dear chap," Hamyadis said.

Suddenly the uncle, sophisticated, kindly.

"My dear chap, you mustn't mind a little horse play. Really you mustn't."

He turned and gave Daisy Miller a deep bow.

"Madam," he said, "pray keep your purse. We gentlemen of the road will never inconvenience a lady."

"I am your debtor, sir," Daisy replied. "Is there no way I can repay this kindness?"

"A kiss from your lips, madam, would outweigh every purse in the country," Hamyadis answered.

Daisy turned and said aside:

"Thank heavens, my husband took the other road."

A murmur of laughter as they kissed.

Mercury dropping down the thermometer tube.

"I'm ready," said Kristen thrusting forward over the edge of the coach.

Hamyadis turned to her. He reached forward and put one hand on the back of her neck. With the other he took hold of the purse she still held and wrenched it out of her grasp. Then he pulled her forward till she was nearly toppling off the coach and kissed her savagely. He jerked her back to her seat and said:

"I hope it makes you happy."

Kristen sat without a word.

"On you go, driver," said Hamyadis. "And I hope for your sake no one has been so foolish as to hide anything on the coach."

"Nothing hidden at all, Mr Highwayman," said Joe Dagg giving his son a poke in the ribs.

Hamyadis turned his horse. Peter Dagg reached under his seat for the hidden pistol. All the passengers crowded to the side of the coach to watch.

Without looking back Hamyadis urged the heavy black horse off. Peter lifted up the pistol, held it out towards the highwayman at arms length and pulled happily at the trigger. There was a heavy explosion. Peter fell backwards. His father laughed. Hamyadis slid forward on to his horse's neck and stayed there while the animal trotted on.

"Are you all right, my boy?" said Fremitt. "The noise seemed even louder to me than yesterday."

"I suppose our friend is waiting for a nice soft spot to fall," said Wemyss.

"He managed on cobbles before," Daisy said.

The black horse scrambled up a small bank. Slowly Hamyadis slipped from the saddle. The horse shook itself slightly as it noticed the absence of a rider's weight. Hamyadis flopped to the ground and rolled on to his front.

"Keep clear, keep clear, please," shouted a voice from behind the coach.

The film lorry came bumping over the ground towards the prostrate figure. Technicians worked busily.

"Stand back," called the man in charge. "We want a close-up."

The lorry halted about five yards away and its camera whirred for a moment.

"Thank you very much, sir," said the director.

Hamyadis lay without moving.

"You'd think he'd done well enough out of that bit of ham without trying it again," said Wemyss.

No movement.

"I think this time he may be hurt," said Smithers. "He fell very differently."

He climbed down and once more went across to Hamyadis.

But as soon as he got within two yards of him he saw that this time it was different.

Very different.

There was a hole in the back of Hamyadis's neck.

FIVE

Smithers knelt beside Hamyadis for an instant and felt for the pulse in his wrist. But without hope.

When he got to his feet and turned to face the others, still bunched together standing on the roof of the coach, he saw that they had realised that this time it was no act.

"We must have a doctor," Smithers said. "But you may as well know that there will be nothing he can do. And I suppose we will need the police."

"Are you in it this time, too?" said Kristen.

But Smithers had no need to contradict her.

"I thought I wanted him to——" she said.

And crumpled into a faint.

It was Fremitt who lifted her back on to the seat and Daisy who loosened her clothes. The others shifted about uneasily.

"Back in the States . . ." said Schlemberger.

Smithers walked towards the coach. He pulled out a large white handkerchief and used it to pick up the Durs Egg pistol still lying on the coach roof where Peter had dropped it.

"Dad," said Peter, "what has happened to Mr Hamyadis?"

"He fell off, lad," said his father.

"But he's dead, isn't he?" asked Peter.

"Yes, I'm afraid he is dead, Peter," Smithers said.

The boy looked at him.

"What was it that killed him?" he said.

"You don't need to know just for the present," Smithers answered.

"And that means," said Richard Wemyss, "that it wasn't an accidental fall. That pistol——"

He pointed to the bundle in the white handkerchief that Smithers held.

"That's enough," said Smithers.

Wemyss looked at him.

Smithers said nothing.

"All right," Wemyss said, "but you'll see."

"You are sure, aren't you?" the major asked Smithers. "Military man, seen something of this sort, pallida mors, you know, want me to have a look?"

"This is a moment when inaction is the only action needed," said Smithers.

The film man who had dismounted from his truck came across towards the coach.

"I could take the vehicle back to Winchester and get you help," he said to Smithers. "Must get on to my news room, too."

"That's a very useful offer," Smithers said. "Or the first part at least."

"I know how you feel, old boy," said the man, "but even if I never mentioned this to a soul the boys would all be here in a couple of hours."

"We shall try to be prepared," Smithers answered.

"Then I'll be—er—off," said the film man.

He walked back to his lorry. Slowly. A glance back. Quickly. With pebbles from the road verge spurting from under the tyres he left.

Silence. But not stillness. Shufflings: animal, tense. And as a background wasp-nest buzzings of talk from the delegates' coaches still parked fifty yards away.

Schlemberger consulted the watch on the inside of his wrist.

"Twelve-thirteen exactly," he said. "I checked with the ship's chronometer all the way over. Doesn't lose a second. Guess we ought to make a note of just when it happened. The homicide squad always——"

A pause.

"But I guess this will be handled by your British police. I wonder ought I to contact the Embassy?"

"You want to claim asylum, I suppose," said Wemyss.

"Now look here——" Schlemberger began.

"Mr Schlemberger," Smithers interrupted.

The senior master. In charge.

"Mr Schlemberger, I think it would be best if you were to send on your fellow delegates to Basingstoke. They obviously will be able to contribute nothing when the police come, and it's scarcely fair that they should be kept hanging about."

"That's pretty right," said Schlemberger climbing down the coach side. "And I'd be all the better for a word with Sam Geifertz. Sam's vice this year."

He was hardly out of earshot when Wemyss said:

"If he gets into one of those coaches and goes hell for leather to catch the first plane home it won't be my responsibility."

"No," said Smithers, "it will be mine. I wish I could take them all as lightly."

"How long do you think it will be before they do come, the police?" Daisy asked him.

"Not much more than half an hour I should say," he answered. "That young man drove away very fast."

"He's got to get his films developed," Kristen said. "I shouldn't be surprised if he didn't forget about the police and go as fast as he can bat to London. You'll have the pleasure of seeing yourselves on T.V. tonight."

"I don't think you quite realise the seriousness of the situation," the major said. "That young man very sensibly drove off in the direction of the nearest police station and away from London. When he comes back with the police it won't be a question of seeing ourselves on television, but of seeing one of us in gaol. Somebody interfered with that pistol."

"I don't think we can usefully discuss it," Smithers said.

"Oh, come, don't let's pretend we aren't all trying to work it out," Wemyss said. "That pistol was supposed to be a dummy. And it killed George Hamyadis. A thing like that doesn't happen by mistake."

"It's surely just possible that it could be a mistake," Fremitt said. "Perhaps the pistols were interchanged."

"No," said the major. "From my collection. I'd know it like my own brother, if I had one."

"There you are," said Wemyss.

"Dad, does that mean I killed Mr Hamyadis?" asked Peter Dagg.

"Now, lad," said Joe, "don't you listen to what you're not meant to hear."

"But Dad, it does. I shot him. I killed him."

Tears, ugly tears, innocent tears.

Joe Dagg put a quick arm round the boy and said:

"You take no notice. It isn't true, lad."

Daisy Miller left her place and stood on the seat opposite to get near him and said:

"Nobody thinks you meant to do it, love. It was all an accident."

Major Mortenson said:

"Why can't people exercise some tact?"

Richard Wemyss said:

"I didn't bring up the subject in the first place."

Kristen Kett said:

"Oh lord, I feel so ill."

John Fremitt said:

"That car has been gone at least five minutes. Or not less than four."

Foster P. Schlemberger, walking back to the coach unobserved, said:

"I guess this is a pretty rotten business."

Smithers made no contribution. But he looked at each speaker in turn with angry speculation.

Nobody after that tried conversation. Slowly Peter's sobs ceased. He sat white-faced, pressed tightly against his father. Overhead the sun moved through the blue sky.

The last of the delegates' coaches roared away towards London, and the coach party was left sitting silent and alone. Driftwood.

And at last the police. First a motor-cyclist blasting the quiet, pulling up at the sight of them with a squealing of brakes, and then sitting astride his machine looking down at them from the slight incline they had come down to meet the highwayman. Poised, ready to act, not acting.

Soon three cars appeared over the brow of the hill behind him. He waved at them and pointed towards the stranded coach. An accusation. The cars slipped slowly down the slope, and came to a halt alongside the coach. From the first of them stepped a police inspector in uniform. He gave the coach a brief incurious glance and turned to the squad of constables tumbling out of the following cars. He gave them sharp efficient orders to cordon off the area, to photograph the body, to move on any sightseers. Each task given equal importance.

Not until all this was settled did he approach the coach. Then he turned to the party and said:

"Good afternoon, ladies and gentlemen. A nasty business this seems to be. My name is Jones, Inspector Jones, Hampshire Police. Can any of you confirm what we've been told?"

"Have you been told it's murder, inspector?" said Richard Wemyss, leaping down from the top of the coach.

"Murder?" said the inspector.

He looked hard at Wemyss, his taut white face, his trembling hands.

"Yes," Wemyss said. "George Hamyadis, travel agent, night club impresario, crook, was shot thirty minutes ago by a pistol that until last night had its barrel blocked. Someone melted the lead and loaded the pistol with a real bullet. And if you ask me that someone is up on that coach there. Now go ahead. It shouldn't be difficult."

"Now then, that's a very serious accusation to make," said the inspector. "What is your name, sir?"

But without waiting for Wemyss to answer he signalled to the motor-cyclist who still watched the scene from the road. The man kicked his machine to life and rode over the bumpy ground to where the inspector was standing. Wemyss watched him. The inspector gave the man a brief message in an undertone and then turned to Wemyss again.

"Now, sir, your name?"

"Richard Wemyss."

"Address?"

With open throttle the motor-cycle charged away up the hill in the direction of Winchester.

"194 Chancery Inn, London, E.C.4."

"Thank you, sir. And now I don't think there's anything much we can do here. I'd be glad if you'd all come to Winchester."

The party was split up for the journey back. Joe Dagg and Peter were allowed to stay with the coach which started slowly off up the hill. Sitting beside them on the box a uniformed constable. A height of incongruity.

The others were split up amongst the three cars, and in a few moments the body of George Hamyadis surrounded by busy policemen was all that remained of the High Flyer coach to London.

At Winchester police station the convoy of cars drew up and the coach party, with the exception of Joe Dagg and Peter, was reassembled in the waiting room. They sat silent on the hard scrubbed bench that ran round the walls. A constable stood by the door, looking into space.

After about twenty minutes the door opened briskly and a man in a blue suit came in.

A nose. More than large: beaked, fleshy, quivering at the tip. The man —about forty-five, thatch of greying hair, eyes pale and speculative—stood peering in following the nose. Darting, prying, poking. Nothing missed. Number of walls: four. Colour: white. Texture: painted brick. Number of bricks: approximately two thousand five hundred.

Number of people: seven. Average number of hairs in each head: counted.

"Good afternoon," he said. "My name is Parker. Detective Inspector Parker, Hampshire C.I.D. I have been put in charge of this business, and I've come to ask for your help. I'm afraid I must apologise for keeping you here. It took me a little time to drive over. But I hope I won't have to keep you much longer."

"I guess I hope not, inspector," said Schlemberger. "I have a conference opening in London on Monday. There are a great many details to fix."

"You must be Mr Schlemberger, Foster P. Schlemberger, isn't it?" said the inspector. "We certainly appreciate your position, sir. Perhaps you would care to spare me a few minutes straight away and then you'll be free to make any telephone calls you want."

"That's pretty handsome," Schlemberger said.

He got to his feet and walked to the door. Awkwardly. And the others looked at each other briefly. Police questioning had begun.

Nobody said anything. The constable at the door stood staring at the same patch of wall. Six minutes passed. Outside voices were heard. The door opened and another constable showed Joe Dagg and Peter in.

"You got back without incident?" said Smithers.

"Nothing that you'd call incident," Joe said. "Only that copper sitting on my box looking as if he was Lord Muck. I don't like 'em. Never did, never have, never shall. It's the way they look at you. As if they were a house surveyor and you were a cracked wall covered up nicely with a bit of new paper."

The joking phrase. No joke.

"Anyhow we got here. We're taking the horses along to the farm where they were last night. So I suppose everything's all right. More or less."

Then silence again. For twelve minutes. Brisk opening of door. Head of constable thrust in.

"Mr Wemyss."

Exit young actor. Not as an actor exiting. And then there were seven.

Wemyss was absent fourteen minutes. Next the major: absent twelve minutes. Daisy Miller: six minutes. Kristen Kett: fifteen minutes. Fremitt: eleven minutes. Joe Dagg and Peter: four minutes. And then there was one.

Smithers followed the constable along a bare corridor. At the end there was a glass panelled door. The constable knocked, opened it and said Smithers's name. He motioned him in.

Detective Inspector Parker was sitting behind a small desk. On it lying on Smithers's handkerchief was the pistol. In a corner a constable sat, a shorthand notebook on his knee.

The inspector pushed a cigarette towards Smithers who refused it.

"I'm sorry to have kept you till last, Mr Smithers," he said. "In some ways I ought to have seen you first. Mr Jones told me you seemed to be more or less in charge."

"No one was in charge, inspector," Smithers said. "Mr Hamyadis appeared to manage everything himself. When he—when the accident occurred, as nobody did anything I asked that young man with the film machine to go for the police. There's nothing more to it."

"No," said the inspector. "But all the same in my experience the man who sends for the police in such circumstances is the one who's going to be useful to you. That's why I waited to see you last."

Ground bait.

"I'm afraid there's little I'll be able to tell you," Smithers said. "I appeared to know less of Mr Hamyadis, or anything of what was going on, than anybody."

A wary fish.

"Of what was going on," the inspector echoed the phrase. An invitation.

"Of the arrangements for the trip," said Smithers.

The inspector sat silent, unmoving except that at its tip the enormous nose quivered. Almost a tic.

"Look," the inspector said suddenly leaning forward, "something was going on. Now, I know you are thinking that whatever it was, it was probably nothing to do with the death of Mr Hamyadis. And you may be right. But I'd just like to know about it all. It'll go no further. But I'm curious. I don't like the feeling that things are happening that I don't know about."

Smithers said nothing.

The inspector leant back in his chair.

"You know what they call me," he said. "All the toughs and wide boys, all the petty criminals and police informers: they call me Nosey Parker. And it's not just because of this."

He hit the nose with his index finger. A thwack.

"It's because I like to know things," he went on. "I like to know everything."

He paused.

"Did you know," he said, "that to get the best out of champagne you want to drink it from a tankard? No? Fact. I was on a case last month. Breaking and entering at a wine merchants. The owner told me, proved it to me. That had nothing to do with the case, but I couldn't help asking questions, and that was one of the things I found out."

"If you want to know about coaches and coaching I'll be glad to do my best," answered Smithers. "But really Major Mortenson is your man. My knowledge is all book stuff. He really knows about coaches."

"Does he now?" said the inspector. "I wondered about that. There was that incident at the inn entrance just along the street from here."

"That was nothing to do with knowledge or lack of knowledge," Smithers said. "That was simply a question of character. The major has a streak of——"

He stopped.

"Go on," said Inspector Parker, Nosey Parker, "a streak of what would you say?"

"I'm sorry," said Smithers. "I've no objection to satisfying your curiosity where I can. But I won't stoop to gossip."

An angry hand flicked chalk dust off an old waistcoat. Which was embroidered fancy dress.

"I appreciate your point of view," said the inspector. "I admire it. But, you know, gossip isn't quite the right word. Not any longer. We aren't just chatting about a handful of your acquaintances: we're looking at murder. Because there can be no mistake about it. Mr Hamyadis was shot, and there shouldn't have been a workable weapon anywhere in sight."

"It's not my job to teach you your businss," said Smithers, "but couldn't it have been a stray shot from some rifle range or something like that?"

"There's nothing like that for miles around," said Inspector Parker. "I checked. And it would be really too much of a coincidence that such a stray shot should hit Mr Hamyadis at the exact moment the pistol was fired from the coach."

"It was the exact moment," Smithers said. "I've thought about it very hard."

"Thank you," said the inspector. "That's the sort of thing I want to hear. That and other facts. Facts about any of the people who were in a position to tamper with that pistol. The barrel had been unblocked, you know."

"Everyone in the party knew the pistol was being left in the coach all night," said Smithers. "There was an altercation about it, and the coach was simply in an open stable. All of us could have got at it."

"Suppose you tell me about the altercation," said the inspector.

"I can tell you the facts of it," Smithers answered. "But you've no doubt got half a dozen versions of those already. If you want my impressions of how the incident showed up the characters of those involved, I'm afraid I shall have to disappoint you. Don't think I'm unwilling to help. It's simply that I can't. Gossip, like anything else, improves with practice. Over the years, in common-rooms I've trained myself not to gossip, and that means not to register the facts on which gossip depends."

"On the other hand," said Inspector Parker, "over the years you've formed hundreds of characters. You can't do that without observing them."

"If I've learnt anything," Smithers answered, "I've learnt not to make a fool of myself. The human boy is a very complicated mechanism, inspector. So is the human adult. In the few days I've seen my travelling companions I've observed nothing about them that I would care to put before anybody else as facts. I'm not that sort of a person. If I don't know something for certain I don't talk about it. I believe it's a necessary qualification in my profession."

"I suppose I shall have to accept that," said the inspector. "I'm all too human: you're a monk. But you may well be seeing more of your party in the next few days. I'm asking you all to stay here in Winchester and to let my men know where you are at least over the week-end. I've booked you back in where you slept last night. A purely voluntary exceptional arrangement. I hope you'll agree to it. Otherwise I shall be chasing all over the country every time I want to ask a question. Now, if you get to feel certain about anything to do with your party, any little thing, I'd like to hear of it."

"Very well," said Smithers. "And can I assume from what you said that our charade is at an end?"

"It is," said Inspector Parker. "I'm afraid it would be out of the question."

The distance from the police station to the inn: five hundred and forty-seven yards. The time taken by Smithers to walk the distance: thirty-eight minutes. Yet he entered the inn yard walking briskly and glancing round. Nobody was in sight. He walked quickly over to the door of the stable where the coach had been kept the previous night. He tried it. It opened easily. With a brief glance inside at the gayly painted High Flyer, its journey ended, he shut the door. Then he walked out into the street and went into a small toyshop two doors away from the inn. He bought a pocket torch and went back to the inn. He moved purposefully along the corridors, putting his head round the doors of the public rooms.

Sitting alone in an armchair in an alcove half-way up the main staircase he saw Peter Dagg, pale, smudgy-eyed, unmoving. The chair too lumpy to sit on; next to it a potted plant, dust on its faded leaves.

"Ah, Peter," said Smithers, "I was looking for you."

The boy looked up. Wild hope.

"Now," said Smithers, "have you ever had any pets?"

"Pets, sir?"

"Yes, rabbits, a puppy, a kitten."

"I did have a budgie once, but it died."

"Was that a long time ago?"

"It was about"—face screwed in concentration—"about three quarters of a year ago."

"I see. And do you often think about it nowadays?"

"Well, no. Though I thought about it very hard when it died."

"And what did it die of?"

"It had too many worms."

"I see. So although the budgerigar died you learnt something. There was no way of bringing it back to life, but there was something to do about the way it died."

The boy said nothing. Thought showed itself on his face, eyes clouded, brow wrinkled.

"Well," said Smithers, "what's the answer?"

"Is there something to be done about—about Mr Hamyadis, sir?"

"If I was to tap at your door late tonight," Smithers said, "when all the rest had gone to bed, would you wake up?"

"Yes sir, I wake quite easily when I'm not at home."

"Could you slip on some clothes and come with me to see something?"

"Yes sir."

A sparkle in the eyes. And a doubt.

"But, sir, what's it all for? Why have I got to see whatever it is, too? Wouldn't it do if you saw it by yourself?"

"No, it wouldn't, Peter," Smithers answered. "You see, only if you're with me can anybody be sure I didn't put the thing where I hope to find it myself. You're very important to me."

"Couldn't you tell me a bit what it is?"

"No, Peter, that's not my way. I don't guess, I wait till I know."

Smithers walked slowly down the broad stairs and ordered a whisky before dinner. He drank it alone.

When he came into the inn dining room he saw that the coach party had been put at their old communal table. He took his former place. The meal was eaten almost in silence. Afterwards the party dispersed with scarcely a word.

In each mind a question. Who? In each mind but one.

Moonlight with its soft shadows etching the cobbled inn yard. The hands of the stable clock, silver now on black, moving. Midnight.

Smithers paused in his walk along an upstairs corridor and glanced quickly up and down. He tapped sharply three times on a door and waited. After four seconds it was opened and Peter put his tousled head round.

"Shall I put some clothes on?" he said.

"Yes, slip on something warm," said Smithers, "and meet me where I saw you this afternoon."

He stood in the shadow of the potted palm. Its dry leaves rustled as his arm, back now in the worn tweed with the faint smell of chalk dust, brushed against it. When Peter came he murmured:

"Go down to the yard and wait for me just outside the door. Don't let anybody see you."

At the yard door Smithers looked carefully round before speaking again. "Follow me," he said, "and watch everything I do carefully."

He walked quietly round the edge of the yard keeping in the shadow of the building. When he got to the stable door he paused and listened carefully. No sound. He looked slowly round the yard and up at the windows of the inn giving on to it. No movement. He signed to Peter to be quiet once more and raised the latch of the door.

Then he heard a sound. A heavy creak from the coach inside the stable.

Without hurry he lowered the latch silently back into place, and walked on tip-toe into the deep shadow of a water butt at the corner of the stable. Peter followed him and they stood waiting. The coach creaked again and the light pat of a pair of feet landing on the ground came clearly to their ears.

Peter sneezed. Loudly in the still night.

From the coach house the heavy crash of a body bumping into the High Flyer. Then a slow grating squeal.

"A window," said Smithers. "Is there one in the coach house, Peter, do you remember?"

"Yes there's a little old one high up at the back."

"Come on then," said Smithers.

He ran as hard as he could. Weak flesh. Along the length of the stabling, round a corner, into a narrow alley between the inn and the shop next door.

The high buildings blotted out the moonlight and it was almost impossible to see. Smithers stopped and listened for a moment. Ahead in the darkness he heard somebody running. Running away from him. He set off in pursuit, but almost at once he knew he was outpaced. His heart was pounding, his head ached, his legs rebelled.

He stopped. Peter panting caught up with him, ran on.

"Stop," shouted Smithers.

The boy paused.

"Can't I?" he said.

"Here," Smithers said, "follow me and don't speak."

He walked out into the street and stopped.

"Whoever that was," he said, "may well have been responsible for killing Mr Hamyadis. Did you see them at all?"

"No," said Peter.

One syllable. An essay.

"Then let's hope they didn't see us."

"Mr Smithers I couldn't help sneezing then. I didn't know I was going to, honestly."

"Perhaps it was a good thing," Smithers said. "I'm going back to the coach now, to look round."

"Can't you tell me what it is we're looking for, sir?"

"Can I? No, I don't think so. Wait and see. We do at least have reason to believe there's something there to find, don't we?"

"Gosh, yes," said the boy.

Adventure. The pages of a comic paper happening.

Again the scrutiny of the inn yard, the lifted latch. And this time, nothing, silence. Smithers and Peter slipped into the dark coach house. The odour of confined air and cutting into it a draught from the opened window. Smithers took the small torch from his pocket and cautiously flashed it round the shed. Cobwebs, dust.

The new paint of the High Flyer gleamed in the thin ray of pallid light. Smithers hoisted himself up on to its roof and stooping to avoid the beams of the stable roof pulled Peter up beside him. At once the boy said:

"Somebody's been pulling the cushions off the back seat."

"There's a cavity there," Smithers said. "Hold the torch."

He thrust his hand into a deep hole at the back of the seat, normally covered by the shiny black leather cushion. Grunting slightly with the effort he moved his outstretched fingers along the whole breadth of the coach. When he got to the far end he gave a sharp "Ah" of satisfaction.

And then heard the latch on the door of the coach house lift. Peter at once put out the torch. They stood exactly as they had been when the noise came to their ears. Statue still. Smithers leaning forward his hand still thrust deep into the recess: Peter crouching, the torch pointing to the spot where Smithers would withdraw his find.

As the door slowly opened Smithers felt the draught from the opened window gather strength. A stealthy footstep. A slight jar of the coach as it was lightly brushed against.

Smithers felt he could hold his breath no longer. He breathed slowly and silently in through his nose. The cold night air from the window. And something else. Something new.

Then he too sneezed.

The cold air.

The door was flung open and rapid running steps pounded across the cobbled yard. Smithers pushed Peter aside, scrambled anyhow off the coach, flung himself towards the open door.

In the soft moonlight the empty inn yard. Cobbles sleeping. Smithers stood looking at the scene.

Peter joined him.

"Well," Smithers said, "did you smell it?"

"Smell?" said the boy.

"Yes," Smithers said. "And now I know what it was. A woman's scent."

"Then was it Kristen Kett?" said Peter. "Or Miss Miller?"

A difference between the two names. A judgement.

"I find it hard to believe it was neither of them," Smithers said. "And what did you think about the first lot of footsteps? Were they a woman's?"

"No, sir."

"I didn't think so either. Very odd."

"And please sir, you did find something behind the coach seat, didn't you? Can you tell me what it was now?"

"Yes, it was just what I expected. Look."

He held his open palm out towards the boy. Plainly to be seen in the moonlight a small automatic. Clamped round the end of the barrel the awkward shape of a silencer.

SIX

"A gun," said the boy. "Was that what you expected to find all the time? Did you expect it to be where it was?"

"One at a time. One at a time. I did expect to find this pistol, yes. And I guessed it must be somewhere near where it turned out to be."

"But what does it mean, sir?"

"It means for one thing, my lad, that you had nothing at all to do with this business. You see, Mr Hamyadis wasn't killed with the Durs Egg pistol. If anybody had wanted to kill him that way they would have been extremely stupid to have relied on you aiming correctly. As a matter of fact I half thought I had seen you jerk at the trigger like a nervous colt."

"I was a bit afraid of the bang," Peter said. "I've never shot with anything before. Is it wrong to jerk?"

"Yes," Smithers said. "You'll have to learn to release the trigger with a gentle squeeze, so that the weapon doesn't move the slightest bit."

"I don't think I ever want to learn."

"Now don't be silly." A gust of irritation. "You can't shut your eyes to things like that. There's a great deal of pleasure to be got out of shooting if you get the chance. Guns will continue to exist whatever you feel about them, so you might as well make use of them in a proper way."

"Sir, why did you say that last bit, about in a proper way?"

"Because somebody has just made use of this little gun in my hand in a most improper way. The piece on the end is a silencer. It doesn't make the pistol completely noiseless, but it does reduce the sound. So if it was fired at the moment you loosed off your noisy weapon, nobody would notice. And this little thing, used skilfully, could be pretty accurate at a short range."

"Please sir, did somebody on the coach fire it at Mr Hamyadis then?"

"I don't think there can be any doubt about that now, Peter."

"And why was the gun with the silencer hidden on the coach?"

"Because the person wanted to get rid of it before the police found out that the Durs Egg pistol had nothing to do with it. Pretending that Mr

Hamyadis was shot by you gave them perhaps twenty-four hours to get rid of the real weapon."

"But why did they need all that long? Couldn't they have just thrown it away?"

"When? Just think what happened. We were all on the coach together until the police arrived and after that we were being watched all the time."

"Sir . . ."

A doubt.

"Sir, Mr Schlemberger wasn't."

"No, that's quite true. He wasn't. That's very good, Peter. Though as a matter of fact I had remembered that Mr Schlemberger walked over to the motor coaches, but you know Mr Wemyss watched him every inch of the way."

"I'm glad about that, sir. Mr Schlemberger's a bit funny, but he's nice."

"And I'm afraid that's got nothing to do with it now. One of the people on the coach shot Mr Hamyadis, and though they may be nice about everything else we can't be sure they didn't have a secret. A secret which made it important to them to kill."

They walked in silence across the moon soaked cobbles.

"Did— And did the person mean to come back to the coach tonight and steal the pistol so that they could hide it, say in the river?" asked the boy.

"Yes, that's exactly it. By tomorrow the police will know what sort of a bullet killed Mr Hamyadis. Then they'll start making inquiries about the gun, and unless I'm very much mistaken they'll find that the automatic with the silencer on that Mr Hamyadis slept with under his pillow every night is missing."

"The Kett told everybody about it," said Peter.

"The Kett?"

A teaspoonful of reproof, quickly administered.

"That's what Dad calls her, sir."

"Well, when you speak of her to me, it's Miss Kett."

"Yes sir, but she did tell everybody, didn't she?"

"She did."

"Sir, what about fingerprints, sir?"

"Good boy. And have you noticed how careful I've been not to handle the pistol too much? The police will find a few of my prints on it, and they may find some others. But you know we were all wearing our costume gloves, so I'd be very surprised if they got anywhere on those lines. All the same I'll put this nasty little weapon very carefully among my handkerchiefs so that the least mark will be preserved. And now, my boy, isn't it time you slipped back into bed? Will you sleep all right?"

"Yes, I will, sir. I was worrying about what I thought I'd done, you know. But I'll be all right now. I'm sorry I sneezed though."

"We each did. It was chilly out."

They climbed the stairs together.

When they got to the boy's door Peter whispered:

"Sir, couldn't somebody have seen the automatic as it was fired?"

"Remember the big cuffs on our costumes. And everybody was looking at the highwayman. Now, off to bed."

"Yes, sir. And thank you, sir."

The door quickly closed.

Smithers walked along the uneven corridor of the ancient inn to his own bedroom. Slow steps.

He entered and locked the door carefully. Then opened the drawer of the rickety dressing table where he had put his handkerchiefs when for the second time he had unpacked in this room. Gently he laid the silenced automatic inside. He undressed slowly. His mind elsewhere.

In bed he lay still, deep in thought while the stable clock strruck quarters and hours. Across the wide oak floorboards of the room a swathe of moonlight from the open window moved as easily as the hands of the clock. When it reached the corner of the bed Smithers slept.

He woke suddenly. The moonlight had almost left the room. A shaft, finger thick only, lay obliquely. Smithers felt every muscle tense.

A noise, slight, unaccountable, alien. What might have been a low snore, ending in a gentle thump.

Smithers checked an instinct to call out. He peered with desperate concentration in the direction he thought the sound had come from. But it was too dark to see anything. Too dark even to be sure from which part of the strange room the noise had come.

Suddenly the finger of moonlight switched off, on. In the darkness Smithers thought of some cosmic mechanism.

An effort of will. A burst of futile anger at the sleepy brain.

A cloud? A momentary mental black-out?

Silently, fiercely, ears still straining, he worried at the mystery.

Then he knew. Something, someone had passed between himself and the moon. Was standing now beside the open window. Had come from the dressing table.

He sprang out of bed, eyes fixed in the direction of the suddenly located window. Against the faint lightness of the part outside the moon's beam he could half see a figure. Dim, unidentifiable, there.

Arms outstretched without a sound he ran towards it. It disappeared through the window. Smithers banged against the sill, thrust out his head. In the full light of the moon was blinded.

For a moment. For three seconds while his ears detected a hurried scuffling. Then he was able to see. In front of him ran a wide roof, scarcely sloping. He looked along it either way. Nobody. Nothing.

He scrambled over the low window ledge and stood balancing without difficulty on the tiles. To his left he heard quick footsteps on boards. He ran in their direction. Six yards. And found himself standing at the wide open window of the main corridor of the inn. He stood looking into the darkness. Somewhere he thought he heard a door softly close. In triumph.

The stable clock struck four. A cold wind stirred Smithers's pyjamas. The pattern of stripes.

He walked back along the creaking boards of the corridor to his own room, turned the door knob to go in, found the door fast against him. Carefully locked by himself.

Wearily he retraced his steps. Barked shins on the corridor window. The slope of the tiles now inexplicably dangerous. His room again mysterious, looming with forgotten objects. He blundered.

The light on at last. Revealing, implacable. He crossed to the dressing table, opened the handkerchief drawer, saw the neat piles of white linen. Nothing else. He shut his eyes. Slowly he pushed the drawer in and home. The noise that might have been a slow snore ending in a gentle thump. He sat on the edge of the bed, shoulders bent, wisps of grey hair awry, naked feet cold and shrinking from the bare boards.

At seven o'clock as the stable clock struck, he telephoned the police station. He was told that Detective Inspector Parker was expected at eight and asked for an appointment.

"So," said the inspector, Nosey Parker, "so you've had a closer look at your travelling companions. What titbits have you got for me?"

"I've got a confession to make," said Smithers.

"Come, you sound so serious you might almost be going to tell me you killed Mr Hamyadis."

"And that would surprise you?" asked Smithers.

With curiosity.

"A little," the inspector answered. "We haven't so far been able to trace the remotest connection between the two of you before he wrote to you as the author of the fourteen volume *History of Travel.*"

"Well, you're right. There's no connection and I didn't kill him. But my confession is serious. I think I've aided the criminal."

"Tell me."

Smithers narrated without concealment the exact sequence of events from the moment he had realised there was someone in the coach house to the final opening of the handkerchief drawer.

"And you took the boy with you as a witness," the inspector said.

"Yes, I had thought I might be suspect, you know."

"You say you had to put out the torch just as you found the automatic?"

"The boy was holding it for me. He put it out."

"Before or after he had seen what you found?"

"Before. It came as a surprise to him when I showed it in my hand as we stood in the inn yard after the second intruder had run off. That must have been when the first person overheard me say where I was going to put the gun overnight."

"When you left the coach house for the second time, did you get any idea who it was running away?"

"No, none."

"And the boy? Did he?"

"He couldn't have done. I was out of the door several seconds in front of him."

"As I thought. So he didn't have you under continuous observation all the time?"

Smithers was silent. Then said:

"No. He didn't. But remember, I wasn't expecting to find anyone else there, much less two people. If everything had gone as I expected he would have been able to swear I had found the gun where I did."

"I see. Now about these intruders as you call them. Did the boy agree with you that there were two of them?"

"I don't remember exactly what he said about it. I became convinced of it only when I thought out how the theft from my room could have taken place."

"How much of the intruders did the boy see, would you say?"

"Very little. I was generally running in front of him."

"But you told him what you had seen?"

"Inspector," Smithers said, "it's no use me pretending that I don't know where your questions are leading. You're insinuating that I persuaded the boy these people were about so that I could make him the victim of a piece of sleight of hand. I think he has been made victim enough already."

"He certainly has," the inspector said. "I had the result of the post mortem late last night. The bullet was still in the body. It was probably fired from an automatic, certainly not from a nineteenth century pistol. But to be quite frank with you this confirmation you have produced doesn't really prove that you are not the person who played the trick on the boy in the first place."

Smithers on his feet.

"It was intended to do nothing of the sort," he said.

"All right. All right," said the inspector.

He sandwiched his enormous nose between the palms of his hands and stroked it slowly.

"Listen, Mr Smithers," he said. "I've mentioned nothing about charging you, and if I believed you had killed Hamyadis it would be my duty to do so, as I dare say you know very well. But I've said nothing, and I believe nothing. Still, I have to consider possibilities. And to my mind the possibility that you are the person I'm looking for is now much greater."

Smithers sat down.

"I suppose you're right," he said. "I came here in a humble enough state of mind. But I hadn't realised what my actions might lead you to think. Let me try and explain myself. I owe you that."

"You told me yesterday that you found it difficult to voice suspicions before you had proof," Inspector Parker said. "I imagine you will repeat that now."

"Inspector, I don't at all like your tone."

"I'm afraid this must be something new to you Mr Smithers: to be at the wrong end of the law. You're not in the ordinary category of criminals and possible criminals, so you're used to policemen as useful, friendly, helpful people. But when it's a case of murder everybody concerned has to be in the category of suspect. And policemen aren't so pleasant."

"Very well," said Smithers. "Is there anything further you want to ask me?"

"No, nothing immediately, I think."

"You know where to find me if you want me."

The hand on the door knob. Then:

"Mr Smithers, if you wanted to show me you're still on the side of the law-abiding, you could."

"I have done nothing to show you anything else."

"You have been anything but helpful."

"I'm sorry. Circumstances were too much for me."

"I wish I could believe that."

"You can, or need not, as you like. It makes no difference to the truth."

"Mr Smithers . . ."

Wheedling.

"You could prove you are on the right side."

"And how?"

"By co-operating with me. By telling me a lot of things I want to know about those people. I've seen one or two of them a second time, at some length. You may have heard. But the more I see of them the more I suspect they are concealing from me. I must break in somewhere. Won't you help?"

The door knob released.

"Certainly not," said Smithers. "If you think you can induce me to pander to an unhealthy sense of curiosity by threatening me, you have chosen the wrong person."

"All right. I can't compel you to tell me. But threats apart, your attitude puts you in a very curious light. Remember that. And now good morning."

"There's one thing, inspector."

"Yes?"

"I want you to have a word with the boy, Peter Dagg. I want to be present. I shan't say a word but I want to see what effect his answers have on you. I've a right to ask this."

"I won't conceal from you that I was going straight up to the inn to see him. But I suppose there's no reason why you shouldn't be present, with the father. But no questions, no hints, mind."

Already the sunlight on the street was warm. In silence their two shadows pointing black in front of them the two men walked along to the inn. The time was 8.17 a.m. A few inquiries by the inspector and they found that Peter was still in his room. A knock on the door. And abruptly without waiting for a reply Inspector Parker, Nosey Parker, jerked it open.

Peter Dagg was still asleep.

The inspector crossed to the bed, listened closely. Smithers smiled. Icily.

"The luck has turned my way a little," he said. "You're convinced of this, I take it."

The inspector shook the sleeping boy lightly. He woke.

"Remember me, son?"

"Nosey . . . Er—Inspector Parker."

"That's right. And never mind about mentioning the pet name: I like it. It shows I mean business. I want to ask you one or two things."

"All right."

The boy sat up in bed. Tousled, bright.

"Inspector," said Smithers, "you mentioned Mr Dagg."

"That's all right," the inspector said. "This is off the record. It won't take a minute. All I want to know is what you and Mr Smithers did last night, son."

And the boy told him. The account unvarnished, with the stamp of truth.

"Just a couple of questions," said the inspector when he had finished. "Did you recognise either of the people?"

"No, I just heard the steps and the other sounds."

"No ideas at all?"

"Honest, no. It might have been anybody, either of them."

"But you're sure the second one was a woman?"

"There was the scent. I smelt it in the coach house. You couldn't mistake it."

"If I bring you samples of scent, would you recognise it?"

"I don't know much about scents and ladies' stuff, but I think I would."

"And you, Mr Smithers?"

"I make the same answer."

"Very well, will you both come down to the station at, say, ten o'clock. You'll be wanting some breakfast, lad."

"Gosh, yes," said Peter. "I'm hungry."

"All right, we'll have to start looking for this gun," the inspector said to Smithers.

He grinned at Peter.

"And one last thing, don't talk about this to anybody."

Breakfast. The coach party all seemed to be late risers. When Smithers entered the dining room he found they had scarcely started. And still nobody speaking.

"Ah, there you are, boy," said Joe Dagg. "Perhaps you and I can have a bit of a barney. I passed a few remarks earlier on about the weather, state of the roads and such like, but I didn't have the luck to meet with much in the way of replies."

Peter, who plainly could think of nothing else but the forbidden subject of the night's adventure, had nothing to say.

"Lord, you gone silent, too?" said his father. "I suppose it's all along of old Hammy. But I can't understand it, straight I can't. I didn't think any of you much cared for him when he was amongst us, as they say, so I don't see what you want all to go clamming up when he ain't amongst us any more."

Smithers sat down with an air of resolution.

"You don't think the way he ceased to be amongst us might have put people on their guard, then?" he said.

"On their guard?"

Light suddenly.

"You mean it being a police job."

A glance over the shoulder.

"Tell you the truth, I'd forgotten all about it. When it ain't something to do with horses, commander, I wander off like."

"It shows how clear your conscience must be at any rate," Smithers said.

Stones in the wall crack. Round the table a stir, a rustle.

"Conscience?" said Dagg. "That's clear enough. And now I suppose all them coppers are going around saying, 'How can we pin it on old Joe?' The lousy bastards."

No joke.

"I'm sorry they aren't here to hear you," Smithers said. "You may not be showing a very high opinion of them, but you are at least manifesting your innocence."

"I suppose you think that going around shouting 'I didn't do it' is enough?" Richard Wemyss said. "I suppose you think that anybody who has the sense to keep his mouth shut is a murderer?"

Loud. Ringing. Not to be avoided. The breach in the wall.

"I simply wonder what there is to keep one's mouth shut about," said Smithers.

"I guess it's important for me, as an American national, not to get involved in a purely British affair," Schlemberger said.

"Very natural," said Smithers.

"If it is a purely British affair," Wemyss said.

"It took place on British soil," said Schlemberger.

"But at least one American national was in a position to do the killing."

Schlemberger laughed.

"I only met the guy two days ago," he said.

"But he had spent a long time in America," Wemyss answered. "What did he do when he was over there? I should like to know. Who did he meet?"

"Now listen——"

But Smithers interrupted.

"Mr Wemyss has put a pertinent question," he said. "It must have surely been something in Mr Hamyadis's past that gave rise to his death. What do we know of that past?"

"I don't think you're right," said Kristen Kett. "I don't see why anybody has to go into his past at all."

"Don't you?" said Wemyss.

"Oh, Richie, don't be silly. We none of us much liked Georgie, but it's obvious one of us is going to be arrested for shooting him. I don't want to make accusations, but I don't think the police are going to have to look far, not once they hear what went on on the coach ride."

"I may be a simple old soldier," Major Mortenson said, "but I see where these remarks are leading. And let me tell you, I'm perfectly willing for the police to know everything that went on during the trip. Hamyadis behaved like a pig towards me, because he knew I needed his filthy money, but even if the police, stupid as they are, believe that that's a ground for murder, thank goodness we still have juries in this country. You can't persuade a jury to convict unless there's a pretty good case."

"That's what frightens me," said Daisy Miller. "The thought that, if it does come to light, there is a perfectly good case against one of the people sitting round this table. I can't believe it, yet it must be true."

"I'm afraid the solution is that one of us is mad," said John Fremitt. "No doubt the police will investigate both the distant past and the immediate past, but I don't see that either will necessarily help them. One of us has lost all moral bearings."

"You may be right," said Smithers, "but I'm inclined to think it's too easy to assume every murder is committed by a madman. We take to that view only because killing on an individual scale has become a comparatively rare thing. In the days when it was dangerous to go unarmed on a long journey people thought of taking life as no more than an extension of taking purses. People, sane people, do have reasons for killing, and sometimes act on them."

"You're quite right, dear," said Daisy. "Madness is something quite different from killing somebody because they stand in your way."

"Excuse me, madam."

The inn head waiter, old, dignified, shop soiled.

"Excuse me, madam, your call is through. Would you care to take it in the office?"

Daisy jumped up, took two steps from the table, returned for her handbag, thanked the major for handing it to her, thanked the head waiter, hurried half-way across the room, stopped, turned round and said:

"I am so sorry. A special call. I won't be a minute. Or perhaps really I'll probably be rather a long time."

She hurried out. The head waiter followed, stooping.

There was a moment's silence. A moment for the review of thoughts, of possibly careless speech. It might have become a clammy fog of reticence again only Joe Dagg said:

"Here, I think I've been a bloody fool about all this."

"I suppose you're going to tell us that you shot Hamyadis in a fit of absentmindedness," Wemyss said.

"Now then."

Joe Dagg whipped round, thrust his burly shoulders across the table, glared at Wemyss.

"You've no call to go saying things like that, lieutenant."

A shout, a frightened shout.

"Perhaps I got a bit too near the truth," Wemyss said.

Joe jumped to his feet.

"Richie, Richie, say you didn't mean it," Kristen Kett said. "Don't let's have a row, for heaven's sake. I've got a head like nobody's business this morning. I can't stand shouting."

They looked at her. She was pale, strained. Under the eyes heavy circles.

"Are you sure you wouldn't be better off back in bed?" asked Fremitt. "I'm sure there's no need to be up, the police will understand."

"What, go up to bed and not know a blind thing about what's going on down here?" Kristen said. "My nerves aren't made of steel. I'd go crackers."

Then a check, a gleam.

"But you're quite right," she said smiling at Fremitt. "I would like to be in bed. I feel just awful."

The schoolgirl, defenceless.

"You wouldn't do me a favour?" she asked.

"Certainly, certainly," Fremitt said.

"Miss Kett," Smithers said, "I don't think you need worry about anything happening, as you call it, down here. The police are scarcely likely to do anything spectacular."

She ignored him, turned to Fremitt with eagerness.

"I knew you'd help me," she said. "You look somehow just like my old dad, bless him."

She got slowly to her feet and began walking out of the room, each foot put down carefully, with effort.

Fremitt got up, hurried to the door.

"You didn't mention what the favour was to be," he said.

"Oh, didn't I? Just to let me know if anything does happen," she said. "Come up and give a little tap to my door. I shan't lock it, and I won't be asleep, just resting."

"But, I'm not sure . . ."

"Please," she said, "then I'll be able to rest."

"Well, as Mr Smithers said, it's extremely unlikely that anything will take place, but if it should I'll see that you get to hear of it," Fremitt said.

"Oh thank you. I knew you would."

Kristen Kett closed the door.

"So it's unlikely that there'll be an arrest today?" said Schlemberger. "I kind of hoped this whole business would be settled before the conference began."

"I know very little about it," Smithers said. "But from what one reads in the newspapers it always seems to me that, unless the murderer gives himself away by the very act of killing, it is almost bound to be some considerable time before the police can eliminate all the possibilities."

"Well, what have they done up to now?" Schlemberger asked. "Of course, I scarcely count in this business, except as a possible witness of some detail or other, but certainly I haven't experienced anything approaching a headquarters grilling."

"That sounds very ominous," Fremitt said.

"So you haven't had any? Has anybody?"

No one owned up.

"I don't want to seem heartless," Schlemberger said. "But it's a matter of some considerable commercial importance that my society's annual conference should go smoothly, especially on the first occasion it's been held outside the boundaries of the United States. Are the police going to do anything?"

"It's quite likely they won't," said the major. "At least, all they will do is to harass us as much as they think they can. That's officialdom for you, everywhere. I dare say it would happen in America just the same as here."

"I don't know about that," Schlemberger said. "But if what you say about police procedure over here is correct, I reckon I'd like to ask a few questions around this table, here and now."

"Questions? What about?" said Joe Dagg. "We don't want prying into people's private lives. What they've done in the past is their own affair."

He eased back his chair, glanced at the door, the windows.

"I can't agree," said Schlemberger. "I'd like a full account from each one of you of your complete antecedents. Then we can see for ourselves who is likely to have met up with this Hamyadis earlier on."

"Listen, wing commander," said Joe. "I think we're all going to have enough on our plates with those ruddy cops, without you beginning. You can count me out."

He marched across the room and left. On the stairs heavy feet thundering.

"You only put yourself in the wrong by not co-operating," said Schlemberger. "But in any case I guess his kid can tell us most of what we want to know. It'd make as good a starting point as any."

"Mr Schlemberger," Smithers said, "I think I may have misled you about the efficiency of our police. Personally I have little doubt that Inspector Parker, an extremely intelligent man, whatever else one might say, will see this business through with the maximum despatch and the minimum awkwardness."

"I'm certainly glad to have you say that," Schlemberger said, "But we all doubtless have our contributions to make. Now, Peter, when did your pop first meet Hamyadis. Can you tell us that?"

Peter looked at his plate, said nothing.

"You don't know?"

No answer.

"Look, don't get me wrong, kid. I'm not trying to put anything on your old man. I only began with him because I reckon he's the least likely. Now then, how about coming across?"

No reply.

Wemyss laughed.

"I think the boy has given us all a lead," he said. "After all only one of us has got anything to worry about, why should we all submit to this rather humiliating business? I worried quite enough about my interview with Inspector Parker last night. I hardly slept at all. You can see from my face, it's all strained, and I got a rotten shave this morning. I couldn't concentrate. Well, now I've had enough. I'm going up to change into some more respectable clothes."

Schlemberger looked at his retreating back with a puzzled frown.

"I think he had not met Hamyadis until the night before your arrival," said Smithers.

"It's easy to say that," Schlemberger answered, "but I'd like to know if he had any possible contacts with him. Hamyadis had theatrical interests, didn't he? That guy's an actor."

"On the other hand, Mr Hamyadis seemed surprised to hear that," Fremitt said.

"Then has he ever been to the States? There's a possible link there. Hamyadis was over there a good many years, I understand."

"If you're counting American visits as a suspicious circumstance," the major said, "I've never crossed the Atlantic in my life, and I first heard of Hamyadis when he wrote and asked me to join this trip in a professional capacity."

Schlemberger looked from Smithers to Fremitt.

"Either of you two gentlemen care to co-operate?" he asked.

"I confess to visiting America," Fremitt said. "Or at least confess is scarcely the word."

"And I have not been to America," Smithers said. "But you may well be right about its importance in this business. It's a part of Hamyadis's life that is unlikely to be much known about."

The door opened and Daisy Miller came in.

"Hello," she said, "breakfast over already?"

"I think the coffee's still hot," Smithers said.

"Oh no, I didn't want any, thank you. I just looked in to apologise for leaving you all in such a hurry. It was a call to my agent in London. It doesn't do to miss things, you know, whatever's happening."

"We were just discussing the past activities of our friend Hamyadis," said Schlemberger. "Do you happen to know what he did while he was in the States?"

"He was in night clubs, I think," Daisy said. "But I didn't meet him till after he'd left. Or, I think that was it. With people you just keep bumping into you don't remember when you first bumped. I get so vague about dates and things, but I think he came over here when prohibition ended, if it did end."

"So he was in the States back in those days," said Schlemberger. "Well, that's news to me. That certainly is news to me."

The didactic, informative, irritating voice.

"And you," he went on turning to Daisy again, "were you in the States in the prohibition days?"

"I think I was," Daisy said. "There was something about sandwiches with your drink, or is that over here? But I was only in the States—such a nice way of putting it—for a few days. The show was a terrible flop."

"Then you didn't have any dealings with Hamyadis?" said Schlemberger.

"I had scarcely any dealings with the States at all, any of them," Daisy said.

The head waiter came in.

"And when did you first meet Hamyadis exactly?" Schlemberger asked Daisy.

"Mr Schlemberger," she said, "I do believe you're questioning me. I'm afraid I didn't do it, you know. I didn't understand all that business about the pistols."

"Excuse me, madam," said the head waiter, "can I get you some more coffee?"

"No, no thank you," Daisy said. "I wasn't having breakfast. I was having some fourth degree. Or is it third?"

"Indeed, madam."

The professional deaf ear.

"I trust your call went satisfactorily?"

The bland attention.

"Very well, thank you," Daisy answered.

The old man blushed prettily, unexpected rose on the parchment cheeks.

"I've never had the pleasure of putting a call through to America before."

SEVEN

"Now, you know," said Daisy.

She looked at them each in turn.

First Schlemberger. The cat not sure that it wants the mouse after all. "I guess you owe us some kind of explanation, I don't know," he said.

Second Fremitt. The chance light shows the red apple is rotten. "I must admit there is some discrepancy, or at least perhaps I should say there seems to be."

Third the major. The pure shock of suddenly finding in the hands a football, a lampshade, a large cardboard box, empty. "I don't know what to make of it. Varium et mutabile semper femina."

Fourth Smithers. The honest boy caught cheating, the annual event. "You chose not to tell us the truth," he said. "You had every right."

Fifth Peter. The stage hand finds the curtain has gone up. "Has something happened?" he said. "I wasn't sort of listening."

"Yes, something's happened, dear," said Daisy. "I've been caught out telling a rather silly lie. Did you know grown-ups did that?"

"I did in a way," said Peter. "There are some things Dad has to——"

He jumped suddenly off his chair and scuttled from the room.

"When I first took to schoolmastering I made the mistake of pretending to boys that adults didn't behave like children," said Smithers.

"I'm sorry," Schlemberger said. "I guess a naturally suspicious turn of mind will come out. It's a question of what you might call a professional disability. I'm sure my British colleague here will back me up in saying that in our walk of life it's one hundred per cent necessary to cultivate all those aspects of the human mind which lead us to see into the actions of others motives which they themselves may not even be aware of."

"I think," Daisy said, "that I'd better tell you all something."

"Are you sure?" said Smithers.

"Well, I'd like to keep my secret, but, you know, I can't. It's just to tell you that I was over in America for rather longer than I said. The show didn't flop, and something personal kept me over there afterwards as well. That thing isn't finished yet, and it's what I was ringing up about. And that's all I'm going to tell you, except to say that in a way it could have been something to do with poor old George, and you'll just have to believe me when I say that it wasn't."

She left.

"You were all for finding out the truth," said the major. "Well, it begins to look to me as if Miss Miller might have known Hamyadis in America. She seemed to protest too much about how little she knew him, even at the time. Now you have found out that much perhaps you begin to see the advantages of leaving all this business to the police. There's a reasonable chance that they'll discover nothing."

"Or, as I prefer to put it," Smithers said, "they are in a position to test the truth of surmises such as we have just been making. As likely as not we are reading too much into reticences and turns of phrase that mean nothing."

"You think the police will be able to judge better than us, do you?" said the major. "I'd be ready to bet on the opposite. But perhaps that's a good thing. By far the best outcome of this matter would be a trial with the defendant found clearly not guilty."

"No," said Schlemberger. "Major, you're an independent man, but there are others of us who have business reputations. It's scarcely right that they should be prejudiced perhaps for all time by a purely transient circumstance."

"Some of the people who could have done this murder are not the sort of person I would choose to spend a holiday with," said the major, "but none of them is the sort of person I would choose to see hanged. The least one can do is to take a small share of suspicion so that no one takes a full share of the blame, as likely as not unjustly."

He left.

Schlemberger shrugged.

"I guess there are occasions when a little personal speaking is an excellent thing," he said. "I'm going to say right now that we must none of us forget that Major Mortenson suffered at the hands of that man Hamyadis."

"Come," said Fremitt, "you must have summed up the major by now. He's a failure. Intelligent as you like, but lacking that necessary stamina. And he's turned a little bitter. We must try to excuse him his outbursts."

An exit line. The door closing. An apologetic half smile, the door closed.

"Mr Smithers," said Schlemberger, "there's something I want to say to you. You're a man whose opinions I have a very high respect for. Of course, in many ways you're a typical Britisher, and you might not expect me to share a great deal with you. But I reckon I can tell what a man is like no matter what dress he wears and no matter what customs he has. Sir, I'd highly value your opinion on a certain theory I have conceived as regards this crime."

"A theory, Mr Schlemberger?" said Smithers.

"Yes, sir. A theory. I don't deceive myself into thinking I've solved this case. There are plenty of loose ends your British policemen will have to tie up, but I've been giving the matter a lot of quiet thought and I'd like you to put the final okay on it."

"And that," said Smithers, "I'm afraid I'm entirely incompetent to do. I feel perhaps I ought to tell you that in ten minutes' time I have an appointment at the police station with Inspector Parker."

He got up from the table. And like Richard Wemyss, like Daisy Miller, like Major Mortenson, like John Fremitt he left.

Without hesitation he climbed the stairs and made for the alcove with the retired armchair and the neglected potted palm. Peter Dagg was sitting there where he had expected to find him.

"Nearly ten," he said. "Are you ready?"

"All right," said Peter.

Neither spoke while they left the inn and turned into the street patterned with bright sunshine. It was only when they had to wait to cross a road that Smithers said:

"You know that what we tell the inspector now will not necessarily mean anything, however it may look to us?"

"I was hoping the scent wouldn't be Miss Miller's," said Peter.

"Even if it is," Smithers said, "the worst we can do is to put Inspector Parker on a right track."

"But, sir," said Peter, "whatever the inspector's right track is, it does mean somebody——"

"It does, Peter," Smithers said. "And it's no use pretending anything else. That's the law, and without it we'd be in a pretty mess."

"Sir, what would happen if it turned out to be the man we heard and nothing to do with the scent. And if that man was—was . . . Well, was somebody."

"Look at it this way, Peter," said Smithers. "If a person is someone we respect very much, we wouldn't believe he would be a murderer, would we? And if he was, in spite of everything, he wouldn't be the person we thought."

Peter did not answer, and they walked into the police station without another word.

As soon as they arrived they were shown in to Inspector Parker.

"Well," he said, "I've managed to find out what scent the two ladies use. In fact I've found out quite a bit about what's popular in that line at the moment, quite a bit."

He gave a sharp sniff and wriggled the tip of his huge nose. Another morsel.

From a drawer in the little desk he sat at he took two buff envelopes and laid them in front of him.

"One moment," he said. "We'd better have a record of your replies."

He jumped up and went out. Smithers sat looking at the desk, barer than when he had last been in this office. The two buff envelopes lay all alone on a folded sheet of pink blotting paper. Smithers saw in clear minute writing a set of initials on each—K.K. and D.M.

"Peter," he said, "look out of the window for me, would you, and see if you can spot a clock? I'm not sure my watch is right."

Peter went towards the window. The door opened and the inspector came in followed by a constable.

"There isn't a clock," said Peter at the window.

"Never mind," Smithers said. "I've an idea we arrived at exactly the time we were expected."

"You did," said Inspector Parker. "On the dot of ten."

He picked up the envelope marked K.K. and brought the great nose down on to it. A sniff.

"Strong stuff this one," he said. "It filters through the paper."

From the envelope he took a small white card, perfectly plain except for the number 1 typed on it.

"Now then, lad," he said. "Have a smell of this and don't say a word."

Peter smelt it. A flicker in his eyes. The inspector passed the card to Smithers without speaking. Smithers smelled at it.

"All right," he said.

The inspector took up the second envelope. Again the nose swooped.

"I think I detect the characteristic odour of unused stationery," he said.

He extracted the card with care. It was exactly similar to the other except for the typewritten number 2. Peter smelt it. A quick frown. He smelt again.

"Okay," he said.

Uneasily.

Smithers smelt. Once.

"You want my verdict?" he asked.

"You're quite happy about it?" said Inspector Parker, Nosey Parker.

"Perfectly."

"Very well then."

"If there is any difference between the two samples I fail to detect it," said Smithers.

Peter's eyes lit up.

"Are they the same?" he asked. "I thought they were."

"What about the scent you say you smelt in the coach house?" said the inspector.

"As far as I can judge it's the same," said Smithers.

"I thought it was as soon as I smelt the first card," said Peter.

"You're quite right, lad," the inspector said. "I had it reported to me that both ladies favour the same scent. It's the season's latest, so they tell me, strongish—if that's the word—and highly characteristic."

"And which were you expecting us to pick as the one we knew?" Smithers said.

"Expecting?"

"Don't let us misunderstand each other, inspector. Was it K.K. or D.M.?"

"There you are," said Inspector Parker.

For the nose a tap with the tip of the right forefinger.

"There you are, Mr Smithers, you haven't learnt yet. I'm not here to help you over the unpleasant business of the boot boy who pinched the half-crown postal order. This is a matter of murder. I can't treat anybody like a gentleman."

"Very well," said Smithers, "if no holds are to be barred let me ask you a question which puts you plainly in an embarrassing position. Do you believe I'm a liar?"

"If I did I wouldn't give you the satisfaction of knowing," said the inspector.

"Let's put it another way, then," said Smithers. "Will you set a guard on the coach tonight?"

"Now why should I?" asked the inspector. "If the automatic was there, it's gone now. If it wasn't there, there's nothing I can do about it."

"Very well," Smithers said. "Come along, Peter."

On the police station steps Peter asked:

"Why did you ask him to guard the coach again tonight? The gun has gone."

"Can't you think why?" Smithers said.

The boy looked puzzled.

"No," he said.

"Well, you can't be expected to work out everything," Smithers said, "though the inspector should have thought of this."

"Is it fingerprints?" asked Peter.

"No," Smithers said. "The coach would have a fair sample of all our prints anyway. No doubt Mr Parker knows that."

"Then what is it he hasn't thought of?"

"Simply that two separate raids on the coach mean two separate things hidden on it, my boy."

"The pistol was one, and—— Is there some money or something there too?"

"I wouldn't say this to everyone," Smithers answered. "You know I don't like to claim things are true until I've more than a guess to go on. But it seems to me pretty likely that there is something hidden there. I don't think it will be money, but I don't know what else it might be. We shall just have to see."

"Does that mean another watch tonight?" Peter said.

"We shall have to try and be a little cleverer this time."

"Please sir, are you sure you want me?"

Smithers stopped in the sunlit street.

"So that problem is still worrying you," he said. "You know I think it would be best to find out one way or the other as soon as possible, don't you?"

"I suppose so, sir."

"But that doesn't make it any easier, does it? We'll see how you feel when I come and call you tonight."

"I think I will come, sir. I'll try to."

After Peter had left him Smithers strolled round the ancient inn. He noticed that the little window looking out on to the alley from the coach house was now tight shut again.

The rest of the morning Smithers spent sitting on a dilapidated bench in the inn yard. He read 74 pages of Volume 3 of Gibbon's *Decline and Fall*. Never once did his eyes rest on the door of the coach house.

When he heard the lunch gong he went slowly indoors. He found a full table. Mealtimes the prisoner's solace.

"You've heard about Hamyadis's automatic?" Fremitt asked.

"I have," said Smithers.

"Do tell us you couldn't have taken it from his cases in the hall," Daisy said. "All the rest of us could have done, and it would be nice to have somebody really innocent."

"Is that what the police think happened?" Smithers asked.

"That's it," said Schlemberger. "Those cases were there for all to see. And in the very early morning after Hamyadis left any one of us could have gotten at them."

"I could have done," said Smithers.

"Oh dear," said Daisy. "Well, come and join the suspects round the table. At least the food's good."

"I don't see how anyone can eat it," said Kristen Kett.

She took some soup. But nothing else.

"Won't you try just some of these vegetables?" Fremitt said. "I can only suppose they come from the hotel garden. Deliciously fresh."

"I would if I could," said Kristen. "But really I feel lousy."

"I know what it is," Joe Dagg said. "I've been doing a bit of thinking during the morning. You can't eat after that."

His plate untouched. The nervous eyes.

"I don't know that you're right there," Schlemberger said. "I have also devoted the morning to re-appraising the situation."

For the second time the serving spoon dug into the piled potatoes.

"It's a curious thing," Major Mortenson said. "This business seems to be having the same effect on me as on our American friend. I'm going to have some more of that excellent salad. Carpe diem."

"Don't you think," Richard Wemyss said, "that we could try to forget about this business? I've been doing so all morning, and with excellent results. I too feel hungry."

"Do you Richie, dear?" said Kristen. "I'm so glad. Mr Fremitt— No, I'm going to call you John—John, pass Richie the potatoes."

"No, no potatoes, thank you," said Wemyss. "I like to be able to wear what clothes I've got. But I will have a little more tongue."

Schlemberger passed him the dish.

"Help yourself, Mr Wemyss," he said. "Eat up. You may not always feel so hungry."

"Oh, I generally have a pretty good appetite," Wemyss said. "I'm careful not to worry. People don't pay enough attention to that. If you force yourself to stop worrying, you eat well, feel better, and look respectable. I sometimes think it should be made an offence to go around looking haggard."

"Now there I cannot agree," Schlemberger said.

He moved his chair three inches away from the table, leaned back in it and looked round the group.

"Worry," he said, "is the driving force behind all success. Nobody ever got anywhere without worry. And the ones who don't worry get to thinking about things they have no business to. They get to start dreaming about sex and stuff. And you know what that leads to."

The overlong pause.

"Sex, when it gets out of hand," said Schlemberger, "leads as often as not to crime. Now I've been doing a little worrying this morning. I've been worrying about my conference. I've been worrying because the death of George Hamyadis is interfering with my business. And in spite of what my young friend here says, I think my worrying has been to some purpose."

The drip, drip, drip of a tap. Nerves stretch.

Kristen—the edge of the table gripped.

Daisy—an unnatural stillness.

Joe Dagg—the chair shifted, once, twice, three times.

John Fremitt—a remark poised, withheld, poised.

The major—food gobbled, eyes elsewhere.

Wemyss—a dull flush mounting the cheeks.

Smithers—a tautening of the facial muscles, a contraction of the eyebrows, a soft, slow drumming with the index finger of the left hand.

"What lies behind all crimes of murder?" asked Schlemberger. "Three things: the love of money, the love of power, the love of woman. Now, in this case I think we can take it that none of the people in a position to kill Hamyadis is likely to benefit under his will. Nor is any one of them likely to gain power by his death. So we come to woman. Now we can't know the details of people's private lives. We can't know who has deceived whom. But there's one thing plain. . . ."

The pause, overlong again.

"We can't blink the facts as put before us. George Hamyadis was during his last days plainly attracted to one member of our party. And that member was as plainly attractive to one other person. It only needs a little worrying over. Doesn't it, Mr Wemyss?"

Wemyss stood up.

"How dare you," he said, "how dare you go prying with your nasty little mind into my private life? What right have you to assume . . . ?"

An unwillingness to express the idea.

"I suggest you leave it at that, Wemyss," said Smithers. "I've some sympathy with your attitude, but I think the less said now the better. Mr Schlemberger, I take it you have stated your case to the full, you've nothing more concrete that you could have added?"

"It's merely the logic of the situation," said Schlemberger.

An excuse. A feeble umbrella.

"And that logic," said Major Mortenson, "is wrong."

Said loudly, unexpectedly, with conviction.

"What's more," the major went on, "I can prove it. I will prove it straight away. Would you ladies and gentlemen do me the favour of accompanying me to the coach house and helping me pull the coach out into the light of day."

"What are you going to do?" asked Kristen Kett.

"I want to demonstrate exactly where the murderer was standing when the shot was fired," the major said.

"The murderer?" said Schlemberger. "Do you know who the murderer was?"

"You'll come to understand when you see what I am going to do," said the major. "Quod erat demonstrandum."

"That's scarcely good enough," Schlemberger said. "If you know——"

"For heaven's sake, you'll find out in a minute or two," said Kristen. "Stop arguing."

She pushed aside her chair and walked to the door. The others followed. The major led them outside and across the cobbled inn yard. They followed in straggling silence. Schlemberger two paces behind, head moving from side to side. Watchful. Ready for the fast one.

Under the major's instructions they hauled out the coach.

Smithers went and stood beside Schlemberger. Two watchers.

The major asked them to seat themselves as they had done on the day of the shooting. Without talking they did so.

"It all began," the major said, "just before the liner docked. I wonder now if any of you noticed it."

"Now he's going to tell a story," Kristen said. "Can't you get on with it?"

"You none of you noticed it?" the major said. "And I worried whether I had given myself away."

A silence. Something momentous not taken in.

"Are—are you telling us you killed Hamyadis?" Wemyss said.

"My dear chap," Smithers said, "hasn't the point of this meeting been plain to you from the start? We're waiting to know why Major Mortenson has chosen this way of making his confession."

"Well," Daisy said, "I'm sure it wasn't clear to me. In fact I'm not sure it's clear now."

"Mr Smithers is quite right," the major said. "From the moment I saw George Hamyadis without a beard that morning I knew I was going to kill him. I'm only surprised it wasn't written all over my face."

"I'm still not sure that I believe all this," Daisy said. "It doesn't seem the sort of thing that happens, a confession like this. Why were you so sure you were going to kill George?"

"Because I recognised him as the man who, under another name, had taken every penny I had ever owned off me at a sort of club in the West End," said the major. "And when I say every penny I ever had I mean quite a tidy sum. My father had died a year or so before and I was a moderately wealthy young man."

"But why did you want to kill him now? Why didn't you kill him at the time? And why kill him at all? Winning at cards isn't all that terrible," Daisy said. "I suppose I'm being very silly but I really don't understand. This isn't a dream, is it?"

"I'll explain," the major said. "It was only when the man had cleared out, changed his name, and grown a beard to disguise himself that I found out that he had won by cheating, and not only me, but hundreds of others. George Bitlis deserved to die."

"George Bitlis? Was that his real name?" Daisy said. "When did all this change happen?"

"He set up his nasty little club when he came over here from America," the major said. "It didn't last very long. It didn't need to. He'd made his money and could afford to become the respectable George Hamyadis."

"And you never found him?" Daisy said.

"He took good care to make it look as if he had left the country," said the major. "There didn't seem to be anything I could do without creating a lot of stink to no purpose."

"I suppose all this is happening," Daisy said.

"How did you commit the actual murder?" Schlemberger said. "I knew all this stuff about the gambling club, but you still have me kind of foxed over the shooting."

"It was perfectly simple," said the major. "I took the pistol from his case where it was put for all to see. I hid it in the deep sleeve of my coat, and I fired when the boy did. Standing just here. Then I slipped the automatic into hiding in the coach. I'll show you."

"Don't bother," said Schlemberger. "It's pretty plain. I guess I couldn't have known it was you."

The major stood up.

"Very well then," he said, "I thank you all for the pleasure of your company. I deeply regret any inconvenience I may have caused. Try to think well of me. Death was too good for that man. And now I doubt if we shall meet again."

He jumped all the way to the ground, stood for two seconds looking up at them, turned smartly on his heel and walked away across the cobbles in the direction of the street.

In the harsh sun a solitary figure.

"One moment, major," Smithers called.

A quick turn.

"Yes?"

"There's one question still unanswered."

"If you must," the major said. "But I ought to be getting along to the police station. Tempus fugit. Though if I can I'll answer. What's your question?"

"I'm unable to work out why you've told us this little fairy tale," Smithers said.

EIGHT

"It certainly seemed like a fairy tale," said Daisy.

The major stood looking at them from the middle of the cobbled yard. Silent. The blue of the eyes no longer hard, suddenly washed out. In the strong sunlight every detail of his clothes stood out.

The leather patches on the elbows of his brown check suit adrift here and there, the trousers ragged at the heel, a button missing from the left cuff, a slight stain at the bottom of the right lapel.

"What do you mean, fairy tale?" he said.

Without conviction.

"Surely, it's plain enough," said Smithers.

"Of course it's not plain to me," Daisy said. "I mean the major's story did sound like a fairy tale all the time, but I just don't know why it should turn out to be one really. And when I do know that, there's all the business of thinking out why we were told it and what we ought to be believing. Somebody please make something clearer."

Smithers turned to her.

"Hamyadis told us while we were waiting for the liner to dock that he had grown his beard in America," he said. "There was no reason to conceal the truth then. Yet the whole point of the major's story depends on the beard not being in existence when Hamyadis came to this country."

The major walked towards them, shoulders thrown back. Too far back.

"I had to make the attempt," he said. "If one day, perhaps when I'm no longer in this world, some of you get to know the truth, you'll see there was no other course open to a man of honour."

"Just one moment," Schlemberger said. "In my business you just get into the habit of not taking anything anyone says at its face value. Surely, if this man Hamyadis, or Bitlis, or whatever his name was, had grown a beard to disguise himself from people in this country who might recognise him as having run a gambling club, why, surely, then he had every reason to lie automatically about the exact date he commenced assuming this disguise."

"It was good of you," said Smithers, "to let Major Mortenson have his say before you pointed out the rather obvious illogicality in my little supposition. Otherwise we would have had to endure even more confusion than we have got at present."

"I—er. That is——" said Schlemberger. "You're a smart man, Mr Smithers. A damn' smart man."

"If the major didn't do it," Kristen Kett said. "Why did he tell us he did? Nobody's explained that yet. And I think we've a right to know."

"I don't really think we have, you know," Smithers said. "And in any case I think the major will disappoint you."

"I certainly will," said the major.

"But you must say something," Wemyss said.

The major turned on his heel and walked smartly into the inn. An unexpected cloud covered the sun and the courtyard was thrown into shadow. A switch turned off.

"I've half a mind to follow the fellow and force an explanation out of him," said Wemyss.

"Please, Richie," Kristen said. "No scenes. You know how rotten I feel. Anything like that only makes me worse."

"All right," Wemyss said. "But all the same he ought to tell us what he meant by it all."

"I guess it's pretty plain to me," said Schlemberger. "The guy's shielding somebody."

"Not necessarily," said Smithers. "In strict logic it's possible that his confession is simply a device to make people believe there is someone to shield."

"So we are still to go on suspecting each other," Fremitt said.

He climbed wearily off the coach. The others followed. One by one without pretence of conversation they went into the inn or out through the archway into the town.

Smithers fetched his *Decline and Fall* and settled down on the same bench in the courtyard. He read 183 pages from the account of Constantine's jealousy for Julian to the summary of the reasons for the Gothic war of A.D. 366. The weather was less fine than it had been. Heavy clouds frequently obscured the sun. Towards the end of the afternoon they began to turn from white to grey.

The shadows passing across the open pages caused Smithers to look up every now and again.

At 2.48 p.m. he saw Joe Dagg come out of the inn door and walk across the courtyard and out into the street. He kept his hands in his pockets and failed to notice Smithers although he passed within six yards of him.

At 3.14 he noticed Schlemberger and Daisy Miller pass by in the street outside. Schlemberger was talking energetically and Daisy Miller a little. Schlemberger appeared to be walking a bit too fast for her.

At 3.59 Wemyss came to the door of the inn and stood for a moment. He examined his hands with great care and after looking at each finger in turn took out a nail file and scraped at the cuticle of his right thumb. He then re-entered the inn.

At 4.03 John Fremitt came out accompanying Kristen Kett. They walked out into the town. Kristen did not notice Smithers, Fremitt put a hand to his hat when he noticed him, and hurried on. As they turned out of Smithers's line of vision Kristen put a hand on Fremitt's arm.

At 4.32 Major Mortenson came in at the archway, saw Smithers, hesitated, and turned back into the street.

At 4.35 a maid from the inn came out of the kitchen entrance carrying a chair and a basin full of fresh picked peas. She settled down in a corner near the coach house and began podding them. Smithers finished his paragraph, placed a marker in the book, and went indoors.

Just before six from an upper window he saw the maid finish the big basin of peas and gather up her things. He walked downstairs. In the bar he found the whole coaching party sitting almost in silence with drinks. He joined them.

At dinner he began discussions on the weather, on the fallibility of human memory, on public school life, on fire insurance, on the theatre. The latter lasted longest: eight minutes. Afterwards they all sat round a table in the bar again and at ten o'clock talked about going to bed. They had nothing to say to each other. No one appeared to have the courage to leave the others. The evening was extremely sultry.

As soon as the others had gone Smithers resumed his watch on the courtyard. By five minutes to midnight nothing had happened. The temperature seemed to be rising all the time. There were three distant rumbles of thunder.

Smithers got up and hurried to Peter Dagg's door.

"Peter," he called quietly.

The boy woke at once.

"Is that you, sir? I'll come now."

As they stepped out into the thick air of the courtyard there was a flash of lightning, by it the hands of the stable clock could be seen pointing to the hour.

"I didn't like to leave watching the coach," Smithers whispered to Peter as the clock chimed twelve silvery notes. "But I thought nothing would happen before midnight. I hope I won't have to keep you out of bed till dawn, but I can't do without my witness."

"Where are we going to hide?" Peter asked.

"Behind the same water butt as last night, I think," Smithers said. "Come on."

Thick clouds hid the moon and there was less need to creep round the sides of the inn yard. Smithers quickly led Peter across to their hiding place. Before they reached it they heard a sound. A tapping, steady and insistent, coming from the other side of a low range of buildings.

"It'll be round in the alley," Smithers whispered. "Follow me and don't get ahead whatever you do."

He set off at a loping run across the cobbles, not daring to go too fast in case the sound of footsteps became audible in the alley.

They reached the mouth of the narrow passage and peered in. Between the two rows of buildings it was pitch dark, but the sound of the tapping still came to them clearly.

Then there was a tinkle of falling glass.

"The window," whispered Peter.

Distinctly in the dark they heard a muttered grunt of triumph.

Suddenly from almost overhead there was a flash of intense lightning.

For an instant the dark alley became a channel of light, mauvish, eerie. And in that instant the figure of John Fremitt was plainly visible.

He was standing on a dustbin he had dragged across the alley and he had a hand through the broken window pane. But the sudden flash of light had made him glance round, and for the fraction of a second that the narrow passage was lit up he and Smithers stared straight at one another.

Then blackness. And complete silence.

There was a crash as the dustbin overturned and the sound of stumbling footsteps. Smithers plunged into the pit of darkness in front of him. Ahead he heard Fremitt, stumbling less now, but still not running very fast. Behind he could distinguish the patter of the boy's feet. But in the muffling blackness none of them was making much speed.

Smithers nerved himself and tried to run full out. For three paces reason prevailed over instinct. Then with a roaring crash he went full tilt into the dustbin where it had rolled into the middle of the alley.

He lay still for an instant.

Peter slowed and halted. He picked his way towards Smithers.

"Are you all right, sir?"

"Yes, only a little winded but I'm afraid we've lost our man. . . . No we haven't, though. Follow me."

Walking quickly and able now to make out more of his surroundings he led the boy back into the inn yard.

"You remember what that alley does," he said. "It turns sharply and runs into a dead end. I expect you could climb out if you were chased. But, if you had time to look about, you would find that there's a small gap between two buildings just in the corner of the inn yard. Over there. Now I don't think our man will dare to come out the way we came in because he'll think we'll be waiting for him. But sooner or later he'll spot this gap and come out there. We'll wait."

"Sir, was it Mr Fremitt?"

"It was."

"But, sir, he doesn't look as if he would have killed anybody."

"Who does, my boy? But, in any case, don't forget two lots of people have tried to get to the coach, perhaps three, if it wasn't Mr Fremitt we disturbed in the coach house the first time. They can't all be murderers. Now, let's watch quietly."

They stationed themselves near the slit between the two buildings and strained to catch any sound.

The second flash of lightning startled them even more than the first. Peter gave a sharp yelp and Smithers dropped the torch he had taken from his pocket ready to surprise Fremitt. The flash was followed almost at once by a crack of thunder like an explosion. And it was raining.

Steadily, dazingly, like a full power shower-bath. Before Smithers had had time to speak he felt the cold of the rainwater touch his skin across the tops of his shoulders.

"Are you all right?" he asked Peter.

He made no attempt to whisper. It was necessary almost to shout to be heard above the slapping of the heavy drops on the cobbles.

"Yes, I'm okay. It was a bit of a shock. Did I scream?" said the boy.

"It doesn't matter," Smithers said. "Do you want to go in?"

"Please, sir, no. I couldn't think of anything not knowing what Mr Fremitt's going to say."

"All right."

Smithers bent down and felt about for the torch. Already there were puddles on the ground. The rain had seeped into the torch before he got to it and it failed to work.

As Smithers straightened up he heard the squelch of heavy footsteps

on the other side of the buildings. Fremitt was making no attempt at concealment and could be heard even above the din of the storm. He gave
a little "Ah" as he found the gap and a moment later he stood in the inn
yard, the rain beating on to his cap and cascading down to his shoulders.

"Good evening, Fremitt," Smithers said.

"Evening, Smithers, what beastly weather."

But a perceptible start. Something uncontrollable before the quick re-
covery. Before the will that had driven him to the top of his profession
asserted itself.

"No, it won't do," said Smithers. "I saw you, you know. Just as clearly
as you saw me."

Fremitt leant towards him. A fine stream of rainwater shot off the tip of
his nose.

"What did you say?" he shouted. "This rain, you can't hear yourself
think."

Politely puzzled. Every feature of his face placarding it. The lift of the
eyebrows, the faint frown, the tilt of the head, the parting of the lips.

"It won't do," said Smithers. "You'd make out what I'm saying if we were
in the middle of an earthquake. It's too important to you."

"I must have got hold of the wrong end of the stick somewhere,"
Fremitt said. "I've simply no idea what all this is about. But I can't stand
here in this downpour talking about it. For heaven's sake, come indoors. I
can't think what you're doing out."

"Mr Fremitt's quite right about one thing, Peter," Smithers said. "We'd
all three be better indoors."

Fremitt looked at the boy.

"Hallo, Peter," he said. "I didn't see you in all this rain."

He turned and led them to the inn door. As soon as they got into the
bare corridor, with the out-of-date calendar, he stopped and said:

"I suppose you intend to ask me what I was doing at the back of the
coach house just now. There was something of the policeman in your
'good evening'."

The rainwater ran off him. A puddle grew on the boards at his feet.

"You'd better take your jacket off, Peter," said Smithers.

"Please," the boy said, "I've only got my pyjama top underneath."

"That'll be all right," Smithers said with a smile.

He turned to Fremitt.

"When I'm not sure I've picked on the offender out of a class of twenty-
five boys," he said, "dumb ignorance always confirms my guess."

"Only in this case there is no question of an offender," Fremitt said.

"You saw me just now in inexplicable circumstances. They are to remain unexplained."

"You're right of course to remind me that this isn't the classroom," said Smithers. "It is, after all, a question of murder."

"And you do well to remind me of that," Fremitt said. "It's dangerous for anyone to indulge in suspicious behaviour in our circumstances. Would you care to tell me what you were doing prowling about after dark in a storm of rain?"

"Shall we say seeking to confirm a hypothesis?" Smithers said. "Seeking successfully."

"The phrase could cover almost any set of circumstances. It's no explanation. But if you're not going to say anything, I can do nothing to make you."

"Though other things being equal," Smithers said, "such an explanation when used about a walk in the dark looks better than when it is used of breaking a window."

"That would depend on the circumstances in which the question was asked. A reply of that sort is hardly likely to impress a hostile policeman," Fremitt said. "My dear chap, you're too old to want advice, but I should consider your position very carefully. Inspector Parker asked me questions about you this afternoon which to my mind could mean only one thing. I am probably betraying a confidence in telling you that, but I feel sure you must have some explanation. Make up your mind to it. Let the inspector know everything, or there will be some hideous mistake."

He turned and walked away along the corridor leaving a trail of drips.

"No," said Smithers as he went, "it won't do all the same. I apply your own words to yourself. Let the inspector know everything. Otherwise I shall."

Fremitt turned the corner as the words were spoken.

"Now," said Smithers. "Upstairs quickly with you, my boy, and a hot bath before you get back to bed."

At breakfast next morning once more nine people sat round a table. Eight murder suspects and a boy.

There was once again little conversation. After the waiter had taken away the bacon plates the major slapped together the copy of *The Times* which had shut him out of the scanty talk and said:

"So another day begins, dies irae, another day of pointless suspicions and uneasiness. I expect we shall most of us have the pleasure of a conversation with Inspector Parker. He tells me he delights in the name of

Nosey Parker. And it's a good name for him. But not for the reason he thinks. It's a good name for him and all his tribe of Government snoopers. You know what this business means to him?"

A pause for an answer.

No answers.

"I suppose you think it means an opportunity to serve the ends of justice, to right a wrong. Not at all. It means a glorious chance to tabulate a few more facts about some more helpless citizens. He had the damned impudence yesterday to ask for my fingerprints."

"And did you give them to him?" Smithers asked.

The major looked at him.

"As a matter of fact I did," he said. "I've lived too long to think I've got any rights left. I simply kow-towed. It's what we all come to in the end."

"I certainly am glad to hear you say this, major," Schlemberger said. "Since I've been over here I've heard a good deal about how corrupt the cops are in the States: I'm frankly delighted to hear your British policemen aren't quite so wonderful after all. I reckon we have the edge on you when it comes to being human."

"Well, sir," said the major, "I'll say nothing about the American police force. I've never been to America and I don't know about it. But wherever else I've met policemen they've been just the same. It's a disease among the higher ranks everywhere. A disease that drove me out of the Indian Army, sir. I had the experience once of knowing a man was guilty and seeing nothing done about tracing him because people in authority had committed themselves by showing trust in him. That's officialdom for you."

"That Inspector Parker," Joe Dagg said. "What right has he to ask about things that happened years ago? Things best forgotten."

Sudden emergence from the long absorbed silence.

"None at all," said the major. "And the man hasn't an idea about this business. You know what he asked me yesterday? If I could tell him where Hamyadis's flat was. He said he didn't know. All he had to do was to look it up in the telephone book and he asks me, and waits till yesterday to do it."

"Ah, there you're wrong, dear," Daisy Miller said. "It isn't as easy as all that. Nobody knows where the flat is. It isn't on the telephone, if you wanted to write to him he gave you his office address, and when he entertained he did it at one of his clubs. It was a complete secret. I don't believe a soul knew."

"I don't think Georgie was as secretive as all that," said Kristen Kett. "He told me an awful lot."

"Did he tell you his address?" Schlemberger asked.

Kristen looked like a pert schoolgirl.

"That's just what the police asked me," she said. "And so I said 'No'. I think the major's right. They're not so clever."

"Of course I'm right," said the major. "I can tell you now just exactly what's going to happen over this business. The police are going to keep us here as long as they dare, and make life as unpleasant for us as they can. And then they'll let us go, and after that no one will hear a word more about 'the coaching death' as those wretched newspapers call it. The whole affair will be quietly forgotten. And no one will think of it enough to blame the police. I've seen it happen before."

"Well, I wish they'd get on with it," Wemyss said. "I'm beginning to need a haircut pretty badly and that blasted inspector keeps on putting off choosing a time for me to slip up to town."

"It's all very well," Schlemberger said, "but I can't afford to have a thing like this hanging over me. It must be solved."

"I suggest one step that ought to be taken," Smithers said. "Miss Kett, I recommend you to give Inspector Parker that address."

"But I told you it was never given to me," Kristen said.

A flounce.

"Come," said Smithers, "this is simply prevaricating. Hamyadis took you to this flat I've no doubt. You know where it is even if you were never given the address. It's your duty to help the police."

"Perhaps I will," said Kristen. "When I'm ready to. But I just wanted to pay the inspector out. He wasn't at all nice to me."

"That's pretty clever, Mr Smithers," said Schlemberger. "But you'll permit a businessman to have his doubts? That's business, you know, to have doubts about everybody and everything. I'd be better prepared to believe Miss Kett's claim if she told me exactly where this flat is."

"All right, then," said Kristen. "It's so easy, but it fooled everyone. It's just at the back of one of his clubs: the Red Cockatoo. He used to say 'Well, I'm off home' and get a taxi. Then he'd drive round about for a bit and end up just round the corner. The flat was above a dry cleaner's and he had it under another name."

"Guess you win," said Schlemberger.

"All the same," Fremitt said, "my sympathies are with Miss Kett." His long silence broken.

"At least they are with her in so far as she does not deliberately hinder the process of law. I must say that. But, on the other hand, I cannot help resenting the attitude Inspector Parker takes. Of course, we have become involved in a murder, I know that, but all the same he pries. There is no other word, or at least I don't think so. And one must do something to defend one's privacy, or anyhow one feels very much inclined to do so."

"My point exactly, sir," said the major. "Though I doubt if you'll have much success."

"It brings me to something I have been feeling I ought to tell you all," Fremitt said.

Smithers leaned forward. Polite attention.

"I have taken the liberty of carrying out a quite small investigation on my own behalf," Fremitt said. "There were one or two things I wasn't satisfied about."

"Well, Mr Schlemberger, you're not the only one," Wemyss said. "We're to have no peace."

Schlemberger did not reply. His knife tracing the pattern of the tablecloth.

"You carry on," said the major. "Though, if you find anything out, don't expect the police to thank you."

"But have you found anything out?" said Daisy. "If I had, I'd behave just like you. I'd hug it to myself as long as I could and then give out hints. Only, of course, when I made my revelation it would turn out to be something everybody had known all along."

"I'm sorry to disappoint you," Fremitt said. "I haven't done more, so far, than half confirm some faint suspicions. I don't think it would be fair to put it more strongly than that. I'm afraid the reason I mentioned the matter at all was much less dramatic. I'm not altogether the dramatic type, if you'll excuse my saying so."

"Well, what was the reason?" Joe Dagg said. "You've got me jittery, colonel. I don't know what's wrong with me, straight I don't. I've got the feeling a copper's going to pop out of that sideboard there and take me off."

They looked at the sideboard. The doors closed. The tomato ketchup oozing from the top of the bottle.

"It's simply that, while I was having a look at the coach house last night, Mr Smithers here and young Peter happened to come by. They caught me making my investigation."

"Oh, lord," Kristen Kett said, "I feel so ill."

She pushed back her chair and rushed out of the room.

Fremitt began to follow her and changed his mind. The others left the table and looked embarrassed. Only Schlemberger stayed where he was.

"Do you think she'll be all right, the poor kid?" said Daisy.

"We can scarcely intrude on her," Smithers said. "She has a bell in her room if she feels really ill. Let's hope we see her at tea."

"I expect we shall," Daisy said.

With unexpected confidence.

"I doubt if you'll see me," said Wemyss. "I'm getting more than a bit sick of these little reunions over food."

But when the gong called them for tea Wemyss was there. So was Kristen Kett, looking pale but no worse. One by one they all trooped in. Bees at a honey pot. Waiting to hear something. In they all trooped, all but Foster P. Schlemberger, president of the American Institution for the Investigation of Incendiarism Incorporated.

NINE

It was Wemyss who spoke about it first.

"For an American Schlemberger is unusually fond of his tea," he said.

No one answered.

"Is," said Wemyss, "or should I say was?"

"Was?"

Kristen was quick. "Has something happened to him?"

"Well," Wemyss said. "He's not here and there's no reason why he shouldn't be. So you can draw your own conclusion: something's happened to him, or more likely he's taken certain action of his own."

"Certain action?" said Smithers.

"Don't you understand?" Wemyss said.

"I prefer to hear it in your own words."

"All right then. I'm not afraid to call a spade a spade. If you ask me Schlemberger's realised that he's not going to get away with this murder after all. He's on his way out of the country. I warned you all, but none of you would take any notice."

"Oh dear," said Daisy Miller, "and it's only by pure chance I haven't been late for a meal so far. It's bad enough coming in and seeing everybody standing up in the middle of what they're eating, but if you know they've just been wondering if you were the one . . ."

"Exactly," said Smithers. "One is free not to eat."

"That's as may be," the major said. "But I tell you what none of us is free to do: to go without information. Look at Joe, look at Miss Kett. They hardly eat a thing, but do they ever miss a meal? I think Wemyss is right."

"You make out a good case, major," said Fremitt. "Though of course Miss Miller spoke with her usual good sense, if I may say so. Ought we to do anything, I wonder."

"Yes we ought," said Major Mortenson.

He jumped to his feet. The man of action.

"Waiter," he called.

The old head waiter appeared from round a corner. Quickly. Very quickly for an old man.

"You called, sir?"

"Get them to ring Mr Schlemberger's room," said the major. "I want to know if he's in the inn, and sharply."

A bark.

The major stayed standing while the sedate old man hurried away. With a natural shambling trot, awkward, aroused, unwaiterlike.

The others sat silent. Wemyss ate some tomato sandwiches.

But everybody knew that sooner or later they would be told that Schlemberger was nowhere to be found.

As they were.

"Very well," said Smithers. "I will telephone Inspector Parker."

"You sound a little grudging, Mr Smithers," said the inspector, appearing round the corner that had concealed the head waiter.

"I was not very anxious to waste your time, inspector," Smithers said. "It seems that Mr Schlemberger isn't in the inn and Mr Wemyss here and others thought it was a matter for you."

"And you didn't?" asked Nosey Parker.

"I didn't when it was simply a question of his being a few minutes late for tea," Smithers said. "But now I'm glad that you know."

"I hope the delay wasn't too long, inspector," Wemyss said. "But I imagine calls to the airports and docks will do the trick."

The inspector smiled.

"I suppose there was some link between them over in America years ago," Wemyss said.

"You have a very flattering conception of police efficiency," said the inspector. "But, you know, it takes time to find out that sort of thing. It's only forty-eight hours since Mr Hamyadis met his death. We've found out a lot since then"—the nose twitched—"but there's a lot more we'll have to find out yet."

Wemyss sat down again and smiled. Faintly, with superiority.

"It was to find out a little bit more that I came up here," said Nosey Parker. "I'm afraid I shall have to ask most of you a lot more questions."

The nose darted, pointed, quivered.

"Now," he said, "who had I better see first? Ah, Mr Smithers, I think. Would you come this way? I've arranged to use the office here so as not to take up too much time."

Smithers followed him without a word into the hotel office.

At the door they were joined by a uniformed constable, notebook in hand.

The inspector stood for a moment looking round the small room. A vacuum cleaner sucking up every fact: the leather topped table, the exact extent of the bare patch at one of its corners where the black leather had rolled back; the varnished oak desk in the corner, and the likely length of time before the broken slat of its roll top would fall off; the swivel chair, the three hard chairs relegated from the dining room, the piles of papers on two of them; the green metal shade for the light; the vase of overblown roses, variety White Moss; the signs of abandoned activity, remote, prosaic, uninspired.

Smithers flicked at the waistcoat of his tired tweed suit with an impatient gesture.

"I take it, then," he said, "that you're not as sanguine as my young friend Wemyss."

The inspector turned swiftly round. He motioned Smithers to the vacant dining chair and took the swivel one himself. The constable lifted the pile of papers from one of the other chairs and propped his notebook on his crossed knee. The inspector offered Smithers a cigarette. He refused.

With elbows on the table and hands clasped in the air Inspector Parker said slowly:

"It's very natural, Mr Smithers, for the public to make mistakes when they become involved with the police investigating a murder case. The mistakes vary. Mr Wemyss makes rather obvious ones, if I may say so. You are quick to spot them. But don't let that blind you to the fact that you are making mistakes yourself."

He plunged his nose into the cavity formed by his hands and stared at Smithers above the linked fingers.

"I never feel obliged," he said, "to give a running commentary on an investigation. But I'm going to tell you one thing. At present I have very little reason to believe Mr Schlemberger was in any way involved. And I will tell you why. Because he has been extremely frank with me. There's not a question I've asked that he hasn't given a full, a very full, reply to."

"I take it, then, you know where he is," said Smithers.

"I don't know," Inspector Parker said. "And I'm not particularly worried. What I do know is that he is very anxious to join the rest of his conference in London. He's concerned about the arrangements. And I've no doubt that what's happened is that he's taken French leave. But I trust him. Now, what about Miss Kett?"

The long sword dance, the sudden jab.

"Miss Kett?" said Smithers. "I first met her three days ago. Though I had heard of her, but not by name, earlier on from Mr Hamyadis. Since then on the whole I have spoken very little with her. She has told me nothing that I recall of herself, except that I did learn that she has a brother, Charles, I think his name is."

Then silence.

"Very well," said Nosey Parker. "If you won't satisfy my curiosity on your own, I shall have to prompt you. You persuaded her earlier today to tell me a certain fact she had hitherto concealed. Now, what exactly is the relationship between the two of you?"

"Just what I have told you, inspector," said Smithers. "I take it you have made some inquiries about me. What is the point then of this pretence of not believing my statements? Surely you know I am the sort of person who tells the truth to the police."

"I would put that last phrase a little differently," said Nosey Parker. "Shall we say: who tells the truth to the police or who stays silent?"

"Well, if we must bandy definitions I would put it at its most finickity: who tells the truth and no more than the truth however unpleasant it might conceivably be to him."

"As you like," said Parker. "I will bear all that in mind as I listen to your answer."

"Very well. There is simply nothing mysterious about my persuading Miss Kett to come and see you. She was foolish enough at lunch to boast of tricking you by using words that appeared to tell the truth while concealing it. I did with her what it is my duty to do with countless fourth formers who preen themselves on the same trick. I pointed out to her that it ended to her own disadvantage."

"I see. Just that. She was being naughty and you made her own up. And the scents business? What schoolteacher's trick of the trade was that?"

"I will reply to that as carefully and precisely as I can," said Smithers. "But first I must warn you, inspector, that I don't at all like the tone of your remarks. If I am to be treated in this hostile fashion I shall have to ask to have a solicitor present. Now, my answer. A simple matter of logic. When I first told you that I had noticed a woman's scent shortly after an attempt was made to remove something from the coach, I had no idea what scent Miss Kett wore. It had not escaped my attention that the presence of such a scent pointed to Miss Kett equally with Miss Miller, but I felt it my duty to hand a fact of that nature on to you."

"But it did escape your notice that your description of the speed of the mysterious woman's flight pointed very clearly to Miss Kett?"

Smithers sat in silence.

"I suppose that does point to her," he said at last. "It had escaped my notice. But, you know, you may not be right. After all, Daisy Miller was in her prime an accomplished dancer as well as a singer. She is on the stage still, though I have not seen her for years. She may very likely be in pretty good training."

The inspector looked at the splotched pink blotter in front of him.

"No," he said. "It's all possible, but it's all—shall we say?—a little unlikely."

He sat again without speaking. Slowly his glance travelled up and down the blotter, the spade nose moving methodically. A mine detector.

"Mr Smithers, I want to apologise to you," he said when the whole blotter had been examined. "I have rubbed you up the wrong way. It was the very last thing I wanted to do. I've no doubt you've told me everything I could reasonably ask you to. Have your solicitor by all means if you want to, but if you do it's very unlikely that I shall have anything more to ask you."

He looked at the blotter once again, wistfully.

"I'll have a new search started for that gun of Hamyadis's," he said.

A finger laid carefully on a large ink blot.

"Dammit," he said, "you're the only one who hasn't been prepared to talk about everybody else for all they were worth, and you're the only one whose opinion I give a fig for."

"And you know why that is, inspector," said Smithers. "It's because I find it impossible to speculate on the human character. To speculate. You'll forgive a schoolmaster for punning? But it makes my point. A personality is too valuable to risk gambling on. No, I have nothing more to say, and, unless I make altogether unprecedented progress, I am not likely to have anything to say in the few days you can reasonably ask us to stay here."

"I suppose I can see your point," Inspector Parker answered. "But I beg you to ask yourself if you are right. We're not in your schoolroom world now, we are dealing with someone who has killed a fellow creature. And while you are weighing and reweighing and making your hair's breadth adjustments that person may kill again."

The tightly clenched fist.

"No," said Smithers. "It won't do. Stop a moment and think about what you have just said. Wasn't it rather impassioned for a policeman? Didn't you go rather far in putting the whole burden of solving the case on the characters of those involved? Haven't the police any other methods? Of course you have, and it is with them that the emergency work of stopping a killer striking twice is done. You know all this. After all, you posted the men who so unobtrusively keep an eye on us all."

The inspector grinned a little.

"Now," said Smithers, "let me tell you something that perhaps you don't know."

"Ah."

Smack. Down on the black leather of the table came the inspector's outstretched hands as he flung himself into an attitude of passionate attention.

"No," Smithers said, "what I am going to tell you has nothing to do with this case. Or at least it may have quite a lot to do with it, but only in common with every case you handle. Because I'm going to tell you something about yourself."

The inspector leant back in his chair.

"Go on," he said.

Smithers took a moment to weigh his words.

"Curiosity," he said, "killed the cat."

Inspector Parker, Nosey Parker, looked at him.

Motes swirled in the broad beam of sunlight coming through the window.

"That's not a threat?" the inspector asked. With bewilderment.

Smithers smiled.

"I had an idea you would find yourself at a loss," he said. "It rather proves my point. Inspector, curiosity has become a ruling passion with you. It was that passion that animated your appeal to me just now. Animated it, and took it clean out of the domain of reason. No doubt this passion in its early stages furthered your career, but let me warn you now. If you are not very careful, it will blight it entirely."

Nosey Parker looked at Smithers. He blinked. As with a child a frown deepening on his forehead betrayed thought.

At last he said:

"Mr Smithers, either you are talking utter nonsense or I was right a minute ago and you are a clever and unscrupulous man issuing a direct threat to a police officer."

"I think I was simply too late," said Smithers.

He got up and without another word left the dusty little room. The inspector made no move to stop him.

The sunbeam motes danced a little faster.

Smithers returned to the teatable he had deserted. The meal was over.

It had provided its dram of rumour. Most of the food lay untouched. Nerves prey on appetite.

Except in one case.

Tucked away in a deep armchair, legs drawn up, sat Peter. In his right hand a wedge of fruit cake.

"Hello," said Smithers. "I thought the few minutes I was away would scarcely be long enough for your tea."

"Nobody else seemed very interested after you went, sir," said Peter. "Super cake."

"Would you be able to drag yourself away from it to come on a little expedition with me?" Smithers said. "For the same reason as before."

"Gosh, yes," Peter said. "And I could take a bit of the cake with me, couldn't I? I'd eat it very quietly."

"That wouldn't matter. This time it will be a bit different. We're going up to London."

"Golly, did old Nosey let you go then? Everybody else seemed to think you were going to end up in clink."

"Did they? That scarcely surprises me. But Inspector Parker, as I think you should call him to me at least, has not, as a matter of fact, said we could go. We're going to play truant."

"That means skipping school, doesn't it, sir?"

"Just that. Reprehensible, no doubt. But I think the time has come to look after oneself."

"Sir, what did Nos—Inspector Parker say to you just now? Did he threaten to put you inside?"

"Do you think I ought to be put inside, Peter?"

"If he said that, sir, he must be daft."

"The trouble is, my boy, he may be. Just a little. That's why we're going. Are you ready?"

"Yes, sir."

"All right then. There'll be a bus stopping outside the hotel in a few minutes which will take us to the station. We should be able to pick up a fast London train almost at once. Just come with me, and when I give the word do what you're told smartly."

Smithers slipped the half-hunter from his waistcoat pocket and checked it against the stable clock visible through the window of the tearoom.

"You've time to finish that cake," he said.

He sat while the boy munched solidly through. Then he strolled out into the hall of the inn. Peter followed and they stood for a while looking at a framed copy of a nineteenth century advertisement for the house. Its glass reflected the busy scene in the street outside. Suddenly Smithers said:

"Right. Off we go. Quickly now."

He walked straight out of the hotel at a rapid pace, the boy running beside him. A few yards away the last passengers of a short queue were heaving themselves aboard the bus.

"Jump in," said Smithers.

Peter leapt on to the platform of the bus, and Smithers followed as the vehicle moved off. As soon as he was in he stooped and fumbled with his shoelace. Getting up he glanced out of the rear window.

"With any luck," he said to Peter, "no one will know we've been away. There's another fast train back which will bring us in just before dinner if we're quick up there."

"What are we going to do, sir?" asked Peter.

"Same rules as before," Smithers said. "You just follow me and notice everything that happens."

Smithers had carried with him the volume of Gibbon he had laid aside when he began tea. A paper stall at the station produced a sensational American comic for Peter. They sat reading as the train sped through the early summer evening.

At Waterloo, Smithers put Peter quickly into the first taxi they saw. He sat well back in the seat.

"Look out, Peter, and see if you can spot any policemen," he said.

The boy craned his neck out of both windows as they left the station.

"Not a sausage," he said.

A note of disappointment.

"Never mind," said Smithers. "I hope to be able to provide you with a small surprise in a few minutes' time."

The taxi took them across the river, round Trafalgar Square and up Charing Cross Road. Then it turned sharp left, and twisted about in the small streets of Soho. It stopped and the driver said:

"There you are, sir."

He pointed to a small grimy red painted sign that hung beside a slit-like door in the same red paint. On the sign in white letters were painted the words 'The Red Cockatoo'.

Smithers paid off the taxi and looked around.

"This should be the way," he said.

He led Peter a short way back along the street and then took the first turning on the same side as the Cockatoo notice board. He took the first turning he came to again and paused.

The street they were in was almost exactly similar to the one where the taxi had put them down. Five small restaurants, two grocers' shops, next door to each other and almost identical, and a music publisher's and a dry cleaner's. Otherwise dingy houses.

Smithers walked slowly up the street. As he got to the third restaurant just opposite the dry cleaner's he stopped short. The place was open in a half-hearted way. Smithers examined the bill of fare hung in the window for a few moments.

"We aren't going to be disappointed after all," he said.

"Is it something to eat, sir?" Peter said. "Dad says you want to watch this dago cooking."

"Do you know any dagoes, Peter?"

"No, sir. Dad steers clear of them. I think he's got a special grudge against one or something."

"Well, wait until you meet some before forming any judgements. And don't jump to conclusions even then. But you won't have to worry on this occasion: I don't think there'll be much eating involved."

He pushed open the door.

"Good evening, Schlemberger," he said. "May we join you?"

Schlemberger looked up at them from the little table near the door. A statue. 'Incomprehension Becoming Incredulity.'

And without the passage of time statue into frenzied machine. A soup plate jerked hard across the small restaurant. With accurate aim straight at Smithers's face.

He ducked, the plate caught him a glancing blow on the ear and broke into pieces on the jamb of the door behind him.

There was only one other way out of the small room and Schlemberger, without waiting to see whether his missile had gone home, took it. Through the service door, leaving it swinging noisily backwards and forwards on its double hinge.

Smithers followed him. Down a short flight of stairs. Into a long narrow kitchen, steamy and rich smelling. At the far end a small door stood wide open. Dimly visible through the thick atmosphere of the kitchen some concrete area steps. Half-way along the room, standing opposite a large stove covered in pans, was a heavily built swarthy man wearing stained white overalls and a chef's cap. In one hand he had a meat chopper and in the other a heavy double boiler. He was swearing in Italian.

As soon as he saw Smithers he shouted:

"Another. My bloody sauce Bearnaise she is spoiled."

He turned and advanced towards Smithers.

With all his force Smithers hurled Vol. 4 of *The Decline and Fall* straight at the cook. It caught him hard between the eyes. He fell on to his back. Smithers ran on, scrambling over the man's outstretched legs and out into the area and up the steps.

He found himself outside the Red Cockatoo. Schlemberger was on the far side of the road shouting directions to the driver of a taxi he had just stopped.

Smithers judged the distance and halted. There was no possibility of making the long diagonal crossing of the street before the vehicle went. He breathed a long sigh.

And as he lifted his head he recognised the taxi driver as the one who had brought him from Waterloo.

He ran into the roadway waving his hand wildly. The driver spotted him and brought the taxi to a stop just as it had started.

"Lost something, sir?" he called across the road.

"Yes, yes, just a moment," Smithers shouted back.

He dodged across. Schlemberger opened the door of the vehicle and abruptly shut it again. At the corner of the street a police constable slowly walked across.

"This gentleman's a friend of mine as it happens," said Smithers. "I won't keep him a moment, but I was carrying a book with me when I got out of your cab, and I'm hanged if I know where it is now."

He got in beside Schlemberger.

"I take it you were watching Hamyadis's flat," he said.

"I guess I was," Schlemberger answered. "But you were the last person I expected to see just then. It kind of surprised me. I'm awfully sorry about that plate."

The taxi driver opened the communicating glass.

"There's that nipper you were with, sir," he said. "I think he's carrying your book. Big blue one."

"That's it," said Smithers. "Call him over, would you? And we'll all go off together."

Schlemberger sat silent while the taxi driver attracted Peter's attention and brought him over. When he arrived Smithers said:

"Are you all right, my boy? I had to trust you to keep out of trouble, but I've been a little worried."

"I'm perfectly okay, sir," Peter said. "The old cookie's still sitting there. If you ask me, he never will know what hit him. I just picked up the book and dodged through after you. It was a super throw, sir."

"Thank you, Peter," said Smithers. "Now jump in and sit quietly while Mr Schlemberger tells us something."

"I'm going to ask you to keep a confidence," said Schlemberger.

"Certainly," Smithers said. "As long as there is no question, you understand, of keeping anything from the police."

"You're sure you want it that way?" Schlemberger said.

Smithers tapped on the glass behind the taxi driver.

"Drop us in Whitehall," he said. "Just about opposite New Scotland Yard will do."

The taxi started off.

"I guess you win," Schlemberger said. "But you will keep this to yourselves?"

"We will," said Smithers.

"All right then. Back in the States I have the reputation for being a pretty tough negotiator. They don't put much across Foster P. Well, someone did put something across on me, somewhere in the transatlantic cables. That someone was our old friend George Hamyadis."

From Peter a gasp. Smithers's hand quick to the boy's knee.

"He didn't put much across on me," Schlemberger went on. "But he did put his organisation across as an honest outfit. All right. So I hadn't been on British soil ten minutes when I began to smell a rat. I guess you all smelt the same one. There's no need for me to go into details."

"Perhaps not," said Smithers.

"All right then. Somebody kills him, and I knew at once I'd put the whole Institution for the Investigation of Incendiarism in a spot. I thought I could lose the presidency. A big scandal could lose me my job. And if I don't have a job, I'm through. I'm a bum, strictly a bum. You see me looking as if I'm doing all right; but every night I say to myself 'Thin Ice' and I think of that automobile coming right down at me and the way I'd have to just drop in front of it. At first I thought there was nothing to do but sweat it out. Until I learnt about that mysterious flat. Then the hair on my scalp really did begin to start doing things. If ever there was a loud noise saying blackmail, this was it. And I began to wonder if the I.I.I. wasn't mixed up in it somehow."

"Just to wonder?" asked Smithers.

"You've got to believe me on this," Schlemberger said. "As far as I knew there was nothing for the guy to get his hands on. But say one of our employees, or officers even, had done something which the guy had got a line on. Well, the police weren't supposed to have found this flat, so I brought a little pressure to bear on that girl, Kristen. And, as soon as I had what I wanted, I came on up here for a quiet look around."

"And you didn't even get that far?"

Schlemberger's gaze, fixed up to this point on Smithers with unwavering forthrightness, dropped.

"I was still casing up the place when you happened along," he said.

"Fortunately that is a point the police will be able to check," Smithers said. "And you know if"—a pause—"they do find anything involving your organisation I think you can rely on their discretion."

"I kept telling myself I was a fool not to do that," Schlemberger said. "Do you know what? I guess that was why I hadn't made a move up to the time you came. Yes, I guess it was a question of that little old unconscious substitution again."

The taxi halted.

Schlemberger looked out.

"This it?" he asked.

"Straight through there and you'll find somebody to see you," Smithers answered.

When Schlemberger had gone from sight he glanced at his watch.

"Well, Peter," he said, "it didn't take very long, did it? I think we'll catch our train all right."

The Decline and Fall had come out of the fight better than the cook had done. Smithers was able to resume his reading on the train. Peter fell asleep suddenly.

He had just had a short conversation with Smithers on the subject of the encounter with Schlemberger.

"Please, sir," he had begun, "did you think it was going to be him after all?"

"Not altogether, shall we say? And what about you?"

"Well, sir, he is an American, sir. And nobody can know about him the way they can know about an Englishman, can they, sir?"

"A good point."

"Sir, was what he said in the taxi true?"

"It was true in a way," Smithers said. "It was what you might call a fable. It told the right story but the people were a little different."

"You mean when he said that bit about some officer of the I.I.I. he meant him?"

"Good boy. I think we can be sure that Hamyadis had 'got a line on' him, as I think he put it. No doubt the police will try to find out how strong a line it was."

"Sir, if it was a very strong line, Mr Schlemberger could be the one, couldn't he?"

"He has certainly got a motive."

Peter had opened his eyes wide at this. Then shut them in sleep.

At Winchester Smithers took no precautions to avoid being seen. He took a taxi from the station and he and Peter entered the hotel five minutes late for dinner.

Just before going into the dining room Smithers said:

"Can you come and watch the coach again tonight?"

"Is it still important then?" asked Peter.

"More so than ever."

"I'll be ready then, sir."

Together they entered the dining room. Everybody except Schlemberger was already there.

"Where have you been, lad?" said Joe Dagg. "You don't want to go wandering off like that."

The snapping nerves.

Peter stopped short. A look of bewilderment. His father shook his head dazedly and said:

"I might have wanted you all of a sudden, see."

"My fault, I'm afraid," Smithers said. "I took him for a ramble. It took us a little longer than we thought."

"That's all right, colonel," Joe said. "I haven't felt much like entertaining the lad lately. But I've got to know where he is, that's all."

"If you were wandering about the countryside," Richard Wemyss said, "I suppose you haven't heard anything of the murder hunt. There was no appeal on the wireless or picture on the T.V. or anything. I wonder if that means they've got him."

"There's certainly nothing I can tell you," Smithers said. "Though I would advise you not to speak in quite the terms you chose."

"The fellow was damn' silly to hop off, if he has hopped off," said the major. "If he'd just sat tight they'd never have cottoned on. Verbum sapienti."

"I shall be glad when it's over one way or another," Daisy Miller said. "The longer it goes on the worse it gets. Even my chatty postman mentioned it when I met him again as I was catching the last post just before dinner."

"If it really is Schlemberger," Fremitt said, "and I am reluctant to believe it can be, it really is about as bad as possible. It almost amounts to a national calamity. There are important issues involved, the tourist trade, dollars. At least so it seems to me."

"Why do you all go on about it so?" Kristen Kett said. "If I've heard you all say that stuff once, I've heard it a thousand times. You've been round and round it all afternoon. Can't you just shut up and wait for the end?"

"A remark which I seem to have heard before this afternoon," Wemyss said.

"Now you leave her alone, captain," said Joe. "She's quite right for one thing. It's over. Talking can do no good now. It's all something to do with gangsters, that's what I think. It all ought to be finished with. The ruddy coppers ought to leave us in peace. And we ought to forget it all."

"Very true, I dare say," said Wemyss. "But as I happened to introduce the subject I think I've a perfect right to point out to anybody that they're being inconsistent in not wanting to talk about it."

"Just leave the kid alone, that's all I asked," Joe said. "She's a bit off colour like. Anyone can see that. So let her be, that's all."

Wemyss moved his chair slightly and leant over the table towards Kristen.

"Tell me," he said, "did your friend Georgie ever talk to you about this gangster Schlemberger?"

"You've asked me that before," said Kristen. "And I've told you he didn't. I've told you and told you and told you."

Joe Dagg scraped back his chair and stood up.

"Listen," he said.

"You know," Smithers said, "I was asked just now if I knew anything about a supposed hunt for Mr Schlemberger."

Joe sat down. Without fuss, quickly.

"I said I knew nothing of a hunt, which was true," Smithers went on. "But after what I've just been listening to I think perhaps I ought to say that while I was speaking to Inspector Parker this afternoon he distinctly gave me to understand that Mr Schlemberger scarcely entered into the police reckoning at all."

Silence. Adjustments of view.

"I knew it was too good to be true," said Daisy. "Not that I wanted it to be true anyway."

Another silence.

"Damn it. Damn it," said Joe. "They'll begin those questions again, poking and prying. Why can't they leave us alone?"

He jumped up from the table and left the room.

The others looked at each other. No more was said while they went into the coffee room. Old magazines were much re-read that evening. Everybody sat in the same room glancing at each other from time to time. Speech at a minimum. There was no surprise when Schlemberger walked in and said the inspector had let him go up to London for a few hours.

Everybody went early to bed. Unlikely excuses for tiredness were given and accepted.

Once again Smithers stationed himself to watch the coach house. He began Volume 5 of *The Decline and Fall*. His watch was undisturbed.

At midnight he went to Peter's room. He stood outside the door hesitating, and then tapped lightly.

No reply.

He tapped again. Opened the door a crack. The beam of light from the corridor fell on an empty bed.

TEN

Smithers slipped the half-hunter from his pocket. Three minutes past midnight. He left the room and sat in the window seat at the end of the corridor where he could see the door clearly.

Eighteen minutes past midnight. Smithers walked back, opened the door again, glanced at the empty bed, shut the door, took a box of matches from his own room, emptied the contents and, holding the box, went along the corridor to Joe Dagg's room. He knocked.

No response.

A louder knock. Still nothing.

Smithers tried the door. It opened. The room empty, the bed still made up. A quick look round. No suitcases. No clothes in the cupboards or chest of drawers.

Smithers went down to the hall and rang up the police station.

"The inspector's here, hold on a minute," said the constable who answered.

A short pause.

"Inspector Parker speaking. Is that you, Mr Smithers?"

"Yes. I rang to tell you that Joe Dagg has left the hotel, taking his boy and all his luggage."

"I see. Hold on a moment, would you?"

Faintly in the background the sound of sharp voices. Then:

"I'm sorry to have kept you. Now tell me all about it."

"There's little more to tell. I happened to run out of matches and I thought Dagg might still be up, so I tapped lightly on his door and then put my head round it. When I saw the bed was unslept in I thought it was odd, so I glanced round the room and found all the clothes gone. The boy isn't there either."

"I see. Anything else?"

"No, I don't think so."

"Would you stay by the telephone, I may want to ring back."

Smithers sat down and waited.

In two minutes Inspector Parker came into the hall, jerking the door open. He was breathing heavily.

"Ah, there you are," he said. "I want a word with you."

A sergeant and two constables came in. The inspector ordered one of the constables and the sergeant to go upstairs. Then he turned to Smithers:

"You don't smoke, Mr Smithers, do you?" he said.

Smithers waved the offer aside.

"I never do."

"Exactly," said Parker.

A spring.

"Exactly. You never smoke. There is a perfectly good electric light in this hotel, and yet you want a match at midnight. There may be some explanation. The boy, Peter, disappears, so you tell us. You have produced him as a witness to some pretty inexplicable behaviour immediately following a murder. You also took him with you to London in defiance of my request to you to stay in Winchester. I get to hear things, you know. Now, I would like your explanation."

Smithers heard from behind him the steady scutter of the constable's pencil across the page of his notebook.

"There is an explanation," he said, "it is simply that I have lost confidence in your conduct of this investigation, inspector. At the same time I have no reasons I could properly put to, say, your Chief Constable. Even if he would listen to someone involved in the case."

Nosey Parker looked at him. A scrum half waits for the ball.

"Very good," he said. "I will tell you Mr Smithers what I think your motive in making that remark might be. It might well be deliberate provocation to force me to make a move before I had proper evidence. Let me make it clear. At present I have not got evidence enough to make me believe you are responsible for the crime I am investigating. All I have is an inexplicable course of conduct."

"Look," said Smithers, "I feel some of the blame for this situation rests with me. I had nothing to do with the murder of Hamyadis. On the face of it, why should I have? So any time you spend suspecting me is time wasted. About that I feel guilty. Can't we sort it out? I have never thought of myself as likely to become a murder suspect, much less so as playing amateur detective. But that is what I have been doing. I have had to do it to protect myself. Simply because owing to your unnatural curiosity you refuse to see my perfectly valid, if a little unusual, unwillingness to gossip in its natural light."

"You went to fetch the boy to witness another stage in your investigation then? I take it that's what you'll say?" Inspector Parker asked.

"You're quick to see all the implications," said Smithers. "I like to think that makes my actions seem all the more credible."

"Hm. . . . That's as may be. What were you going to do half an hour ago that the police in their ignorance had omitted?"

"It's not a question of ignorance. You know that. It was simply that I believed you had made a mistake about me personally and I was, if you like, trying to prevent some of the consequences."

"Stop a minute," said Nosey Parker. "Keep off the business of my so-called excess of curiosity. I don't understand it and I don't believe it. What I find easier to understand is the game of knowing more than a mere policeman. It's common enough. Stick to that. Give me the facts about that, and I'll see if they hold water."

"You're making a mistake," Smithers said. "I leave technical matters to the expert. But I won't press the point. As to what I was going to do, I was keeping a watch on the coach. Whoever wanted to get something from it has not succeeded yet, and they are pretty anxious about it."

"So you come back to that," said Inspector Parker. "If you can do no better I'll find it hard to believe you. Don't you want to tell me what you were going to do? Do you still believe you can outsmart us? Or are you simply trying to see if we're interested in a red herring?"

The sergeant came quickly down the stairs.

"Well?" said the inspector.

"Gone, sir," said the sergeant.

Inspector Parker looked hard at Smithers.

"You're perfectly certain, sergeant?"

"Trabert, the man I put on duty here tonight said he saw Dagg about 11.45. The room's been pretty well tidied up. There wouldn't have been time to do it between then and the time we got the call. He must have had everything packed when Trabert saw him and have gone a minute or two after."

"Probably just making sure where Trabert was when he noticed him," the inspector said. "What about the boy?"

"Clean sweep there too, sir."

"Are you working on the prints?"

"Yes, sir. Long way to go, of course, yet, but no sign of anything but the boy, his father and what looks like a maid so far."

Inspector Parker turned to Smithers again.

"We don't believe much in subtleties in the force," he said. "I'm keeping an open mind, of course, because Dagg's one of the sort that take badly to policemen. On the other hand, he had something to hide or I'm a Dutchman. In any case from now on we concentrate all our energies on finding him. We won't forget that gun though. As to what you've been doing, I don't pretend to know. Good night."

As he went out he passed a constable coming in carrying a case.

"Tell Sergeant Hanks I want you to relieve Trabert and I want to see Trabert at the station right away," he said.

Smithers walked slowly upstairs and went to bed. He had been short of sleep since the murder and though the inn was noisy with police comings and goings all night he slept soundly.

Round the breakfast table set aside for the coach party, the murder party, two empty places.

"I happened to discover last night that Joe has left and has taken Peter with him."

An announcement from Smithers.

He sat down and began his breakfast.

"This time it must be all over," Kristen Kett said. "I can't stick it much longer. Why can't they tell us we can go back to London? Think of going and meeting people and forgetting your troubles."

The child's nose pressed against the sweet shop window.

"I think we're all a little anxious to be on our way," said Schlemberger. Wise uncle.

"I guess I'm not the one to talk," he continued. "I've had my little jaunt. But all the same, I'm mighty glad to see the case is cleared up."

"You think it is?" asked Fremitt.

"Look at the facts," Schlemberger said. "Number one: the guy's gone. That in itself should be enough for anyone. You can't get over a plain fact like that. Then there's number two: he was as nervy as a cat since the murder. I keep my eyes open. I was just watching what was going on. Right. Number three: from what I've been able to piece together there was no present Mrs Dagg and hadn't been for a good while, but there is a Dagg Junior. Add to that a great deal of prejudice against foreigners and what do you get? That his wife had run away with one a long time ago. Add to that one other fact: that Hamyadis had shaved off his beard. What's that add up to? You can see it now as well as I can. He recognised Hamyadis as the man who had seduced his wife. A pretty hard case, I'd say."

"It's a good case, sir," said Major Mortenson, "but there have been others."

"That's a pretty charitable sentiment," Schlemberger said. "But let me add one more circumstance I didn't think it necessary to refer to just now. Let us call it the incident of the major's confession. That's a piece of the jigsaw all right, and it's got to fit. Major, won't you tell us right now that you confessed to keep your old friend Joe Dagg out of trouble. Didn't you borrow your account of the beard business from him, from the truth as he told it to you in his trouble?"

The major looked at Schlemberger across the table. Bright blue eyes glittering.

"I prefer to make no comment on that," he said.

"I guess perhaps you couldn't," Schlemberger said.

"Has nobody considered the possibility that Dagg has not run away?" ask Richard Wemyss. "Kristen seems to be in a dreadful hurry to pin the crime on to the first person she can and hurry back to London, but personally I'd rather be sure. And after all, there's no hurry. We're very comfortable here."

"What do you mean about Joe not running away?" Kristen said. "Richie, I don't know what's got into you lately. We used to be such friends, and now you seem to say anything you can just to upset me."

"Not just to upset you, dear," Wemyss said. "Just to keep the record straight. Joe Dagg may have been murdered, you know. It would account for his disappearance just as well as this flight from justice everybody is so keen about."

"The police have discounted that theory," said Smithers. "Joe apparently packed before he left."

"Well, then," said Wemyss, "he may have gone off for other reasons. Just because he's not here, it's too easy to say he must be the murderer."

"I certainly agree we must avoid jumping to conclusions," Fremitt said. "He had an obvious dislike of the police. He was the sort to be so scared that he might run off. We ought to keep open minds, or at least to wait as long as possible before saying we know, or think we know."

"Personally," Wemyss said, "this disappearance clears the man in my eyes."

"Oh dear," said Daisy, "the longer this has gone on the less I've understood. If anyone was to ask me, and thank goodness no one ever does, I'd say that because someone—— No, that's too complicated—I'd say that because poor old Joe has run away it must mean he was the one who killed George. And I'm sure he had good reasons whatever they were."

For Daisy's surmise quick official confirmation.

Hardly had she finished speaking, leaving a silence, when Inspector Parker came in.

"Good morning," he said. "I hoped I might find you all together. I dare say Mr Smithers has told you the news."

A sharp survey of faces. The thrush on the lawn misses nothing.

"I see he has. Well, we haven't located them yet, but we have found most of their clothes and personal possessions hidden in a suitcase at the farm where the coach horses are. With other evidence this has led us to believe that they are very likely not attempting to leave this district. There's a pretty wide expanse of downs round about and it wouldn't be hard to hide out there at this time of year. There are dozens of odd little hollows and pockets of land they could use, beside copses here and there or even ditches."

"Why are you telling us this, inspector?" asked Smithers.

"I have my reasons," the inspector said. "To begin with we don't as yet know a great deal about Dagg's state of mind. He may be just thoroughly frightened and on the run, or he may not be. He may be desperate and ready to act."

"I suppose one of us is likely to know something he'd rather we didn't," said Daisy.

"Exactly," said the inspector, "there's been one murder and I intend to see there isn't another."

"You mean the man may be waiting to kill one of us?" Wemyss said.

"It's possible."

"Then I think you ought to know that he and I have quarrelled on a number of occasions. I always thought him pretty overbearing, and I'm afraid I didn't bother to conceal my opinions. In the circumstances I think I ought to get back to London as soon as possible. I'm ready to go this morning if you'd prefer it."

"I think you'll be rather safer here," said the inspector. "I have made certain arrangements. And in fact they were what I came up here to speak to you about. For the immediate future I want you all to stay in one party."

"It hasn't occurred to you, inspector, that that may expose some of us to danger even more effectually?" said the major. "I don't care one way or the other myself, but, dammit, there are ladies in the party."

He looked at Daisy. Kristen smiled, faintly.

"I'm well aware of the possibility that Dagg isn't our man," Inspector Parker said. "But my first job is to find him, and for that purpose I intend to enlist your aid, all of you. If he is hiding somewhere around, there is one thing that is certain to attract his attention and very likely to make him come out into the open. Because I don't disguise from you that he has only to lie absolutely low to elude us for some considerable time."

"I guess we'll all be happy to co-operate, inspector," said Schlemberger. "You just give us the broad outlines of this plan and you can rely on us to fix the details."

"Your part is comparatively simple," said Inspector Parker. "What I intend to do is to get the coach out again and to go for a series of rides round the town. In this sort of country Dagg is almost certain to spot it sooner or later, and it's my guess that he won't be able to leave the coach alone. When he moves we shall be ready for him."

"I suppose you want me to drive?" said the major.

"Please, if you would be so good," said the inspector. "I'm relying on you to see to all the technical side of the business."

"And you want us to dress up again?" said Fremitt.

"If you please."

"I take it this amounts to an order," Wemyss said.

"Not at all. I can't order you to do a thing like this. It's simply a request, though I must tell you that any refusals will be noted."

"I was just asking," Wemyss said.

"I see. Well now, major, how soon would you be able to make a start?" "Today?"

"As soon as it can be managed. I want to see Dagg as quickly as possible. That's why I'm doing this instead of a full scale search. It ought to be quicker if it comes off. What is the first moment you could be ready?"

"In about an hour, I suppose," the major said. "The horses would have to be fetched."

The inspector looked at his watch.

"It's now 8.45," he said. "Shall we say 10 o'clock promptly in the yard here. I'll let you have some labour if you want it, major."

Faded gold on faded blue, the old clock above the inn stables pointing at ten. Shadows not yet deep but dusky with the promise of heat to come. The mellow stones of the inn. The worn cobbles. A small crowd: twelve school children and two below school age, five servants from the inn, two passers-by, two police constables.

And in the middle of the square the High Flyer coach to London, journey postponed, indefinitely.

Major Mortenson, in full rig approved by a leading theatrical costumier as that of the proper period, sat on the box, the reins from the four matched greys held loosely. Waiting to board the vehicle the passengers. Three fewer than before.

"Right you are then," said the major. "If some of you gentlemen help the ladies up, we'll be off. Inspector Parker asked me to start as soon as possible. He's given me a route. We make a sort of circular tour. It should take us most of the morning. We don't want to tire the horses."

They clambered up, took their places, looked at each other, looked away. The major gave a flick to the reins and once again the coach moved off. No cheers.

Out of the narrow archway into the street. The major driving slowly, carefully.

They headed at once for the countryside and attracted little attention. A few people stared. Sometimes children ran along beside them for a short way. Faces at windows every now and again. Dogs barking.

No conversation among the passengers.

After twenty minutes Smithers said:

"Major, you didn't give us details of our route. Was that by design?"

"Our route's none of my choice," said the major.

"No, you told us: the inspector asked you to follow it. But did he say we weren't to be told where it would take us?"

"He didn't, no."

"Come, major, sooner or later my suspicions will be confirmed. There's nothing to be gained by not telling us all now. I'm right, am I not?"

"You are. I tried to argue the point, but your policeman is nothing if not obstinate."

"What's all this mean?" asked Kristen. "There's nothing but mysteries. Can't someone speak out?"

"It's just that this is the way we went when the coach left the town the day George was killed, dear," said Daisy.

"Guess it's a police reconstruction," said Schlemberger. "Pretty smart dodge to get us all there."

"It is and it isn't," the major said. "We go past the spot all right, but we don't stop."

"There's been no police car following us as far as I could see," said Fremitt. "I've been a little surprised at that. Perhaps we are exaggerating."

"Oh, don't deceive yourself," Wemyss said. "They're watching us all right. You can see the whole road easily from a few key points in this sort of country. All you need is men with field glasses and we're covered almost as well as if there was a policeman with us."

They stared uneasily at the various vantage points they could find all too quickly.

"What are we going to do when we reach—that is when we come to . . . ?" said Fremitt.

"The place where poor George was killed," said Daisy. "It's difficult even to think about it, isn't it?"

"I don't see why we've got to go past there at all," said Kristen. "We could go round, couldn't we?"

"Not now," said the major.

"Well then, couldn't we go back? Say I didn't feel well. I don't. I feel like hell. We'd have to turn back then."

"And go another day, I'm afraid," said Smithers. "I've no doubt the inspector chose this route with care, he won't be put off all that easily. No, I recommend that we go past and behave quite naturally as we do so."

"It would be nice," Daisy said, "but we do know already where we're going, don't we? We won't be able to help thinking."

"You're right, of course," Smithers said.

No one spoke while the coach under the hot sun clopped steadily on. The countryside implacably familiar.

"Very well," said Smithers. "I propose to take off this absurd hat at the brow of the incline and to keep silent until the place is out of sight."

"I don't see why," said Wemyss.

"I do it as a gesture of respect to a human being suddenly done to death," said Smithers. "There is no need for you or anybody to follow my example if you prefer not to."

Smithers looked straight in front of him. All the others except Daisy looked down. Daisy looked round at each of them in turn.

Nothing more was said till they crossed the brow of the gentle hill and looked once more at the place where George Hamyadis died. Smithers took off his hat. All the other men did the same. Daisy bowed her head. Kristen after giving her a quick glance from under her eyebrows followed suit.

Two miles further on the major turned off the London road.

"We make a wide sweep round now," he said, "and rejoin the main road just before we get back to Winchester."

The words were the first spoken since Smithers's declaration. But they broke the ice. Comments were made on the countryside and the heat of the sun. The major answered a series of questions about coaching. Smithers was asked about the history of the period. Daisy told a story about the difficulties that occurred when a coach had to move across the stage in one of her musicals.

Uneventful.

Only when they came to the villages was there any excitement. Then there was an onrush of children. Thin cheers. Laughter. Anxious mothers. Giggles from teenage girls. Terrified hens squawking and swerving.

At the last village before they joined the main road again one daring boy even leapt on to the back of the coach as the major took it at a sedate pace through the scattered onlookers. Smithers, who was sitting on the back bench, turned round and told the boy to get down.

"Your name Smithers?" said the boy.

"You see," said Kristen who overheard, "I knew it. They all know all about us. They're just standing there and saying, 'Look at the murderers'."

"I don't think anyone would believe we united to kill Hamyadis," Smithers said. "And now lad, down you jump."

"Is your name Smithers?" said the boy.

"Yes, it is, but down you get."

"This is for you," said the boy.

He thrust a sheet of paper screwed up into Smithers's hand and jumped from the coach. Smithers got to his feet and peered back, but the boy had run off between two cottages and was nowhere to be seen.

Smithers sat down again and looked at his fellow passengers.

None of them appeared to have noticed what the boy had done. With some difficulty Smithers unrolled the paper in the palm of his hand and glanced down at it. There were a few words laboriously written in pencil.

"DEAR SIR. SORRY DAD ASKED ME TO. HE HAS NOT SAID ANYTHING. MUST STAY. PETER."

While the coach travelled a hundred and fifty yards Smithers sat thinking. Then he said:

"Stop a minute, would you, major. I want to attract the attention of the police."

The major pulled the horses to a halt.

"What's happened?" said Schlemberger.

"I've had a note thrust into my hand by that boy that may have some bearing on Dagg's whereabouts," Smithers said.

He stood up and waved.

Nothing happened.

"You were given no signal for the police, I suppose, major," he said.

"You don't think I'm in their pay, do you?" the major said.

"No," Smithers said. "You've spoken too convincingly of your distrust and dislike of policemen for that. I simply wondered if they had made any arrangements to be summoned in a hurry."

"Not as far as I know," said the major.

Smithers turned and looked behind him again. Inspector Parker had just come out of the last cottage in the village. Smithers waved to him.

"What is it?" the inspector said.

Smithers handed him the note. He read it and signalled violently to someone in the cottage. A constable came running out.

"I don't know whether you saw a boy jump on the back of the coach for a few seconds," Smithers said. "He handed it to me."

"On my blind side, I take it," the inspector said.

"If you were in that cottage it would be."

"You'd recognise the boy again?"

"Almost certainly. Miss Kett saw him too. Perhaps she would."

"Ah, the obliging Miss Kett. Would you be able to identify the boy again, Miss Kett?"

"Identify him. I scarcely looked at him, the damn' cheeky little pest," said Kristen.

"Did anybody else see this boy Mr Smithers says got up behind the coach?" asked Inspector Parker.

"I thought there was some excitement or other," Fremitt said. "But Smithers was between me and whatever it was."

"I see. Well, I don't think I'll trouble you any more about it. If the boy was here no doubt he's run off."

"He ran very sharply between those two cottages," said Smithers.

A declaration of fact.

"I'll get you to describe him later and ask the local constable if he sounds familiar," said Inspector Parker. "In the meanwhile I'll consider all the implications of this note."

The major flicked at the reins and the coach started off again. Smithers briefly told the story of the note. They were back at the inn in time for lunch. Not a meal missed.

Round the table a little talk. Conversation. People asked polite meaningless questions. Remarks answered in general terms. But no one asked Smithers any questions. No one answered any of his remarks unless addressed directly. As they were finishing a message was brought from Inspector Parker. He said the afternoon coach trip was cancelled.

Smithers left the table and went to his room. There he undressed carefully and went to bed. He set his alarm clock to wake him in time for tea.

He did not stay long over the teacups. Again there was little said.

When Smithers had drunk a single cup of tea he left and walked at a rapid pace down the street to the police station and asked for Inspector Parker.

In the inspector's small office he said:

"I've come to do two things. First I would like to give you a description of that boy this afternoon."

Inspector Parker called a constable to take notes and Smithers gave a description of the boy. An extremely detailed description.

"We ought to be able to recognise him if we ever come across him," Nosey Parker said.

"I imagine he was from the village. Peter must have seen the coach, been told its probable route and gone down to the village to see if he could get a message to me," said Smithers.

"I had worked out that that was meant to be the pattern," the inspector said.

"And that brings me to the second thing I came here to do," said Smithers.

"I'd been wondering about that."

"I want to make a complaint."

"Oh, yes?"

"This afternoon you treated my report to you about this boy with such obvious disbelief that everyone in the party now suspects me of the murder."

"I see."

"I want you to do something to rectify that."

"Mr Smithers, I don't think I commented on your account in anything but a proper manner. Plainly, if I haven't your confidence you can't expect me to give you mine. If the consequences are what you say they are the remedy lies in your own hands."

"Let me get it quite clear," said Smithers. "In order to satisfy your morbid curiosity with a lot of gossip, based on the merest guesses, you are prepared as far as you dare to allow these people to believe I am a murderer."

"I won't in any way exceed my duty."

"That goes without saying, inspector. I don't deny your ability. I merely say you have allowed yourself to be carried away. You can't really believe a lot of hearsay and guesswork can help you solve this problem."

"The more I know the better chance I stand."

"Not if what you know isn't true."

"There are truths and truths. A half truth, a quarter truth may be of use to me."

"But what I could tell you, and what the others must have told you, could not even be described as quarter truths. You can't tell me you want inventions, because that is what you'll get and have got."

"I want everything."

"Exactly. Anything anyone tells you becomes sacred in your eyes because it's something, not even a fact, just something you can grip, to feed your curiosity. Well, you will get facts or nothing from me."

He walked out of the office.

For the rest of that evening he sat in the inn lounge at some distance from his fellow coach passengers. The pages of Vol. 5 of *The Decline and Fall* flipped over with the regularity of a machine. One by one the others left for bed. When the last pair had gone Smithers closed his book and walked quietly out of the inn into the cobbled yard. Once more he settled himself behind the water butt near the coach house door.

The cloudless summer sky was brilliant with stars. The moon, according to Smithers's diary, would not appear till nineteen minutes past midnight. The hours passed. From the inn the last signs of activity died away. The air was still and warm.

At last above the roof of the main building came the soft glow of moonlight. By it Smithers consulted his watch. 12.25. The light grew brighter. At 1:30 the rim of the moon itself appeared over the roof and the velvet shadowed yard began to divide into areas of lightness and dark.

Smithers watched, assessing the effects of this change. The shadows now provided better concealment. To eyes used to the bright moonlight they appeared almost impenetrable. Almost, but not quite.

Smithers peered into the densest of the black patches. And quietly straightened his back, flexed his muscles.

A flick. Noiseless. Scarcely visible. Something passed from the big shadow to the next patch. And again.

Smithers breathed slowly, soundlessly.

The figure slipped from one shadow to another. Nearer. A man. But oddly shaped. Smithers peered. At last. Coaching clothes. The caped coat, with a scarf round the head. Colourless in the moonlight, anonymous. The door of the coach house creaked slowly open. Smithers leant back against the wall.

The caped man slipped in. Smithers glanced at his watch. 1.34. He heard new faint noises. The groan of the coach bodywork. A slight ripping sound. Then silence. Smithers held his watch where the moonlight fell on it. The door of the coach house creaked again. Once, quickly, 1.40.

For a moment the man stood in the moonlight looking at something in his hands. Dagg? Conceivably. Too short surely for Schlemberger, too heavy for Fremitt. Much too short for the major.

Something in the tilt of the head in spite of the scarf wrapped round it. Wemyss.

ELEVEN

At last Wemyss moved. He turned to walk past Smithers's hiding place and Smithers was able to see that he was holding a large white envelope.

Smithers let him get just past. And darted. Grabbed the envelope and ran. In an instant round into the narrow passage where he had laid his ambush for Fremitt in the rain.

The whole alley was in deep shadow. The tall buildings on either side cut out all the moonlight. Smithers loped along, his eyes fixed on the back wall of the stables. Soon he found what he was looking for. A faint gleam from the coach house window. He half crouched now as he ran holding out his arms, and almost at once he felt the dustbin he had tripped over before. He sank to the ground beside it and sat hunched over his knees. For a moment he held his breath and then forced himself to exhale slowly and silently. At the second breath he heard Wemyss. Blundering steps. Muttering. Then:

"Who's that? I say, who's that? Where are you?"

Smithers kept silent, still.

"What the devil do you mean by it? Who are you?"

Still, silent.

Footsteps.

"Are you there?"

The steps stopped.

"Damn. Damn. Damn."

A long silence.

Then slow steps again. Moving away, round the corner, back in the direction of the inn.

Carefully Smithers eased himself up and peered in the direction Wemyss had gone. Nothing to be seen. Very quietly he walked off in the opposite direction. At the mouth of the alley he stopped and stood quietly for three minutes. Then he stepped cautiously out. The deserted street. A chocolate box scene in the moonlight.

Smithers slipped the bulky envelope he had taken from Wemyss into an inner pocket. He made no attempt to look at it. Quickly but quietly he set off up the street. He took the first corner, stopped and listened. No sound. He set off again. Another corner, another wait. Still no sound. He headed for the outskirts of the town.

Not until he was clear of buildings did he stop again. Then he sat down on a roadside bank and took the envelope from his pocket. It was large, stiff, and expensive looking, sealed with a heavy blob of green wax. It appeared to contain half a dozen documents. On it were written just three words: Miss Kristen Kett.

Smithers recognised the writing at once. He had seen several letters signed in the same large ornate hand. Signed George Hamyadis.

Making no attempt to open the envelope Smithers sat for a quarter of an hour holding it in front of him as if mesmerised.

When he got to his feet his face wore a hint of a smile.

He set off to walk through the moonlit countryside. He was walking at the first hint of day, and walking when the sun rose into a cloudless sky. When he got back to the hotel breakfast was almost due.

Smithers went straight to the reception desk and rang. When the clerk appeared—the washed out cotton dress, a pattern of small flowers almost faded away—he said he had something he wanted to put into the hotel safe. The girl took him to the little office where he had talked with Inspector Parker just before his trip to London. She opened a small safe let into the wall and Smithers asked for an envelope. The girl found a dusty buff one lying on the table. Smithers put Hamyadis's large white envelope into it, wrote his own name on the outside and handed it to the girl. He watched until the safe door was shut and then went upstairs, washed and shaved. He was down to breakfast on time.

At this meal late arrivals caused no comment, but no one ever missed it entirely, not even Kristen who ate nothing and sometimes did not even finish a single cup of tea. And each newcomer had their question. This morning when Smithers entered the room he found Fremitt there alone.

"I slept all the night," Fremitt said. "You didn't wake up and hear anything, I suppose?"

"As far as I am concerned the night brought no news," said Smithers.

"I didn't really mean that. Or perhaps I did. This business is upsetting, thoroughly upsetting. Or at any rate I find it so."

Next Daisy came in.

"Good morning. Anything happened?"

"I was just asking the same thing, more or less," said Fremitt. "The answer's a blank as usual."

After Daisy, Schlemberger.

"Here we are at another day. I sure hope the police get somewhere to-day. There was talk of dragging the river to look for the gun, seems a mite crazy to me. Still, they must do something. I guess they don't work nights, or do they?"

"They seemed to be quite alert the night Dagg left us," Smithers said.

Next the major.

"Bit late on parade, I see. Overslept. Hope everyone else managed to get off. No night alarms, eh?"

"We're just where we were," said Daisy.

"Ah well, another day, new hopes. Nil desperandum."

Richard Wemyss. White, drawn, not well shaved.

"Morning. Nobody asked for me I suppose? Where's Kristen?"

"Not down yet, I think," said Smithers.

Wemyss said nothing. Everybody ate. A little later the door opened and Kristen came in.

"Hell, I feel lousy," she said. "Any letters for me?"

"I didn't see any," said Fremitt.

"No," said Kristen. "You're not very good at seeing letters, are you?"

"I'm afraid I must confess to getting one every morning myself," Fremitt said. "Mrs. Fremitt is an excellent correspondent. And then of course she is worried too."

He spoke quickly.

"I suppose you didn't see any letters for me, Richie?" said Kristen.

"I've got better things to do than run around after you," Wemyss said. "It's time you understood that. I'm not here to obey your every whim. I'm here because you asked me to come and like a fool I agreed. And now look at me."

"All right, all right," Kristen said. "I may have asked you to come, but you were damned glad to take the job."

"I was nothing of the sort. I did you a favour and it's the last one I'm going to do you. Do you understand that?"

"I think I do," said Kristen. "I think I understand very well. You've let me down."

"Let you down——"

Abruptly Wemyss checked himself.

"Listen," he said, "there was nothing for me to let you down about. Nothing at all. Get that into your stupid head. And if you take my advice you won't go discussing your private affairs in public."

"My private affairs, I like that. I shall discuss what I want to, where and when I want to."

"All right then. Let's begin. There are one or two quite amusing things to discuss. Names for instance."

For a moment Kristen was silent.

"Now don't start that," she said. "Georgie used to play that game."

"And look what happened to him," said Wemyss.

"Are you saying I killed him?"

"No, I'm not," said Wemyss. "I'm not such a fool as to say that to anybody's face. All that I was saying is that you've got something you wouldn't want talked about in public."

"You're only saying that to make them all suspect me. To think I trusted you, Richard Wemyss. But you're not right, I've got nothing to hide."

"Oh, haven't you, Christine Kettle," said Wemyss.

Kristen put down her cup with a rattle. Tea spilt in the saucer.

"How did you know?" Kristen said. "Nobody was meant to know. They said it would spoil my career. I hate you."

She jumped up and ran fom the room.

"Silly idiot," said Wemyss.

Too forcefully.

"She pesters me," Wemyss said. "She's pestered me ever since we began this damn' trip, and I can't stand it any longer."

He got up and left them.

"Tell me," said Smithers to Daisy, who was sitting between him and the major, "how silly is she?"

"Silly enough, I think, to believe that if she did become a star she could keep that secret, and that it would matter very much if it came out."

"You know," said Schlemberger, "that I find interesting. Exceedingly interesting."

"In our profession, Schlemberger, we're accustomed to dealing with businessmen who know more or less what they're doing," said Fremitt. "But elsewhere it doesn't do to credit everybody with as much common sense as one trusts one has oneself."

"That's not exactly why I found Miss Miller's observation interesting, though," Schlemberger said. "I was rather reflecting that what wouldn't on the face of it appear to be a motive for murder might, given it was believed by someone in the lower intelligence brackets, possibly become such a motive."

"My dear chap," said Fremitt, "I don't think we need go looking any further for the person the police want. It's surely stretching things a bit far to abandon someone who, after all, has absconded, in favour of any theory, however ingenious."

"I suppose," said Smithers, "we are cast for our role of decoys again this morning."

"I was asked to have the coach ready by ten again," said the major.

"Don't hurry, major," said Schlemberger. "With all due deference to my distinguished English colleague I strongly suspect that after I've had a word with Inspector Parker the coach idea will go."

"I suppose it is evidence in a way," said Daisy. "Though I'm sure there was something in a play I once did on tour about evidence not being what anyone was heard to say. But perhaps I've got muddled."

"I'm afraid you have a little, dear lady," said the major. "The police will certainly want to hear our good friend Schlemberger's theory. Though whether they will altogether welcome another likely suspect I can't say."

But the major appeared to be wrong.

Before Schlemberger had had time to get in touch with Inspector Parker he appeared in the dining room himself and inquired for Kristen.

"I've one or two things I want to ask her," he said.

"She's up in her room, I expect," Smithers said. "She left us rather hurriedly just now, and she frequently complains of feeling ill."

"I'll go up and see if she's available," the inspector said.

He turned and left them among the breakfast debris. Broken toast, half-emptied cups, plates sticky with marmalade, the smell of grilled bacon no longer fresh. As he reached the door he said:

"Oh, by the way, Mr Smithers, we found your boy. The village constable recognised him at once from your description. The lad says he was given the note by a boy he had never seen before and dared to hand it to you. In the circumstances I'm giving up the decoy business."

"I had imagined a liquorice bootlace or some such must have changed hands," Smithers said. "But Peter is evidently economical."

The inspector closed the door.

"Do you know," said Daisy, "yesterday I got the distinct impression that Nosey Parker didn't believe a word you were saying about that boy and the note. I was so cross that I hadn't seen whether there had been a boy or not: I would have loved to have known if you were lying. You did it so well."

"No," Smithers said, "I'm afraid I have no talent for acting. Beyond perhaps deceiving a fourth form into thinking I am 'in a wax'. You were hearing no more than the literal truth, and even that apparently did not sound altogether convincing."

"We discussed you as a murderer behind your back," Daisy said. "The others were being reluctantly convinced, and I was wondering whether it was really best to have the murder committed by someone you liked, so that it could be done for a good reason, or whether it should be someone you didn't mind about and no reason in particular."

"Now I must disassociate myself from every word of that," the major said. "I won't deny to you, Smithers, that I considered the possibility. It was thrust upon one. But never let it be said that I plumped for you. I have been at pains, I hope, to plump for no one."

"I have observed your scrupulous fairness, major," said Smithers. "I'm glad its scope extended to myself."

"I'm sure Miss Miller was joking," Fremitt said. "That is, joking about us. Her sentiments about the identity of the murderer are such that they must have occurred to us all, more or less."

"Anyhow," said Daisy, "now you know what it's like, Mr Smithers. And so do I for that matter. Tell me, what did everybody think about my piece of mysteriousness? Were they all just waiting for the arrest?"

"It was certainly a factor that had to be taken into account," said Schlemberger. "I guess I'm in a better position to see the ins and outs of an affair like this than most. After all whether it's a case of murder or suspected arson it's all a question of detecting fraud. Now there's one principle you've got to stick to right hard when it comes to a fraud case: and that's that everything must fit in. Your piece of mysteriousness, as you called it, certainly did worry me at times, Miss Miller."

"Well, I'm glad you're happy about it now," said Daisy.

"Miss Miller," said Smithers, "I think we all owe you a debt. It was high time we had this conversation."

"You mean you think it might give us some clues?" said Schlemberger.

"You still feel the need of clues then?" asked Fremitt.

"I haven't arrived at anything more than a strong hypothesis," said Schlemberger. "There's an awful lot of facts unaccounted for. Miss Miller has been good enough to remind us that she is still a figure of mystery, and there are other things."

"And I thought you had forgotten that I hadn't explained," said Daisy.

"I take it," said Smithers, "that you don't feel yet that you can."

"I don't see why she should," the major said. "A woman is entitled to her mystery."

"That's a fine sentiment, major," said Schlemberger, "but perhaps just a little British."

"As I see it," Smithers said, "it's a question of whether one is prepared to accept Miss Miller's assurance that her reticence has nothing to do with the murder. It's a decision for each to take for themselves."

"Though I may add," said Fremitt, "that the decision can be made easier if one has other facts at one's disposal which may tend to minimise its importance. And there are facts, which may or may not be relevant, which are known to some of us and not to others."

"If one is convinced these facts are not relevant and if they concern someone else it would not be right to reveal them," said Smithers.

"No, I disagree," Fremitt said. "I have half wished for some plain speaking for a long time now. The opportunity has arisen. I am determined to clear the air."

"Let us then confine ourselves to facts," said Smithers. "To tangible facts and their explanation."

"Certainly. And here is one fact. The second night after Hamyadis's death Smithers and I met some time after midnight in a downpour of rain in the vicinity of the coach house. The boy, Peter, was with Smithers."

"I grant that fact," said Smithers. "And I concede that both of us ought to offer explanations of such unlikely conduct following so quickly on a murder."

"Are you prepared to do that now?" asked Fremitt.

"I think so," said Smithers. "But I am a little worried by the way you have put your initial proposition."

"Very well," Fremitt said, "then let me add that Smithers and the boy saw me break the little window at the back of the coach house and that I intended to enter it. Now, why were you there, Smithers?"

"Simply because I had been there the night before and had seen two separate people attempt to enter the coach house," Smithers said. "One of them was obviously determined to find the automatic used to kill Hamyadis. As a matter of fact I found it myself later and it was then stolen from my room the same night. But that is not the point at issue. The question that worried me was what the second intruder wanted. So I watched again."

"I was not that second intruder," Fremitt said. "Do you believe I was?"

"I don't know. One of the attempts on the first night was made by a woman, but you could have been the man I half saw."

"Tell me," said Daisy, "did you know it was a woman because of her scent?"

"Yes."

"I wondered why the inspector asked me about my scent. He was so off-handed."

"Or Kristen Kett," said Schlemberger. "It begins to add up."

"Fremitt," Smithers said, "have you any comment to make now?"

A pause.

"Yes, I think perhaps it would be fairest if I did. I think I ought to tell you that Miss Kett asked me to find something—I won't say what it was, except that it wasn't a gun—on the coach. I failed as you have heard."

"So if we were looking at it as a matter of strict logic," said the major, "it could have been the Kett girl herself searching the coach on the first night. But if she had preferred to ask someone to act for her, then the case against Miss Miller looks stronger."

"Let me ask the question," Smithers said. "Did anyone here act for Miss Kett on that first night?"

Silence.

"Young Wemyss is most likely I guess," said Schlemberger.

"I certainly think he ought to be asked," Smithers said.

As they left the room in a body the major, glancing round to see if there was anybody to overhear, said:

"There's a possibility I don't think we should neglect. It's conceivable that the girl looked for the gun herself and provided this other business as a red herring."

"I wonder what that inspector's asking her up there?" Schlemberger said.

They walked in a group through the downstairs rooms of the inn. Wemyss was sitting outside the windows of the lounge on one of the benches in the cobbled yard. They went out and assembled round him.

"We're having a bit of a talk," Schlemberger said. "I proposed the idea before but everyone walked out on me then. Still, better late than never."

"If you mean you're bandying accusations," said Wemyss, "I've not changed my opinion. I've nothing to say about this business and I don't wish to hear anything about it."

"Nevertheless," said Smithers, sitting down beside Wemyss and looking up at the others, "it is a matter which concerns you. And so I propose to continue our conversation and you can listen or not as you like. But let us be fair and pursue some line you are not immediately connected with."

Wemyss looked up. None of the others moved. Wemyss took up his paper again.

A poor actor.

"Major," said Smithers, "in the light of our present talk have you anything to tell us about your attempt to confess to killing Hamyadis?"

"I suppose the inference is that since I confessed falsely to the murder I must know who was responsible and wish to take the blame from them," the major said. "Dulce et decorum, eh? That must be what you've all been thinking these last few days."

"Do you know," Daisy said, "I'd forgotten all about it. I'm awfully sorry, major, when it was your big scene and everything, but so many things seemed to happen."

"I'm delighted to hear it, my dear," said Major Mortenson. "It helps me to make my point. The more we look into this the more it looks as though any one of us could have done the business. And that was precisely what I intended to show you by my little demonstration beside the coach. Knowing I had not killed Hamyadis I simply intended to prove that it could look conclusively as if I had. It was a warning."

"A likely story," said Wemyss.

"An unlikely one," said Smithers, "and as such making all the better claim to our credence."

"It could fit," said Schlemberger. "It could be a case of the guy who's too clever."

"That covers rather too much, I think," said Smithers. "Let us put it rather: the man who finds it necessary to express a simple logical thought in terms of wild imaginative exaggeration. Do you read P. C. Wren, major?"

"A very fine writer, sir."

"He frequently makes use of such characters, and seems to honour them."

"All the same, Major Mortenson," said Schlemberger, "I contest your point. Someone killed Hamyadis. A patient investigation into every suspicious circumstance will very likely show us who. I propose to pick up our little inquiry at the place we left it off just now. Mr Wemyss, did your friend Kristen ever ask you to find something for her in the High Flyer coach?"

Wemyss slowly raised his head and looked at Schlemberger.

"I've not the least idea what you mean," he said.

"Right," said Schlemberger, "that answers one question. I think that we can assume it was Miss Kett herself looking round the coach in her own interests, whatever they may be, on the night after the crime."

" 'Assume,' sir," said the major. "You've chosen the right word. I've seldom had to listen to such a lot of barefaced assumptions. You assume Wemyss here is telling the truth, you assume the girl has the guts to do her own dirty work, you assume a hell of a lot."

Wemyss stood up. He faced Major Mortenson.

"Are you calling me a liar?" he said.

"I think we'll go no further," said Smithers.

A chill.

"It was going to be quite exciting," said Daisy. "But I suppose you're right. When it comes to it it's always rather horrid."

Wemyss, almost pushing past Fremitt, strode back into the inn. At the door he met Inspector Parker.

He turned and looked at the group by the seat and said loudly:

"Perhaps you are about to hear the official answer to your sordid speculations. I sincerely hope so, and I don't much mind which of you it is who goes down to the police station."

The inspector stood aside to let him go in, and drew the tip of his right index finger slowly across the side of his enormous nose.

He walked across to them.

"An accusation of murder leading to a breach of the peace might well be criminal," he said. "I hope nobody has been indulging."

"We were talking about the murder," Smithers said. "There had to come a time when we did. Unfortunately things got out of hand."

"There was some plain speaking?" asked Nosey Parker. "Has anybody got anything further they would like to tell me, I wonder?"

There was a short silence. Then Daisy said:

"I think you're being very unfair, inspector. Just because you haven't been quite frank with us you seem to think we haven't been quite frank with you. And don't pretend you have been frank. I've just found out what all those artless questions about my scent were leading up to. I'm a little disappointed in you."

Inspector Parker looked at Smithers.

"I see you have been talking well and truly," he said. "But I came out to ask Miss Miller if she would be so good as to look in on Miss Kett. She was complaining of feeling ill when I left her just now. I don't think it's a case for a doctor, but a little womanly sympathy would no doubt be appreciated."

"So she wouldn't tell about her scent," said Daisy. "I can't say I altogether blame her."

Inspector Parker looked down at his feet, small and neat in brown shoes.

"I'll bid you good morning then," he said. "I've a lot to do. We're dragging the river this morning. It's just possible the person who disposed of the gun didn't take many precautions."

The long nose suddenly flicked up and the inspector darted a look at them all.

"And with any luck," he said, "we'll have Dagg and his boy to talk to before this evening. There's someone who will have something to say. And the boy too."

This time the look was for Smithers alone.

"You don't take Peter's note at its face value then?" Smithers said.

"I've no comment to make," said Inspector Parker.

He turned on his heel and walked quickly out of the archway turning in the direction of the police station.

"I must go and see Kristen," Daisy said.

The others parted without a word.

Each went to occupy themselves somehow or other. Filling in the long hours. Deadening the waiting. Looking for some distraction. Avoiding the question poised over them all.

Aimless walks through the town, coffee lingered over in cafés, papers read to shreds, cigarettes smoked, small purchases carefully made, clock golf, crosswords.

Smithers sat on the bench where the discussion had ended. He was reading the concluding pages of Volume 5 of *The Decline and Fall*. Volume 6 in his well-worn edition lay beside him. The sun was warm. The pages turning regularly.

Under the reign of Ommiades the studies of the Moslems were confined to the interpretation of the Koran, and the eloquence and poetry of their native tongue. A people continually exposed to the dangers of the field must esteem the healing powers of medicine, or rather of surgery; but the starving physicians of Arabia murmured a complaint . . .

"Please sir, please sir."

"Yes, what is it?" Smithers said without taking his eyes from the page.

"Please sir, I've been telling you for the last five minutes, sir, I've come back."

Smithers looked up.

Peter.

TWELVE

Smithers closed the book.

"I thought I might see you before long," he said. "Does your father know?"

"No, he doesn't, Mr Smithers, sir," said Peter. "Was I wrong to come?"

"That depends on why you came."

"I thought about it a lot," said the boy. "Dad kept saying that he supposed he'd done it now and the rozzers would pin the murder on him if they caught him, and he said he'd had to get away from them for me. I think that was why I thought it would be best for me to go."

"Then I don't think you were wrong," said Smithers. "But tell me again, as carefully as you can, just what your father said."

The boy hesitated.

"You can tell me, you know," said Smithers. "I'm only here to help you reason it out."

"Well, he didn't say much really," Peter said. "He did a lot of talking but it was mostly the same things."

"I see. About the police pinning it on him?"

"Yes. At first I thought that that must mean he hadn't done anything. Then he would say something a bit different, and I'd begin to wonder if he hadn't done something. You did know I was wondering about him and the murder, didn't you?"

"You couldn't have helped it with all the talk you must have heard. The important thing was not to make up your mind unless there was something you couldn't escape, and you did that."

"I still can't make my mind up," said the boy. "Sometimes I wish I could, one way or the other."

"That's what we all feel," said Smithers. "But we shall just have to keep on patiently looking at everything until we get the right answer. That's why I have to ask you these questions. Now was there anything else he said?"

"He said a lot about keeping out of harm's way."

"I see."

"And he said it wasn't the same for him as the others, and that if he went who would I have."

"Who would you have?"

"Well, nobody really. My mum was dead a long time ago."

"No aunts? No uncles?"

"No, Dad hasn't got any family. He's what they call an orphan."

"Yes. And what else did he tell you up there?"

"There was something else, something I didn't understand," Peter said.

"Perhaps I can help over that."

"It was something like being necessary before the fact."

"An accessory before the fact?"

"Yes, I think that was it. Please, Mr Smithers, what does it mean?"

"It means knowing about something bad before it was done and allowing it to happen."

"I see."

The boy sat still in the warm sun. After a while Smithers asked:

"Well, what do you think? Can you still escape it, or not?"

"He didn't say he really was a nec— an accessory before the fact. It all came in with the bit about it being pinned on him. He said it was something he would never have even thought of."

"Did he say much about that?"

"No, I think he only talked about it once. That was why I wasn't sure how to say the long word. Most of the time it was about keeping out of harm's way."

Smithers sat without speaking for a moment. Then he slapped the two volumes of Gibbon together and said:

"All right. But have you thought about what you're going to do now that you have left your father?"

"Will I have to go to the police?"

Puppy dog beg.

Smithers said nothing.

"Dad did keep on about 'You've always got to steer clear of the rozzers'."

"What do you think?"

"I suppose I've got to see them really if I did leave him. But Dad has got something to hide, I know he has."

"But you are here, aren't you? Come along, I'll walk you down and we'll sort out what you have to say."

Peter was in the police station for about half an hour. Smithers was still standing on the pavement opposite when he came out. Peter crossed over and joined him.

"It was all right really," he said. "In fact old Nosey was pretty decent. Oh, I'm sorry: you said I wasn't to call him that."

"I know when not to hear a thing."

"I asked him if he thought Dad had done it."

"You know he isn't allowed to answer that question."

"Yes, he told me. But he said I wasn't to worry."

"Very sound advice."

"He asked me if I'd seen you, sir."

"And you told him you had?"

"Yes, so he asked me what we'd talked about, and I told him that too. It was all right to, wasn't it?"

"Perfectly."

"He asked me if you'd told me anything about what you'd been doing while I was away. It was a good thing you hadn't, because I wouldn't have told him."

"Do you want to know now?"

"Yes, please."

Smithers gave him a factual account of his activities and ended:

"I won't tell you what I think is in the packet Mr Wemyss had because, for one thing, it's only a guess. But I will give you this warning. Don't mention it to anyone. It wasn't the reason Mr Hamyadis was killed, but if anyone knew I had it, they might go to considerable lengths to get it back."

"I won't say a word."

"Now then, come along and let's get some lunch."

"I've got to see all of them again, I suppose."

"Yes, but I will simply say you have been to the inspector and that will be enough."

When Smithers made his announcement there was silence. Only Kristen had any comment.

"But he can't run away and come back here like this," she said.

"The inspector sent him back," Smithers said. "I propose to keep an eye on him for the time being."

"I suppose his father will just come in and sit down for tea," said Kristen. "The bloody police. They don't know what they're doing. That foul inspector bullied me half the morning and made me feel sick, and with a policeman there scribbling it all down. It isn't fair. Why can't they concentrate on catching the man they want?"

"That," said Smithers, "is all you will say on that subject."

Heads lowered all round the table. Exercise books toiled painfully at; discipline.

But nothing could have prevented the glances at the window as the meal was almost over. Halted at the traffic lights in the road outside two open lorries, sitting neatly in them policemen. Serried. Purposeful.

"I suppose they're on their way to the down," said Smithers. "We must be prepared for the consequences of any act. Peter, you and I will spend this afternoon watching the dragging operations by the bridge. It is concerned with facts at their most tangible."

They had no difficulty in finding the place where the police were carrying out their search of the river at that moment. As they approached they saw a knot of people all looking down at the water. A motor coach was parked nearby and the majority of the crowd looked as if they were on holiday and were delighted to get an extra attraction free. Their numbers were added to by two errand boys leaning on their bicycles and three people dressed with more formality than the coach party, active in being in the crowd but not of it.

Smithers and Peter joined the group and soon found themselves on the ancient bridge wedged against the lichened stones. The crowd had grown shortly after their arrival. A troop of schoolboys on holiday tacking itself on to the edge, milling and shoving. The forty people shifted and strained to get a better view of the activities below them. A buzz of chatter. And the unbudging stones.

Below the river flowed steadily and broadly, the force of the current creating a slight wave as the stream parted at the heavy piers washed smooth by the water of centuries. The river had been marked out with light cords tied to poles stuck in each bank with other cords in the direction of the waters' flow held up here and there by bobbing corks. Some of the marker poles had small pieces of coloured rag fixed to the top and fluttering in the occasional puffs of summer breeze. A sports day. The crowd pushed, chattered, laughed. The sun shone.

There was even a scorer's table. It was set up about twenty yards from the river's bank and at it sat Inspector Parker and a sergeant. A telephone line ran up to the table. The inspector in the intervals of directing the river search made frequent calls.

Nothing of holiday in his anxious watch over the searchers. There to find a murder weapon.

The work was being carried out systematically. One party of three men on each bank in shirt sleeves and wearing waders dealt with the waters' edge. Six divers, in bright bathing trunks with flippers on their feet, goggles, and breathing tubes worked section by section over the rest of the river.

Every now and again one would break the surface holding out some object in front of him. There would be a gasp from the crowd, people would point and then the audible sigh of disappointment when as the mud and weeds fell away the find would turn out not to be a gun. After several false alarms the crowd began to thin. In the hot sun the search went on steadily. One of the divers at the furthest point from the inspector's table sketched a little pantomime and when he had attracted some attention produced with a flourish an old boot. There was a round of applause led by the remaining members of the holiday outing. Value for no money.

An ice cream van drove up and soon attracted a short queue of buyers.

From the river stirred now to dirty turbulence more slime covered articles were produced. Smithers turned to Peter.

"Well now," he said, "how do you feel about all this?"

"I can't help being a bit excited, sir."

"No, neither can I. I keep thinking that at any moment one of these men might, just might, bring up that gun that you and I saw in the moonlight outside the coach house. A solid object for the police scientists to work on. Each time one of those divers bobs under I hold my breath."

"Look," said Peter, "there goes another of them. I wonder . . ."

They watched the hooked tube of the diver being dragged erratically about the patch of water marked out by the lines.

"Do you think you can tell if he's found anything by watching the way it goes?" said Peter. "Sometimes they seem to stick in one place ever so long and then I begin to think the man's trying to pick something out."

"Look," said Smithers, "he's quite still now. And there's one of his legs splashing. He's kicking to get down a bit deeper."

The hooked tube was pulled under the water. The small square of river stilled. Then quite unexpectedly the diver's head broke the surface.

"He's got something," Peter said.

"And what's more I think he's pretty sure it's what they're looking for," Smithers said. "Do you see he's not holding it up. He's clasping it quite closely to him so that no one up here can get a proper look."

"And he's coming out," said Peter.

Quickly the rest of the crowd spotted the man. Talk stopped. Faces peered and craned as the man still holding something close to his body and cupped in his hands loped towards the inspector's table. The sergeant stood up and took a half pace towards him. The man put the object on the table and all three examined it eagerly.

Abruptly Inspector Parker flung himself back in the kitchen chair he was sitting on and gave a huge shrug of his shoulders. The gesture conveyed everything. Failure.

The diver picked the slime covered find off the table and hurled it at a bed of nettles behind. But instead of going in the direction of his throw it shot out of his hand and landed on the river bank immediately under the bridge. Against a background of short grass there was no difficulty in seeing what it was. A toy cowboy's six-shooter.

Peter was trembling.

"I thought it was all over one way or the other," he said.

"You know, even if they do find it it may not help them," said Smithers.

"But it would be something," said the boy. "I do so want to know."

Smithers looked down at him. His hands were holding hard on to the rough stone of the bridge parapet.

"Peter," Smithers said, "I have a name in my mind and it's one that need cause you no worry."

"You know, sir?"

Sunlight through storm clouds.

"No, Peter, I have guessed. All that business of the two things hidden in the coach put me off for a while, but, when I realised what all that was probably about, the rest of it suddenly became quite clear."

"Please sir, aren't you going to tell Nosey Parker?"

"He wouldn't be interested in my guesses. And that's all it is, remember, a guess. If I went to him with it the most likely thing to happen would be that he would discount the whole idea. And if I'm right, and I think I am, by telling the inspector I would simply have impeded the course of justice."

"I know you're not going to tell me."

"No, Peter, not a guess."

A long pause. The boy's clouded eyes.

"But, sir, what will happen, then? Won't anybody ever know?"

"I think they will, Peter. You see it isn't just that somebody decided to kill Mr Hamyadis, shot him, and then stopped. It's something happening that's still going on. The person I'm thinking of is still trying to improve on what they did. And that's where they are going to make their mistake."

"And you'll catch them, sir?"

"I shall be on my guard."

They looked down at the river again. The searchers were now almost at the end of the marked section. The crowd was thinning. The outing party had opened packets of sandwiches and were sitting on the parapet facing away from the river. One of the waders beckoned to the sergeant. He went over and they had a short discussion by the river's edge. The sergeant peered despondently at the muddy water at his feet and went back to the table. Inspector Parker stood up.

"Do you think they're calling it off, sir?" said Peter.

"They seem to have covered most of the area," Smithers said. "And I don't think anyone in a hurry could have thrown the gun even as far as they have marked."

Inspector Parker walked down to the river's edge. The sergeant took some papers from the table and followed him.

"Yes," Smithers said. "It looks as if they're calling it off."

The sergeant, the man in waders and the inspector all talked together for a few moments. They looked down at the water. The inspector nodded.

But, instead of wading out of the river, the searcher abruptly plunged his hand into the water at his feet.

There was a splash as he snatched something up and buried it in a sheet of paper the sergeant held out to him. The sergeant bundled it up in a flurry of excitement.

Inspector Parker shook the wader's hand. Enthusiastically.

"Right everybody," he called.

Peter looked up at Smithers.

"They have found it after all, haven't they?" he said.

"They have," said Smithers.

News for the news hungry tea table. Though as it turned out everyone who came to it had already heard the story that had gone buzzing round the town. Only to Kristen was the account of the finding of the gun something largely new. But she displayed little interest.

"We all know Georgie was shot, don't we?" she said. "What good does finding the gun do? Why don't they arrest someone?"

"So you are anxious for an arrest?" said Schlemberger. "That surprises me a little."

"Look, I don't like it here," Kristen said. "The whole atmosphere makes me feel rotten. I want to go back to London, away from the whole lot of you."

"That's kind," said Richard Wemyss.

"Oh, Richie, why do you say things like that? You've changed. We used to be such friends. I'm sure we will be when we both get to London again."

"So you don't expect Mr Wemyss to be arrested," said Schlemberger. "You know it would very much interest me to hear who it is you have your eye on."

"Have my eye on?"

"Yes, who do you expect the police will arrest? We'd all like to know."

"I've no idea who they'll arrest," Kristen said. "I've had other things to think about. It's the job of that nasty inspector to make arrests, and I wish he'd get on with it."

"You know I think that's a very sensible point of view," said Daisy. "I only wish I could stick to it myself. But I keep on and on wondering all the time. I try to work it out sometimes, but, of course, I only get in a muddle. Somebody tell me: is it important that they've found the gun?"

"It might be certainly," Fremitt said. "It depends if the forensic science people can bring up any fingerprints. I suppose it must have been fired with gloves on. I think we were all wearing them, but it may have been touched with the bare hand when it was stolen from Hamyadis's cases in the first place."

"Hocus pocus, sir," said the major. "Come, do you really know anything about fingerprints?"

"Not a great deal I must confess," said Fremitt. "But in my own line we employ scientists and they can tell us pretty well what caused any fire. Remarkable work in its way."

"Remarkable deception," said the major. "I'll tell you how it's done. It's quite simple. The secret of the whole thing can be put in two words."

"Be careful, major," said Schlemberger. "Let me warn you I am a hundred per cent on the side of my colleague in this. Those scientific boys have put over some pretty good stuff."

"Then you listen as well. It's high time you learnt some sense," the major said. "Two words, that's all. And what are they? Just: stick together. Now, come, admit it, neither of you know very much about the methods these people employ. You can't possibly check their work. So you are bound to believe what they choose to tell you."

"No, it won't do, major," Fremitt said. "You perhaps don't know it but often enough these experts disagree. They don't stick together."

"So," said Major Mortenson, "the experts tell contradictory stories and you still believe them. And what's more, in spite of their contradictions, they still stick together. Not one of them ever gives away the show. They never admit that they're just taking wild guesses. If they've guessed differently from the other chap, they invent scientific nonsense to account for it. They simply play into each other's hands."

"That may be," said Smithers, "but the correctness or fallibility of the police scientists doesn't really concern us now."

"But I thought the major said it did, and he was very emphatic," Daisy said.

"He did," Smithers said, "but, however emphatic he is, I don't think he will induce the police to abandon their methods, and if they get any results from them be sure they will act on them. That is our immediate concern."

"Do you know, it's odd," said Daisy, "but now it looks as if it might all be over soon, I can't believe it."

"They might find nothing on the gun," Smithers said.

"I suppose they haven't had any luck in their other search," Wemyss said. "If you ask me they're on a better wicket there, even though that's a pretty chancy one."

"Peter," Smithers said, "you know that sooner or later everybody is bound to want to talk about your father. You must have had short nights out on the downs; how about going off to bed straight away?"

The boy thought for a moment.

"All right," he said.

At the door Smithers said to him quietly:

"Don't forget what I told you this afternoon. Now I feel a little surer."

"I won't forget," said the boy.

"I suppose you think I oughtn't to have mentioned his father like that," said Wemyss when Smithers came back.

"Yes, I do," Smithers said. "Nothing we can say will make much difference. Sooner or later the police will pick him up."

"You sound very despondent about it all," Daisy said.

"I suppose I am," said Smithers. "This is a nasty business, whatever happens."

After a while Richard Wemyss said:

"I'm going for a walk. I can't stand this. Kris, will you cheer up a bit, try and look decent and come with me?"

Kristen jumped up. The others sat in silence until she came downstairs again five minutes later and joined Wemyss. She was walking more jauntily than she had done since the murder.

"I could have done it once," said Daisy. "And I would have done too. But nowadays I have to sleep the glooms off. And I'm going up to try."

"I'm ready," they heard Kristen say from the hall. "Ooh, I wonder if there are any letters for me. I thought having all this publicity would stir up a bit of fan—— Hallo, Richie, here are two for you and both from America. I didn't know you knew anybody over there. In fact you denied it the other day. I bet this means you're the murderer, but don't worry I won't——"

"Give me those letters."

Wemyss's voice was low but it carried clearly to the group round the tea table.

Through the open door they watched him take the two letters, rip them open and read them over quickly. Then he laughed.

"That's one in the eye for you, Kris," he said. "Fan mail, and from America too. A couple of teenagers who saw my elegant profile in an advertisement for Scotch."

"But both on the same day," Kristen said, her voice as loud as his. "I still think it's fishy. Poor old Richie, now you're in my power."

"Not really so odd," Wemyss said. "It so happens they've just released the film. I expect I shall get a flood of them from now on. But if you're still prepared to risk a walk with someone you suspect of killing your ex-boy friend, come on."

They left together.

"I ought to go along and see if the horses are all right, come to that," said Major Mortenson. "I need a brisk walk. You can cast off depression easily enough if you keep active. Mens sana, you know."

"And I must go along to that little office and have an hour on the phone with Sam," Schlemberger said. "Poor Sam's a mighty worried man."

"I'm sorry to desert you too," Fremitt said. "But I promised Mrs Fremitt a daily letter and I find I need rather a long time to compose it. One doesn't know what to say and what to conceal."

"Don't worry about me," Smithers said, "I have my book, I shall be quite happy."

Fremitt looked at him for a moment.

"There's something——" he began, and then stopped. "No," he said, "I may be wrong. Another time will do if necessary."

Smithers picked up his Gibbon.

The tea was cleared away and he sat on reading. The flick, flick of the pages, the silver chime of the clock over the stables striking each quarter.

Six, a quarter past, half past. . . . Seven. . . . Seven-thirty.

Smithers jerked up his head and listened intently. Then he dropped his book and ran up the broad stairs. Along the corridor. No doubt now.

Screams.

High pitched screams. Perhaps a woman, more likely a boy.

He swept open the door of Peter's room. The boy was sitting up in bed, pale as a ghost, wide-eyed, screaming.

THIRTEEN

"Peter," said Smithers sharply.

The boy went on screaming.

Smithers took a glass of water from the hand basin and flicked some of it into Peter's face.

The screams stopped.

"Now then," said Smithers, "was it a nightmare, or what?"

"No sir, it wasn't," whispered the boy. "I'm sure it wasn't."

"Steady then. It was something that frightened you, was it?"

"Yes."

Almost inaudible.

"Well, there's no need to be frightened now, is there? I'm here."

The boy looked cautiously round the room.

"And no one else is, nothing else is. You're perfectly safe. Now then. Lie down again and keep warm and then you can tell me all about it. Steady a minute, your pillow's on the ground, I'll pick it up for you."

"Then it was true," Peter said.

Voice suddenly clear and loud.

"What was?"

"Look," Peter said, scrambling round in the bed, "I've got my pillows. There were only two and here they are. That's a different one."

"It must have been left in here. There's nothing to get scared about in an extra pillow."

"No sir, it wasn't left. Somebody tried to smother me with it, sir."

"Now Peter, it was simply a dream. You buried your head in your pillows and dreamt you were being smothered."

The boy sat silent.

"Sir," he said, "what about the extra pillow? I know it wasn't here when I came to bed because I looked for my pyjamas under my pillows and they weren't there so I know I only had two pillows."

"It may have been lying down there where I picked it up all the time."

"No, it couldn't have been. I would have walked on it when I came back from the window and—— Sir, I never told you about what I heard."

"What you heard? What is all this?"

"It was nothing to do with—with the smothering bit, sir. This was different. Or I think it was."

"Now you're getting confused. Try and forget all about it."

"No, sir. This bit, what I heard when I leant out of the window, sir, wasn't a nightmare. I could see them both as well as hear them talking."

"See who? You're getting me into a fine old whirl."

"Mr Schlemberger and Mr Wemyss, sir. I heard them first of all. They must have woken me from a bit of a doze. They were quarrelling. I couldn't help hearing."

"Didn't you say you went to the window?"

"That was after, sir. At first I didn't know what to do because I didn't think they would go on like that if they knew I could hear. Then I thought I would go very quietly and see if I could shut the window without them seeing."

"But you did listen?"

"I wasn't going to, sir, honestly. But as I leant out to see if they would spot me shutting the window I heard one thing Mr Wemyss said. And then I knew I had to hear as much as I could. It was going to be proof for you, sir."

"Proof for me? What do you mean?"

"Proof about who did the murder, sir. You see I heard Mr Wemyss say loudly and sort of nastily, 'Then I shall have to go to the police, after all a man has been killed.' "

Smithers said nothing.

"Was I right to listen to the rest?" asked the boy.

"Yes, yes, I think you were. You had better tell me, as nearly as you can, what you heard."

"It was mostly Mr Wemyss talking," said the boy. "Mr Schlemberger was sort of upset. At first he said 'No, no' a lot of times, but then he stopped."

"And what did Mr Wemyss say?"

"Well, after the bit I told you about he said he would go to the police again, and Mr Schlemberger asked him how he knew. Mr Wemyss said he had taken a tip 'verb sap'—I don't know what that means—and he had written to both Mr Schlemberger's wives. I think that's what he calls his exs, sir."

"Yes, go on."

"Mr Wemyss said a bit about it was a good thing his block of flats sounded so legal. I didn't understand that, but he did say it."

"He once said he lived in a place called Chancery Inn. It sounds like law chambers but I believe it's only flats. Go on now, and be very careful. What you heard may be quite important."

"I wasn't dreaming, was I, sir? The bit about the chancery proves it."

"All right. Go on."

"He said he had written and told Mr Schlemberger's wives that if there was any connection between him and Mr Hamyadis it might 'be to their advantage'. I remember that bit, sir."

"Yes, it sounds quite likely. And then?"

"Then he said he had had letters from both of them this afternoon, sir."

"He did, did he?"

"Yes. And they both said their private eyes had said there was a connection. Please sir, a private eye means a 'tec, doesn't it?"

"It's American slang for a private detective."

"And the next bit I didn't understand either. Mr Wemyss said it two or three times. It was 'prohibition'. I think that was it. 'Back in prohibition days' I think he said."

"That was the time when alcoholic liquor was forbidden, prohibited, in America. Lots of people broke the law to have it."

"It must have been bad for the pubs, sir."

"It put them all out of business. But go on. What did Mr Wemyss say about prohibition?"

"I'm not very sure, sir. But I think it was that Mr Schlemberger had seen that Mr Hamyadis wasn't troubled by fire inspectors in his warehouse. And something about 'hooch'."

"'Hooch' means drink, illicit drink. I think I see the picture. Mr Hamyadis when he was in America must have gone in for the drink business in prohibition days. And Mr Schlemberger helped him by keeping fire inspectors away from the warehouse where he kept his supplies. It all hangs together. Now, tell me, what did Mr Schlemberger say to all this?"

"He said 'Give me time,' and something about how he would be finished if anything came out. He said he would step under a car."

"Yes. Anything else? Did he say he wasn't responsible for Mr Hamyadis's death?"

"He did say that. Yes sir. He said, 'You aren't so crazy as to think I did it,' and Mr Wemyss laughed."

"I see. And what did he say when Mr Schlemberger asked him for time?"

"They argued a bit about it and Mr Schlemberger said twice, 'I don't have that much money here,' and Mr Wemyss said, 'Very well then 48 hours, not a minute longer,' and that was all."

"Now, what about this pillow business?"

"That was after, sir. I got back into bed when they had left because I wanted to think it all out. And I fell asleep, sir. It was while I was sleeping. Suddenly I felt something come down on my face and when I woke up it was all black and I couldn't breathe properly. I kicked out and hit something. It felt like somebody. I tried to yell out but I couldn't. And then everything went dim and suddenly I woke up again and I was all alone. And then you came in?"

"You're sure of all this?"

"Yes sir, really."

"And you've no idea who it was who was holding the pillow over your face, if that was what happened?"

"I think it was that, sir. Thinking about it that's what it felt like. But I don't know who it was at all."

"Man or woman?"

"Whoever it was, sir, was pretty strong."

"Still you're not all that big, are you?"

"I suppose it could have been a woman, then."

"They didn't say anything?"

"No. I think I would have heard because the pillow was only pressed tight on my mouth and just covering my eyes."

"Anything else about it that you can remember?"

"Yes sir. I've just thought. It was a person, sir, because they took hold of my wrist. Just before it all went dim, sir. I remember it was funny because they didn't hold tight, not as if they were trying to hold me down. I couldn't understand it and then—— Did I faint, sir? Is that what fainting is?"

"You lost consciousness, Peter. It happens when you get no air to breathe."

"It isn't very nice."

"No, I expect it isn't. But never mind, it's all over now. How do you feel? A bit cold? You look it."

"Yes, I am a bit shivery. That's funny because before I thought it was going to be too warm to sleep."

Smithers draped an extra blanket on the bed.

"Do you mind if I ring up Inspector Parker and ask him to have a word with you about the smothering. I don't think you need mention the other business."

"No sir, I don't mind. If you think he ought to. I'm glad I don't have to say about what I heard. I don't think the inspector would believe it."

"No, he quite likely would not, but people mustn't be allowed to go about playing tricks, and he's the man to put a stop to that. I shan't be a minute."

Smithers ran down to the telephone, left a quick message for the inspector and ran back to Peter's room. He found him huddled up with the blankets round his shoulders.

"Could you stay with me a bit, sir?" he asked.

"Certainly, I'll be here until the inspector comes anyhow. I've asked him to come straight up. Would you like a cup of hot milk or anything?"

"No thank you, sir, just as long as you're here I don't mind."

They sat in silence for a little. Peter yawned.

"Can you keep awake until the inspector comes? He oughtn't to be long," Smithers said.

"I think I can. It's funny, just a minute ago I didn't feel sleepy at all, and now suddenly I'm awfully tired."

"That's a good thing. You'll be able to have a good long sleep and feel as right as rain in the morning. Either a policeman or I will be somewhere quite close."

"I'm feeling warmer now," said Peter.

A long yawn.

"Please sir, was what I heard the proof?"

"Not quite the proof, Peter, but it did provide me quite incidentally with something that confirmed my guess, though nothing that would convince the police. But I think I hear the inspector. Waken up a bit if you can."

Smithers went to the door and let Inspector Parker in.

"He's very tired," he said.

The inspector looked at him.

"I was in two minds about coming."

"Talk to him and you'll see."

In answer to the inspector's questions Peter sleepily repeated almost word for word what he had told Smithers about the attack.

The inspector asked him three extra questions checking points, and then said:

"Well, lad, it looks as though someone did try something a bit odd on you. I'll put a good solid copper on duty just outside for tonight, and in the morning I'll sort it all out. Good night."

"Good night," said Peter.

When they looked at him as they closed the door he was asleep.

"I'll tell you straight away that I believe the boy," Inspector Parker said when the door was shut.

"He's one of the sort that never thinks of telling lies," Smithers said. "Though when they're put up to it they'll do it well enough."

"But in this case I don't think he was put up to it. Though I had the possibility in mind."

"I expected that, but I thought the boy's story would convince you."

"I'll put a man on duty here as I said, and I'll have to make one or two inquiries about this pillow, though it looks just like the others on the bed. Where is your room by the way?"

"Three doors along," said Smithers.

"Here?"

"Yes."

"May I go in?"

"Certainly, though I don't see——"

The counterpane had been roughly jerked back and only one pillow lay at the head of the bed.

"I see now," said Smithers.

"It doesn't really tell us anything," Inspector Parker said. "You can go on wondering about bluff and double bluff until the cows come home."

"Thank you."

"You'll have to find yourself another pillow for tonight I'm afraid. This will have to be gone over. It might provide a clue of some sort. And now it's about time they serve dinner here, isn't it?"

"Yes."

"Then I'll be able to see everyone. We'll drop in at the reception desk and ask them to hold the meal back for half an hour. And then I'll commandeer the office again and see each one of you in turn. Where were you, for instance, all evening and how did you come to find out the boy had been attacked?"

Smithers told him.

"All alone in the deserted lounge?"

"Yes, from the time the boy went to bed to the time I heard him scream, a few seconds after half past seven."

"Thank you. Would you wait here till I have seen the others?"

Smithers sat down again in the lounge. He noticed a constable standing just outside the open door. He picked up Vol. 6 of *The Decline and Fall* from where it had fallen when he heard Peter's screams. He flicked through the pages aimlessly, then sat up straight in the chair, found his place and began reading.

He had read eight pages when Daisy came in.

"What a dreadful thing," she said. "The inspector told me you heard him screaming, poor kid. Is he all right now? Should I go up?"

"He was sound asleep when we left him and there's a friendly looking constable on duty just outside the room, so I don't think we need worry," Smithers said.

"Well, that's a good thing. I feel a bit guilty about it all. My room's not so far from his and I was in there, but I didn't hear a thing. I haven't been sleeping too well lately. I lie and worry you know. It's silly but I can't help it. And when I went up to lie down after tea I dropped off and slept like a log. The inspector asked me could I prove it? I was a bit naughty, I'm afraid. I said that if it had been five years ago I would have had a witness. It made him blush. It was silly of me: I should have said ten years."

"I must admit it's a matter of some relief to me," Smithers said. "You know that it was my pillow that was used. If everyone else had appeared to have an alibi I should have been in an awkward position."

"It's time this business was cleared up," said Daisy. "That's plain nasty, who ever it was trying to pin it on a nice old thing like you."

Pink. Smithers blushed pink.

Kristen came in.

"We're none of us safe in our beds now," she said.

"Did you have an alibi, dear?" asked Daisy. "Neither of us did. We were wondering whether we shouldn't provide each other with one."

"I did sort of," Kristen said. "Only he kept pointing out that there would have been time for me to do it after Richie and I came back from our walk. I went upstairs for a bit and naturally I can't prove I stayed where I was."

"Did your walk last long?" said Smithers.

"Now don't you start. Old Nosey Parker went on and on about that. I told him I didn't know. Do you think that every time I go out of this hole I look at the time? I told him it was more than an hour. Of course I know it was less, but why should I make it worse for myself?"

"Three-quarters of an hour?" Smithers asked.

"I tell you I don't know. It was about three-quarters, I suppose."

Next Schlemberger.

"I guess that inspector's pretty riled," he said. "That oughtn't to have happened. The way he spoke to me I reckon he knows he slipped up. He wanted me to alibi myself every minute of the time."

"And could you?" said Daisy.

"Could I hell. Sam was in a worse mess than I thought. I was in that little office on the telephone till just a few minutes ago."

"Then you have only to get your friend to corroborate that," Smithers said.

"That would be just fine. Only I put in so many calls to help Sam out I got all messed up. Some of them took a long time to go through, too. Your British policemen may be wonderful, but boy, your telephone system could do with a look-over. Anyhow, there it is. Parker was pretty quick to point it out to me: I could have slipped out of that office for ten or five minutes and no one any the wiser."

Then Fremitt.

"A terrible business, a terrible business. As I see it this puts a quite different complexion on the whole affair, or at least it alters my outlook on it. Of course, Mrs Fremitt and I were never blessed with children, but I have always liked them, and now this."

"I suppose you've got an alibi," Kristen said.

"An alibi? Oh, I see what you mean. Well, yes, I have got an alibi as it happens. A pure coincidence. And a most lucky thing for me. I was writing my daily letter to Mrs Fremitt meaning to catch the last post and I'm afraid I fell into a doze. I find with increasing years I am apt to drop off if I sit down for any length of time in the evenings."

"If the inspector accepted that, I wish I'd told him I'd been asleep all the time," said Kristen.

"Oh, no, that wasn't it at all. You see, I woke with a start, realised it must be late, just signed the last sheet as it lay in front of me, slipped it into an envelope, which luckily I had addressed before I began to write— my usual custom—and hurried down the road to the pillar box. Most luckily I arrived at the box just as the postman was clearing it. We had a little chat, about the weather, I think it was. And as it so happens the collection is taken up at 7.30. So at the time of the attack, or what I understand from the inspector to be the time, I was actually out of the hotel."

"But——" said Daisy.

She stopped.

"You were going to say?" Smithers said.

"Oh, nothing really. Only that that must have been my friend, the chatty postman. But it seemed rather a frivolous remark. Anyhow I'm glad someone's got an alibi."

"I tell you someone who is necessarily deprived of one," said Schlemberger, "and that's the kid's father. I don't know how he feels about things but he could be pretty sore."

"Would he dare come down into the town like that?" said Fremitt. "And how could he be sure of finding the boy where he did?"

"He might guess he'd be sent to bed early after being out nights," Schlemberger said.

"True, true. The thought of that was one of the things that disturbed me most while he was away. I'm sure it's not wise to be out of doors even on a summer's night, if you can help it. The dews are treacherous, treacherous."

Next Major Mortenson.

"Well, I have just had the satisfaction of playing a game of vice versa with Inspector Parker. I put a few questions to him. He is in no position to defend himself after this unfortunate incident. I put him through the hoop, and it's just as I thought: he's in more of a fog than ever. Things are twice as complicated now."

"Perhaps you were in a better position than us to criticise, major," said Fremitt. "If I understood Miss Miller rightly, few if any of us have anything in the nature of an alibi."

"Alibi?" said the major. "Never thought of that. The inspector did try to ask me a few tom-fool questions about times and where I was, but he was having too good a roasting to get anywhere much. But as I was down at the farm grooming the horses most of the evening I imagine I have got an alibi. What time did this business happen?"

"Almost exactly at half past seven," said Smithers.

"Let me see then. Yes, I suppose I'm all right. I happened to notice that one of the horses looked as if it had been ridden, bit sweaty and dust covered. So I went back into the farmhouse to ask about it, and I checked the time with their clock. Didn't want to be late for dinner. We agreed that it was just after twenty to eight then. And as it's about fifteen minutes' brisk walk across the fields to the farm and more if you go by road I think that pretty well establishes it."

"You were alone with the horses, then?" asked Smithers.

"I was. There's nobody much about at the farm at this time of day."

"And did the people there admit to having had the horse out?"

"No, they said they hadn't. But that's what I expected. Only mentioned it to show them I was up to their tricks. They're looking after the animals most of the time and you've got to rely on them really, quis custodiet, what."

Smithers smiled.

"I suppose the inspector asked you about the various forms of transport along the road to the farm," he said.

"He did his best to, through the strafing," the major said. "But he got no satisfaction out of that. There's one of his own men at the crossroads leading off to the farm. He'd have spotted me going by. So it looks as if you'll have to let me off. Anyone else equally blessed?"

"Mr Fremitt is and we don't know about Richie," Kristen said.

Soon they did.

"Well, Kristen," he said at the door. "I felt it my duty to warn the inspector that you're really quite a strong girl. I thought he might have been deceived by this wilting flower act you've put on since the murder."

"What do you mean 'warn the inspector'?"

Kristen put out an arm behind her looking for support. It came in contact with the back of an armchair and she sat down quickly.

"Just in case he thought you hadn't the strength to smother the boy," Wemyss said. "By the way everybody: the inspector's compliments and we are free to take dinner now."

"Are you making out I did it?" Kristen said.

"No, but a certain discrepancy in our accounts of our behaviour came to light, and after that I thought I was duty bound to let the inspector have every relevant fact that had come to my knowledge."

"What relevant facts?"

"Simply that you are quite a strong girl really. I don't think anything else I know about you is relevant, or not as far as I can see at present."

Kristen sat still without replying.

"Miss Miller," Smithers said, "may I have the honour?"

He held out his arm for her to take and began leading her from the room. The others turned to follow.

"All right," said Kristen loudly, "so what you told the inspector and what I told him don't agree. I suppose it never occurred to you that he might believe me and not you."

"I'd be quite happy about that," Wemyss said. "You see I told him we were only out for twenty minutes before you lost your temper over some triviality and rushed back in. You apparently said we had been out much more than an hour. If you're right I've got some sort of alibi."

"Twenty minutes, that's a damned lie," said Kristen.

At the open door Schlemberger turned and looked at the two of them left in the lounge together.

"I'd be interested to hear about that alibi, Mr Wemyss," he said. "I happen to have collected most of the rest, I'd like to know yours."

"I said that as far as I can remember I had wandered about around the hotel without seeing any one in particular," said Wemyss.

He joined Schlemberger.

"I must say it's most unfair of the inspector to keep us all from our food. I'm extremely hungry," he said.

When the soup was being cleared Kristen came in.

"I'll just have a little salad," she said to the waiter.

She sat down without a word, looking down at her plate while the waiter served her. She then picked up her knife and fork and began cutting up her salad.

"It seems to be warmer than ever this evening," said Smithers.

"It was certainly beautifully fine all day long," Daisy said.

"I don't trust this heat," said Fremitt. "It thins the blood and in the winter months one suffers for it."

Jog, jog. One more step, another.

Kristen went on cutting up her salad. She had made it into a fine mince but worked at it as hard as at the start. She did not attempt to eat.

They went until the end of the meal without mentioning alibis, the attack on Peter or the murder. As they got up to go to the lounge for coffee the head waiter came in and said:

"Inspector Parker has telephoned. He would like to see you all again in about a quarter of an hour. He asks you not to go out."

A loud voice. With hostile overtones.

When the coffee had been left for Daisy to pour out Major Mortenson said:

"I think we should have a short discussion before we see this chap again. If you ask me, he wants a lot firmer handling. Obviously it's doing no good keeping us all here. Anyone of us may be attacked the way the boy was. If we put that to him firmly enough he'll have to come to some modus vivendi."

"I don't think we are in quite as much danger as it would appear," Smithers said.

"Come now, why not?" the major said. "Here we have this dastardly attack on one of our party. We can't tell where the fellow will strike next——"

"If fellow is the word," said Schlemberger.

"Come, you don't think this is the work of a woman, do you?"

"It could be. Nothing that has been done could not have been carried out by a female hand, and if we go by suspicious circumstances, well, I don't want to pick out names, but the women in our party are in just as bad a case as many of us men."

"Well, sir, I won't argue. It would be invidious in the present circumstances, and in any case it doesn't alter my point. The simple fact is we are faced with someone who has just struck again and is very likely to strike once more. We'd all of us be better off in the open. It's merely a matter of a united front before the inspector."

"Only I think you are wrong about this person having just struck again," said Smithers.

"What do you mean? You're meant to have seen the boy. Was he attacked, or wasn't he?" said the major.

"He was attacked——"

"Well then, let's get on with the matter in hand. The fellow will be here at any moment."

"He was attacked," Smithers repeated, "but not with the intention of inflicting any serious harm."

"That was certainly not the impression I got from the inspector," said Schlemberger. "He described the attack to me very graphically as the kid had told him. Whoever did it seemed to have pressed that pillow down pretty hard. By the way, I understand the pillow came from your room."

"It did," said Smithers. "I rather think I was singled out for that honour. But tell me, did the inspector say anything about the attacker holding the boy's wrist?"

"Why, yes, he did in a way. It was a kind of trick question, I guess. He asked me something or other and I said it didn't make sense to me and then he said the boy's wrist had been held. I didn't get it at the time."

There was a murmur of agreement.

"He did the same to me," said Daisy. "Only I thought it was just another of those things I don't understand, like cross-sections and ju-jitsu."

"It seems, then, most of you know," said Smithers. "Peter's attacker shortly before the boy lost consciousness grasped his wrist. Not tightly to hold him down, there's not much need to use a lot of force with a boy of Peter's age, but lightly. Isn't it obvious why?"

"Not, naturally enough, to me," said Daisy, "unless he was feeling Peter's pulse or something."

"Exactly," said Smithers. "Feeling the pulse, making sure they didn't go too far."

"Are you implying the attack was a fake?" said the major.

"Yes," Smithers said.

The door opened and Inspector Parker came in.

"I sent a message up to you all," he said, "because I am not satisfied with the answers I got to my first questions about this attack on Peter Dagg, or so-called attack."

"But that's what Mr Smithers——" said Kristen.

Inspector Parker looked at Smithers.

"Evidently, inspector," he said, "the same point struck us both. The attacker felt the boy's wrist because he wanted to make sure he didn't kill him."

"Just so," said Parker. "So the matter appears in rather a different light and further questioning becomes necessary. Mr Smithers, I'll see you first if I may."

The inspector took Smithers into the hotel office where the now familiar constable was ready with his notebook.

"That was a curious thing to have done," he said.

"What was?" Smithers asked.

"Faking an attack."

"Have you any idea who did it?"

"Meaning you resent any implication it could have been you. This is not the first time I've had to point out to you that we are dealing with something more serious than the second bootboy's kleptomania."

"And yet the two cases, if I may say so, have something in common."

"Oh yes, I'm not here to discuss it all in a nice quiet way with you, but I grant you that. Mania. It begins to look a bit like it. The bootboy collects the head's mortarboard, two gross of mixed chalks and Jones minor's white mouse: our criminal goes in for mock murder. But I'm concerned at this moment with such details as times, locks on doors and the carrying power of sound."

"The times I have already given you," Smithers said. "Thinking them over I see no reason to amend them. As to locks, yes, my room was locked, but the key was hanging on the board in the hall where it could easily be taken unobserved and the window was wide open. You remember I told you someone had come into the room that way once before and taken the gun you later found in the river. The same person could easily have done it again."

"And, since you are so prompt with your answers, what about the carrying power of sound?"

"Both the lounge and Peter's room look out over the yard there," Smithers said, "and both windows were open. But you will have to check all that in the morning when Peter can scream for you."

"You don't wish to change your statement on that point. Perhaps you had left the lourge for a moment and had gone upstairs?"

"But I hadn't. I sat there reading from the moment everybody went after tea till I heard the screams."

"All right. Would you ask Mr Wemyss to step in?"

"Certainly."

"Oh, by the way, did you get yourself another pillow?"

"I haven't bothered, why?"

"Because we will need that one for several days possibly. The forensic people seem to think there could be something in the nature of minute particles or a faint odour left from the very firm contact of the hands in pressing down like that."

"I hope they succeed."

"Nothing more to add?"

"Nothing."

"No details you would like to correct?"

"No, none at all."

"Thank you. Then I'll see Mr Wemyss."

"I'll let him know."

Smithers went back to the lounge and delivered his message. He then picked up his book and made for the door.

"Excuse me, sir," said the constable standing just outside, "would you mind staying in there for a bit? Inspector Parker's instructions."

"Not at all. I quite understand," Smithers said.

He went back and joined the group sitting where they had been having coffee.

"Perhaps you'll find something for us to talk about," Daisy said to him. "You're generally so good at that. Our friend in blue out there has rather put the damper on us, I'm afraid."

Smithers looked round the party. With the exception of Kristen, who was fidgeting with the clasp of her bag and smoking a cigarette in quick vigorous puffs, everybody was sitting sombrely inactive.

"I don't think this is an occasion for polite conversation," he said. "There comes a time when even the vagaries of the weather are eclipsed in interest."

"Though it is extraordinarily hot," Fremitt said. "I don't like it. Frankly, I don't."

"Even the heat has some bearing on the matter," Smithers said. "Windows are left open; it is easy to get in and out of locked bedrooms."

"It's certainly an unpleasant thought," said Schlemberger. "I don't mind admitting I feel a mite uneasy."

"Then it's time the whole stupid affair was cleared up," Kristen said.

She stubbed out a half smoked cigarette in an ashtray beside her, already nearly full of butts, broken, red-smeared.

"I wish it was. I really wish it was," Daisy said.

"Do you?" asked Kristen.

She jumped up and moved across till she was standing looking down at Daisy.

"If you knew what a struggle it was to keep even moderately cheerful, dear," said Daisy.

"I would have thought you might be pretty cheerful," Kristen said. "You know, I've been doing a bit of thinking recently. Up till a little while ago I didn't much care, to tell the honest truth, who had killed poor old George. He deserved it if every anyone did. But then I began to see that, whoever did it, the innocent were going to suffer."

"Poor little Peter," Daisy said.

"I didn't mean that," Kristen said. "I meant us. The people who are suddenly going to find themselves arrested, put in prison, up at the Old Bailey, and all for nothing. For something they hadn't done. For someone else. No, it's certainly time someone spoke the truth. Isn't it, Daisy?"

"Are you suggesting that Miss Miller hasn't been doing that and doing it damn' gallantly?" asked the major.

"Plainly she is," said Smithers. "I would like to hear more."

"Well, I wouldn't. It's filthy. To hear a lady attacked in this manner and not to do one's utmost to put a stop to it," the major said.

The thin face colouring slowly, stormily.

"No, let's hear," said Daisy. "It's only fair."

Kristen backed away from her.

"I don't know," she said.

"I should think not," said the major. "Now listen here, my girl, I shall expect an apology from you in due course. For the present we're confined to this room so you can't leave us, as I think you ought, but you can remain silent and you will."

"She has said too much already," Smithers said.

He too got up from his chair.

"Now, Miss Kett," he said, "your duty is to finish what you began. If you know the truth, it must be spoken."

Not an order. A statement of the inescapable.

"All right," said Kristen, "I will."

She took another cigarette from the open case next to the ashtray and lit it for herself with an unsteady hand.

"All right. I'm not afraid. You killed George, Daisy, you know you did."

FOURTEEN

"Well, of course, I didn't do it," said Daisy.

"You think you can get away with it," Kristen said. "And I'm not surprised. You thought it all out so carefully."

She was suddenly much calmer. She went to stub out her cigarette, saw her ashtray was full, looked round, spotted another and carefully ground the lighted end into it. Then she turned and half leaned and half sat on the edge of the open window facing the group.

"I suppose you all believe I'm pretty stupid," she said. "Oh, don't think I haven't noticed your attitude towards me. And come to that, I may not have appeared so bright these last few days, I've been feeling too rotten one way and another. But just now I suddenly realised that that damned policeman wasn't asking me all those silly questions just because he liked to put the screws on a pretty girl. I suddenly realised he actually thought I killed George."

"I don't think he necessarily did, dear," said Daisy. "He kept on at me in the most extraordinary way, too. He can't think we both did it. I'm sure it's just his manner. Though it is upsetting."

Kristen smiled.

The smile at once made the reason for her comparative success in the film world obvious. It was not warm and left her eyes hard, but it transformed her face into something alive. Animal and seductive.

"Keep it up," she said. "Keep it up to the end. The star. Always a kindly hand. You know what it all really is?"

She turned from Daisy to the rest.

"It's pure bloody Number One from start to finish. But how the big act has taken you all in. You were a matinée audience if ever I saw one."

"Now then," said Daisy, "be as rude as you like about me, dear. But you shouldn't say things like that to the others."

Kristen ignored her.

"Of course she had to have you eating out of her hand if what she had planned for so long was to come off," she went on. "And especially the major. The dear old major. How long before the trip started had she got to work on you, major?"

"I don't know what you mean," Major Mortenson said. "You should be made to hold your tongue. It's damn' disgusting."

"That's right, major, gallant to the last," said Kristen. "Do you know, now I've begun on this, I feel better than I've done for weeks. Funny isn't it? But let's get on. Between the two of them they cooked up all that stupid business with the pistols. Then there was the beard trick. You all fell for it. The major's confession. And Daisy going on and on about it being a fairy story, and no one cottoning on. Don't you see? The bit about the beard was just put in to make everybody convinced that the murder was done on the spur of the moment. Of course, Daisy knew Georgie was going to shave it off, and she warned the major to look surprised when he saw it had gone. You poor clucks, hasn't it dawned on you that she'd been planning to kill him for years?"

"This is perfectly fantastic," Major Mortenson said. "We can't go on sitting here listening to a lady being insulted to her face in this manner. Is the girl non compos, or what?"

"I suppose you mean looney, major," said Kristen. "Well I'm not, I'm far from it. I'm the only one with the guts to see through all this flapdoodle and fog you and your precious Daisy have been putting up between you."

White. White fingers with muscles gripping the arm of the chair. Every muscle in the major's body taut.

"Now, now," said Kristen, "don't get in a bate. You've got worse to come."

She paused. Leant back out of the window rocking slightly on her hips.

"All right, on we go. Get this. Ever since George Hamyadis walked out on Daisy Miller years and years ago she has had it in for him. And she just waited till he thought they were friends again. She deceived him like she deceived the rest of you. He even thought it all was forgotten and invited her for this coach trip for old times' sake. Then she knew her chance had come at last. She heard about the major and got to work on him. The only thing she overdid was answering the questions about how long she'd known George. I wasn't feeling too good but even I noticed her changing the story."

Kristen jumped back into the room, pirouetted round and stood looking at them all.

"Haven't you forgotten one thing, dear?" Daisy said.

"Now we're coming to it," Kristen said.

She glanced once round the room.

"Go on," she said. "Prove me wrong. I'd be glad to hear it."

"Prove you wrong," said Daisy. "Not my line. I was just wondering about my famous call from America. Couldn't you work that in?"

Kristen laughed. A deep relaxed animal laugh.

"Game to the last," she said. "All right, that fits in too. She hadn't reckoned on all this talk about the States and when it began she suddenly thought that the one thing which would really put suspicion on her might be dug up. She was trying to make sure it wasn't."

"One moment," Daisy said.

Her hands fumbled on her lap knocking her handbag on to the floor.

The major jumped to his feet and picked it up. He held it out to Daisy. She waved it away.

"Listen, dear," she said to Kristen. "I don't mind all this other business. It isn't true and it can't hurt me. But be careful now. If you have really found out something, just ask yourself what it would be like to be in my place."

"Hasn't she gone far enough?" said the major. "There ought to be something that can be done to someone who does a thing like this."

"Go on, Miss Kett," Smithers said.

"So we're getting near at last," said Kristen.

All the vitality that a minute before had ebbed away flooded back again. She stood over Daisy poised like a racing swimmer.

"You know," she said, "it's all going to come out whatever you feel like. I noticed how you wouldn't let Georgie kiss you the first time. But tell me, when you pointed his own gun at him after he had just kissed you at the second time, did you look back to the days when you and he were married?"

"Married," Daisy said.

She plunged her face into her hands. Her body shook uncontrollably. Sobs, gusts of laughter.

With an effort she looked up at them.

"I shall never be able to explain," she said. "She's so wrong."

Kristen a runner checked in full stride. She slowly sat down on the arm of a chair.

The door opened and Wemyss came in.

"Nosey Parker's having a field day," he said.

There was silence. Daisy was quiet now. Slowly she looked up at them and shook her head.

Utter negative.

"I got quite a gruelling," Wemyss said.

Daisy turned to him. Blinked.

"Did you?" she said. "That must have been nice."

Her voice a clear small stream after the floods.

"Nice? You've got an odd idea of what's nice. But you'll see. He wants you next."

Daisy sat still.

"Your turn," said Wemyss. "The inspector wants to interview the celebrated Daisy Miller."

"Oh, me," said Daisy. "The inspector. At the police station, I suppose."

"For heaven's sake," said Wemyss. "In the office here. Remember? He's seeing us each in turn. Do you want me to show you the way?"

"Thank you, that would be very kind," Daisy said.

She looked from side to side, saw her handbag, took it from the table where the major had put it down, fished a handkerchief out and dabbed at her eyes.

Wemyss held the door open for her. With overdone courtesy.

When she got to it she turned and said:

"You know there won't be any explanation when I come back. I'm sorry. But you'll just have to think that about me, or work out what it all means. I've nothing to say. Nothing. And now, I think perhaps I can find my own way to that little office. Thank you."

She went out.

Wemyss looked out after her.

"What in hell's name was all that about?" he said, walking across and flopping into one of the wide chintz-covered armchairs.

"You'd better ask your friend Miss Kett," said the major.

Kristen shook her head.

"Don't bother yourself for me," Wemyss said. "I couldn't care less."

During the rest of the time Inspector Parker conducted his questioning in the little hotel office—the dustiness, the curling leather of the table, the varnished oak—they sat silent.

Daisy was away for only four minutes. She came back and sat down where she had been before without a word. Kristen huddled now in her huge chair did not even glance up at her. Even when Schlemberger, the last to leave, returned and said the inspector saw no reason for them to stay any longer Kristen sat on. Her face was pale again, her eyes without sparkle.

On his way to bed Smithers saw the avuncular constable whom Parker had stationed outside Peter's room sitting on a tall hard chair, his legs pushed out a little in front of him, surreptitiously.

"The inspector said I was to call you if the kiddie cried or anything," the constable said. "I hope that's all right."

"He said me, not Miss Miller?" Smithers asked.

"Yes sir. I suppose her being an actress he didn't think she'd know much about youngsters."

"I suppose so. Though I am more accustomed to them at fourteen or more when tears have to be concealed. At eight it's a different matter."

"I took a look in, half an hour ago," the constable said, "he was sleeping like a babe then. He'll be all right."

"Yes I think so. Good night."

"Good night, sir."

Broad blue uniformed shoulders eased against the sharp back of the chair.

When Smithers came past again an hour before breakfast next morning the chair was not occupied. He tried the door of Peter's room. It was unlocked. Inside the boy still slept. The pillow round his head smooth and uncrushed.

Smithers walked out of the inn and headed for the country. He stepped out at an even pace along roads where there were occasional signs of the start of the day. Cows going back from milking, the windows of a cottage being opened.

As he turned to go back in the direction of the hotel he heard the roar of a heavy engine and glanced ahead to see whether there was anywhere for him to step off the road. But before he had gone another three paces, from behind a tall clump of elms a helicopter appeared, moving slowly, clumsily, ominously.

Smithers stood and watched it as the roar of its engines deafened him. The machine was only some twenty feet from the ground. In it were three men, a pilot at the controls, another man in Air Force uniform holding a map at arm's length and Inspector Parker.

He must have seen Smithers at the same moment as Smithers saw him. His start of surprise was clearly visible. He turned and spoke to the pilot. The machine rose suddenly to twice its previous height, and then drifted slowly down to the field at the edge of which Smithers stood.

"You're out early," the inspector called to Smithers.

"And you're up high," Smithers said as the inspector reached the other side of the hedge.

"Well, I suppose you know what we're doing, but I wonder what you're doing?"

"Walking. And as for your flying I can put two and two together. No doubt your quarry will think it's unsporting."

"Unsporting? Has young Peter been saying any more?"

"No, we prefer not to speak of it much. That's simply my own impression."

"To be taken at its face value?"

"How else?" said Smithers.

"As a move in a game," the inspector said. "But I intend to catch my chicken first. Then I'll judge for myself."

He turned to walk back to the helicopter.

"I never thought you would do otherwise," Smithers said.

Over his shoulder the inspector called:

"Did you know these things were invented by Leonardo da Vinci?"

"As a matter of fact I did," said Smithers.

But his words were drowned by the increasing roar of the machine's engine. The inspector heaved himself aboard, and in a moment was hovering twenty feet above Smithers's head again.

The helicopter flew on. Smithers watched it for a few minutes moving forwards and backwards left and right over the countryside.

He turned his eyes from the blue morning sky to the ground at his feet. Among the tangled stems of grasses ants were busily criss-crossing their way to some place important to themselves.

He was five minutes late for breakfast. But instead of going into the dining-room at once he went up to Peter's room again. He found him spooning water from his hand on to his golliwog hair.

"Good morning," Smithers said, "and how do you feel this morning, my lad?"

"All right, thank you," said Peter. "Was it silly of me last night?"

"Certainly not," said Smithers. "Though as a matter of fact it now looks as though the person didn't mean to harm you but just to give the appearance of doing so."

"Then that's all right," said the boy.

He looked at himself in the mirror, and struck at his hair with the brush another two or three times.

Smithers inspected the wash basin.

"I see you've done your hair," he said. "But did you do anything else?"

"Well, no, I didn't," said Peter. "You see first of all I thought I might have to stay in here all day to be safe. Then when you told me it was all right, I didn't think it was worth going back to wash."

"That's scamping," said Smithers.

Peter began to wash, and went on with increasing thoroughness. They went downstairs together.

"By the way," Smithers said at the door of the dining-room, "I saw Inspector Parker up in a helicopter this morning."

"A helicopter? Pretty super. What was——"

The cold douche.

"It's no different really, you know," Smithers said. "That's what makes the inspector such a good detective: he doesn't scamp."

"Is he really a good detective?" asked the boy.

"Very good. Except for one thing, I should say."

"But not as good as you, sir."

"I happen to be a schoolmaster. You remember that."

"Yes, but you do know who did it, don't you? And the inspector doesn't."

"We don't know what the inspector knows, and neither of us can act until we have proof."

"Will you have proof soon, sir?"

"Now why should an ancient old schoolmaster be able to find proof of who committed a murder?"

"You will though, sir, won't you?"

"If you promise never to think of me as a detective again, I'll tell you something."

"I do promise, sir, really I do."

"All right, I'll accept that, a little against my better judgement. I have begun to get proof, but only begun."

"Then I don't care if the mouldy old 'copter does find Dad," said Peter.

"I thought you were entitled to a little moral support," said Smithers opening the dining-room door.

"You've got to hand it to the inspector," Schlemberger was saying. "He doesn't hesitate to use the latest equipment. A helicopter's pretty thorough."

"Have you heard this latest development, Mr Smithers?" said Wemyss.

He leant back in his chair and looked fixedly at Smithers at the same time waving a half eaten piece of toast in his right hand.

"I saw the machine earlier on," said Smithers. "Now, Peter, what are you going to eat?"

Wemyss looked at the boy for an instant and then put his toast back on the plate and helped himself to more marmalade. There was already a pile on his plate.

"Let the boy choose his own breakfast," said Major Mortenson.

Exasperation.

There was two seconds absolute silence.

Then Daisy said:

"Good morning, major. So you've joined us at last."

"Joined you? What do you mean?" asked the major.

He shook his head. The dog from the river.

"That was the first word we've had out of you," said Daisy.

"Oh, I'm sorry. Damnably rude of me. Truth is I've got a lot on my mind."

"You've got butter on *The Times,* too," said Daisy, "only I didn't like to tell you before."

The major hoisted the open sheets of the paper into the air till he could see the large smear of grease across the back.

"Damn and blast," he said.

The paper landed in a shapeless mess on the floor behind him.

"Why the hell have people got to keep on interfering?" he said.

The remark was not addressed to Daisy.

No one offered to reply.

The major cut savagely at a flabby piece of toast. It resisted his efforts. Abruptly he banged his knife down on the plate and turning to look directly at Smithers he said:

"You're an interfering old maid, sir. You've been causing trouble and annoyance ever since Hamyadis's death, and your actions yesterday brought untold distress to a lady unable to defend herself."

Smithers picked up a letter lying beside his place and began to open it.

Everyone else had stopped eating and all were looking silently from the major to Smithers and back again.

"He isn't an interfering old maid."

Peter.

Totally unexpected. The note of boyish indignation.

"Now, Peter, this is something you would be better to ignore," Smithers said.

"But, sir, you're not an old maid."

The boy turned to the others.

"He's a super detective," he said.

No one spoke.

Then Richard Wemyss laughed.

"Oh, yes he is," said the boy. "I'll prove it to you. Who do you think it was who snatched the mystery package from you when you had pinched it from the coach? It was Mr Smithers, so there."

FIFTEEN

Round the table after the noisiness of the major's attack on Smithers, sudden watchfulness. Silence.

"Oh, dear," said Daisy, "I can't even remember what it was you said now, Peter, and I don't think you had better repeat it. It seems to have been some sort of a revelation, and I haven't the least hope of ever knowing why."

"Do you propose to hand me back that packet?" Wemyss said to Smithers. No hint of overtones.

"I think it was not addressed to you?" Smithers said.

"Oh, sir," said Peter. "I forgot. I forgot everything you said. I forgot about you being a schoolmaster and not a detective and I forgot about having to have a secret about the letter."

"I don't think any great harm has been done," said Smithers. "In fact I was probably a bit over timid about things. It's almost always best to speak out."

"Are you sure, sir?"

"Yes. You see, we all understand each other a little better now. I told you I was no detective, and that's certainly true. But I hesitated to tell other people that I had had to take an active role in this affair in my own defence. And that was probably wrong. Now I suggest we might go for a walk in the town."

"Smithers," Fremitt said, "could I have a word with you before you leave the hotel?"

"Peter, I'll meet you in twenty minutes at the front door," Smithers said. Fremitt led him to the lounge without a word.

"It's a matter of some difficulty," he said as he opened the door.

He gave Smithers his quick smile, and then abruptly looked theatrically sombre.

"Anything I can do, I'm only too happy," Smithers said.

"Mr Smithers."

From a deep armchair its back towards the door, Kristen, who had gone into the room as soon as she left the breakfast table and had been sitting with her legs tucked under her, jumped up. She looked more animated again. A faint flush of colour on her cheeks. A litheness of movement.

"Mr Smithers, I was just thinking about you. Isn't this a piece of luck?"

"That's very flattering," Smithers said, "but I'm afraid Fremitt and I have a little business to conduct. Perhaps I may see you in the course of the morning?"

"No, don't go," Kristen said. "I—I've actually got something to say to you, something quite important. Mr Fremitt can hear too, if he wants. He's a friend."

Smithers glanced at Fremitt.

"As long as I can see you for just a few minutes before you go out," Fremitt said, "otherwise it's of no consequence."

"Are you going out?" Kristen said.

"I was going to take young Peter for a walk round the town," Smithers said. "I don't want him to see too much of this helicopter. So a knowledge of history will prove to have a practical use, and we'll have a conducted tour."

"It must be wonderful to know about the past like that," Kristen said. "Winchester is very old, isn't it?"

"In parts," said Smithers.

"I thought it was. I haven't been into the town much. I seem to have spent most of my time up in my room, but I thought I saw a lot of old buildings. Do you know all about them?"

"No, indeed," Smithers said. "I merely hope to be able to distract the boy for a morning."

"Now you're being modest," said Kristen. "I bet if you wanted to you could go on for hours about it all. I'm keen on it too, you know. I was in one of those historical films once. It was before I made my name, of course. But it was pretty fascinating, I can tell you. All about the French Revolution. Could I come with you this morning, do you think?"

"I'm afraid you wouldn't find Winchester as interesting as the French Revolution," Smithers said. "But I mustn't keep Fremitt here waiting. You had something you wanted to say to me?"

"Oh, well, I did," said Kristen. "But perhaps I ought to wait till I feel I know you a bit better. I'll tell you after our walk, shall I?"

"If you would prefer me to go," Fremitt said. "I have to finish reading the paper, I'll sit in the hall."

"It's not really anything I couldn't tell you," Kristen said. "Only somehow I don't want to say it in public, as you might say."

"I perfectly understand," Fremitt said. "I'll see you in a few minutes, Smithers."

He left them.

Kristen walked across the room and sat on a small sofa tucked into a corner.

"Come and sit down," she said.

Smithers looked at the other chairs dotted about the room and went and joined her on the sofa.

"That's right," she said. "Relax, make yourself comfortable. It's nice to be able to take things easy once in a way, isn't it?"

She humped herself round so that she was half lying sprawled across the sofa.

Smithers smiled.

"Is this the way they conduct business in the film studios?" he said. "No wonder my boys complain that they can't afford to go to the pictures very often."

"But this isn't business," said Kristen. "You are a funny man. Everything doesn't have to be serious, you know."

"I daresay I'm a bit set in my ways," Smithers said. "But you did ask me to join you to discuss something that was quite important."

"Well, I have got something quite important to tell you," Kristen said.

She turned and smiled at him. Slowly.

"But give me a chance," she said. "I told old John it was a bit difficult for me."

"Old John?"

"Mr Fremitt. He said I was to call him John once, and then asked me not to do it in public. He's another funny old stick if you like."

"Another?"

"Oh dear, perhaps I shouldn't have said that. But I can't help it you know. When something comes into my head, out it pops. You must have noticed."

"I can't say that I have."

"That's because I haven't been my real self. Not ever since poor old Georgie copped it."

"It's true," Smithers said, "that we had had very little opportunity of getting to know one another before that event."

Kristen swung herself towards him. She was wearing a tight blouse, buttoned low and tucked hard into the top of her skirt emphasising the figure.

"That's exactly what I feel," she said. "It was too awful all this happening. We could have been such friends, you and I. I know you're a lot older, but I feel we're both interested in the same things, the past and all that."

"I was thinking rather more in terms of the whole party," Smithers said. "We were the barest acquaintances before we were all thrown together into this situation where we were bound to mistrust one another."

"I don't know about that," Kristen said.

In spite of the rebuff she kept her position leaning near to Smithers.

"I don't know about that. I don't think we all of us mistrust everybody. You can tell about some people, I'm sure of that. I don't distrust you, for instance, not one little bit. I'll prove it to you."

Smithers recognised a whiff of the scent he had smelt first in the coach house then on the inspector's cards.

"Look," Kristen said, "you've got my packet of letters, haven't you? Well, I don't mind. It's in safe hands. That's all that worries me. I'm much happier for you to have it and us to be friends than for me to have it and not to have anyone I feel I can turn to."

She put her hand on to Smithers's.

"Let me give you some advice," said Smithers.

He made no attempt to move his hand.

"Would you?" Kristen said. "That's what I've wanted all this time. Someone who could tell me what was the sensible thing to do. I'm all on my own."

"I'm afraid my advice is going to seem hard then," Smithers said. "It's simply that you can't afford to trust anyone in our party. Neither myself nor anyone else. No one has been exculpated. Any one of us might be a murderer."

"No," Kristen said.

The word a sigh.

"It's lovely of you to say all that," she went on, "but I know I can trust you."

Her face was close to his.

The door opened.

Fremitt's voice came from behind it.

"I'm sorry to interrupt, if indeed I do. I went off for a few minutes and was afraid I'd missed you."

Kristen darted a look of irritation at the door and flung herself back into the far corner on the sofa. Smithers sat still.

"I'm not sure whether Miss Kett had finished saying what she wanted to or not," he said.

"It can wait now," Kristen said.

A low voice for Smithers.

"The main thing is we know we can rely on each other."

"Well," Smithers said, getting to his feet, "remember what I told you. And, now, Fremitt, shall we take a stroll in the yard before it gets too hot?"

"I'll see you later," Kristen whispered.

"No doubt we'll meet at lunch," said Smithers.

As he and Fremitt stepped out into the bright morning sunshine Fremitt said:

"I hope I did right to leave you with that girl. She seemed to want to confide something to you."

"She found it difficult to broach the subject," Smithers said.

"She's an odd creature," said Fremitt. "Sometimes I find her quite pleasant, but lately . . . And there was that most regrettable scene."

They walked out into the sunshine in silence.

"You had something to tell me?" Smithers said.

"Yes, yes, of course. I mustn't keep you. I have got something which I do want to—to put before you," said Fremitt.

He strolled a few paces across the cobbles without saying anything more.

"I presume it is something connected with Hamyadis's death?" Smithers said.

"Connected with? It's the very root—I feel having some sort of alibi for the time of the attack on—on the boy, on Peter that is, I can in some measure speak frankly."

But no frank speech: silence.

"I find this extraordinarily difficult to say."

"I promise you whatever it is need go no further," Smithers said.

"Quite so. Quite so. Though if I am right it ought to. And I am afraid it will come as a very great shock to you."

"A remark parents very often make when they feel obliged to reveal their son's behavior during the holidays."

"That's it," said Fremitt.

But once again he said no more.

"Come," Smithers said as they turned to walk back across the yard, "you have aroused my expectations to the point where you are bound to satisfy them."

Fremitt stood still.

"Peter," he said. "Peter killed Hamyadis."

"I would be interested to hear your reasons for thinking that," said Smithers.

"I have been going over the whole affair in the last day or two," Fremitt said. "At first, I admit, I imagined it to be no business of mine, but something someone said gave me the notion that unless the matter was gone into very thoroughly by somebody used to sifting such things the mystery might never be solved. The whole thing might be terra incognita for ever."

"I see," said Smithers.

"So I gave it some thought, and eventually hit on a point hitherto overlooked, I venture to think."

"Go on."

"Simply that an old fashioned pistol, of the sort that was supposed at first to have killed Hamyadis, is loaded differently from a modern weapon."

"Loaded differently? Ah, I begin to understand."

"My dear chap, take it calmly I beg. It's a monstrous thought to be faced with, but if it is so one must grapple with the fact."

"You are going to tell me that an old fashioned ball need not have been loaded into that Durs Egg pistol."

"Exactly. It could have been loaded with a bullet from, for instance, an automatic of modern design."

"I think you had better state your case in full," Smithers said. "I cannot, I must admit, conceive of any motive for what you have hinted at."

"Certainly I will be explicit," said Fremitt. "I owe you that at least. And I am not, of course, suggesting that a boy of—what is he?—eight or nine could have wanted to kill a man like Hamyadis. The possibility does not bear thinking about. But what may not have occurred to you is that he would have a very natural desire to transform what he might have looked on as a toy pistol into a real one. And unfortunately we had all been told that to do just that was child's play. Child's play: it's a horrible thought."

"Yes," said Smithers. "It is a horrible thought. But go on."

"Well, assuming the boy performed this simple operation, he would next want to fire this real gun. And as far as we know there were no bullets of the period about. But here again there's a terribly unfortunate set of circumstances. The boy, and all of us, knew that other bullets were about: the bullets in Hamyadis's own automatic. And on the morning of the murder these were put in a place where they could easily be got at."

Fremitt looked at Smithers. Quick concern. And looked back at the cobbles under their feet, steadily. The crystalline particles lying in the cracks between each worn stone.

"I have no doubt at all that he wasn't thinking what he was doing," he said. "It was his first chance to test out his childish idea, and he took it. There can be no question of moral responsibility. He's a bright and intelligent lad; he could have done it all, but at that age there cannot be any realisation of the consequences."

Smithers said nothing.

Fremitt stopped their slow pacing and took him by the arm. Urgently.

"My dear chap," he said, "I know it may seem a reductio ad absurdum, but isn't that the best way out? Something has occurred which means that one of these people we know, quite well, has killed a fellow human being. Isn't what I have just suggested to you the kindest possible solution?"

"If it were correct I suppose it might be," Smithers said.

Fremitt dropped his arm, and said:

"I thought I would give you a friendly warning before it was too late. I've noticed you seem to have made rather a favourite of the boy. Very good of you. But you must think twice about it."

"I will. Thank you."

"I hope you don't feel offended at anything I have said. There was a moment, I know, when our aims conflicted, but all that is happily settled."

"Having come to the conclusions you have, it was extremely good of you to tell them to me."

"Not at all, not at all. My duty really. Well, I must be off. To tell you the truth I find the full heat of the sun a little much at the peak of summer. I prefer, when I can, to stay indoors until the early evening."

Fremitt glanced quickly at the deep shade of the inn doorway and then quickly back to Smithers.

"Then I won't keep you," Smithers said. "Thank you again."

As Fremitt left Smithers looked up at the stable clock. Hard to read in the glare. He waited till the hands had moved on exactly five minutes and then he went into the hotel again and made his way to the front hall.

Sitting on a high dark wooden chair was Kristen.

"Hallo," she said, "are you looking for the boy?"

"As a matter of fact I was," said Smithers.

He noticed that Kristen while he had been talking to Fremitt had made a complete change of clothes. She was now wearing a summer frock, frilly and full. As she stood up he detected the smell of eau de Cologne. Her lipstick was a delicate pink.

"He gave me a message for you," she said.

"Indeed?"

"He said, would you mind if he didn't go with you this morning?"

"I see. Did he give you any reason?"

"He said—— Well, no, he didn't actually give any reason. Just would you mind."

"Thank you. Did you wait here all that time to pass the message on? It was very good of you."

"Oh, that's all right, I wanted to see you anyhow."

"Again?"

"This isn't about anything like that," Kristen said. "I thought that perhaps if you were free you could spare a little bit of time to tell me about Winchester. You did say you would, you know."

"Did I? Well, then I'll do my best. But if you wouldn't mind waiting a few moments I have one piece of business I want to do before I go out."

"Oh, don't go. Anyway don't let's go out straight away, it's so hot out just now. I'll tell you what we could do. I bought some picture postcards of the famous bits the other day. You could tell me about them first and then we could see them later on, it will be all the more interesting."

"You know," Smithers said, "I'm no expert on local history. If you want to find out about old Winchester you would do best to look it up in a reliable guide book."

"Not a stuffy old guide book," Kristen said.

She took hold of Smithers by the elbow, firmly.

"You can't really see me settling down to have a good read of a guide book, can you?" she said.

She bustled him out of the hall to the foot of the wide stairway.

"No," she said, "I want you to breathe some life into it all for me. You could, you know. You're awfully sympathetic when one gets to know you."

They climbed the stairs.

"Now, I'll tell you what," she said. "We'll just have a look at my collection of picture postcards and then, when I'm full of a sense of the past, out we'll go."

She flung open the door of her room.

It contained much the same furniture as Smithers's own, but Kristen had imposed on its neutrality a strongly feminine atmosphere. The air was heavy with a mixture of sweet smells. The dressing table was cluttered with cosmetic bottles and jars. A trail of spilt face powder ran across it. One of the drawers was not pushed home. It had jammed on the corner of some frothy peach coloured garment. The wardrobe door was slightly ajar showing a thick row of dresses, and a litter of shoes.

There were signs of hasty tidying. Out-of-date newspapers, paper-backed books and letters had been piled together in tilting heaps. On the low table by the window the marks left in the dust by hastily moved objects showed up in the sunlight. A clean packet of picture postcards lay beside an ashtray full of lipstick coloured stubs.

"Now, do sit down and make yourself comfy," Kristen said.

She steered Smithers to a low armchair and then stationed herself on the edge of the bed by the door.

"Now, where did I put those postcards?" she said. "I must have put them somewhere safe because they're so precious to me. Are you like that? Do you hide things away when they're very important, and then not know what you've done with them?"

"Are those the ones?" said Smithers, pointing at the packet.

"Why, so they are. Right under my nose all the time. Aren't you clever to spot them like that? But then you are clever. That boy was quite right when he said you were a super detective."

"Tell me," said Smithers, "what exactly was the message he gave you for me. I'd be very grateful if you could remember it word for word."

"I'm afraid you haven't a hope. I can't learn things, you know. They made me go and act at some theatres in the provinces once for the publicity. I never could learn the parts: that's why they had to call the whole thing off in the end. Quite right too. It's just lowering yourself to go to places like that. The dressing-rooms often didn't have hot water. But now you're making me talk about myself, you naughty man."

"We were talking, I think, about young Peter. I'm a little surprised to hear he's decided not to come with me. I'm anxious to know exactly why."

"Oh, but you can't ever know why a boy of his age takes it into his head to do something. He probably forgot."

"But he left a message with you."

"Did he? Oh, yes, of course he did. I told you, didn't I? And you went all old world courtesy about it. I think it's lovely, I do really. You don't get much of it today. That's why I really prefer older men. They know how to treat a girl. Now, you tell me all about old Winchester. There are my little pictures."

Kristen darted across the room, picked up the packet of cards, ripped off the wrapper and fanned the photographs out on the dressing table beside Smithers.

They were a series called 'Beauty spots of the Downs'.

"Now, isn't that silly," said Kristen. "I was in such a tear I must have grabbed the wrong lot. Never mind. You just tell me about what we're going to see."

She sat on the edge of Smithers's chair.

"Look," he said, "I'm quite anxious about Peter. I don't suppose he's come to any harm, but I want to see him fairly soon. If you've got anything to tell me, tell me now and then I'll go and look for him."

"Oh, you silly man, all you can talk of is whether you're looking after that boy properly. Of course you are. Now relax."

She ruffled his hair.

"Come on," she said. "Admit it. It gives you a thrill to be here with me, doesn't it? There's no need to be starchy, you know. I can keep my mouth shut. You're a man, I can see that, in spite of your tatty old clothes and everything. Why don't you and I have a nice cosy little chat?"

Smithers turned in the chair and looked up at her.

"You're very sure of yourself, aren't you?" he said.

Kristen slid down the arm an inch until her hip was resting against Smithers's shoulder.

"Why shouldn't I be?" she said. "I've got all the equipment, haven't I?"

A murmur.

"In a way, I suppose you have," Smithers said.

Kristen leaned towards him.

Rat-tat. A sharp knock at the door.

"Who the hell's that?" said Kristen.

The door opened and Peter came in.

"I've got a copy of *The Stage* for you," he said. "Bit of luck, the first shop I went to had just one left. But I couldn't find you when I came back, so I thought I'd try up here."

"Thanks very much," said Kristen. "Here. Here's sixpence. Now off you go."

"Will you be able to show me the history bits of Winchester tomorrow, sir?" asked Peter.

"I'll be able to show them to you almost straight away if you want," Smithers said.

"Would you really, sir? Jolly super. I thought you were going to spend the day out of the sun or something."

"No, no," said Smithers. "I really prefer being out on a day like this to being shut away indoors. I'll see you later perhaps, Miss Kett."

"You can't go like this," said Kristen. "Listen, Peter, you come back in half an hour. Mr Smithers and I have got to have a little talk, see? You can come back later and there'll be another sixpence for you."

"What have I got to do this time?" Peter asked.

"I'll tell you later," said Kristen.

The door pushed to.

Kristen turned, leaning against it.

"All right," she said, "so I did push him off out of the way. I did it because I wanted to see you alone. I wanted to desperately. I'm frightened, Mr Smithers. This murder. Do you think they'll pin it on me? You can save me, I know you can. You're so clever."

She put her hands on Smithers's shoulders.

"You will save me, won't you?"

"I don't imagine there's anything much to save you from," said Smithers.

She looked up at him, tears in the eyes.

"But there is, there is. They're all against me, all the rest. You're the only one I can trust. They'd get together and make out a case against me, I know they would. And you'd be the only one who could see through it."

"What would they have against you?" Smithers asked.

"I knew you'd help," Kristen said. "I knew you would, I knew you would."

She laid her head, the heavy mass of blonde hair, on Smithers's chest. Her back heaved as if with sobs.

"There's that packet," she said. "That might be one thing. I think I had better have it after all. It would be safer if I saw it and then destroyed it, wouldn't it?"

"Safer for whom?" said Smithers. "Now listen to me, my girl. You've behaved pretty badly all through this business. I happen to believe that that packet has very little to do with the murder. But your insistence on having it when it was hidden in a place so much connected with the killing has caused untold trouble to the police and everybody. It's also been responsible for getting me into the inspector's bad books. So it stays with me until I say you can have it. And you behave yourself from now on. Do you understand that?"

Kristen stood her arms hanging at her sides, eyes looking at her feet.

"I'm not always like that," she said. "These last few years I've got into the way of it: I've had to. But sometimes, when I see myself doing something like what I was trying to do to you just now, I hate myself. I really do."

Tears. Not glycerine, but salt.

SIXTEEN

Smithers found Peter waiting for him in the uncomfortable, ornamental chair in the hall.

"Ready for our walk?" he said.

"You were an awfully long time," said the boy.

"Well, first Miss Kett wanted to see me, then Mr Fremitt did, and then Miss Kett wanted to see me again."

"Why did they suddenly want you in such a hurry?"

"To tell me stories."

"That would be something about the murder," Peter said.

"I shouldn't have tried to evade it."

"Was what they told you true?"

"Only in bits."

"I see. When is it all going to be over, Mr Smithers?"

"I know how you feel. It's high time it was over. But I think something may be happening."

"What sort of a thing?"

"A fish may be swimming towards some bait. Have you ever been fishing?"

"Of course I have."

"Well, you know what tricky creatures fish can be. You can't be sure of them till they've taken a good hard bite."

"You will tell me when that is, won't you?"

"I will. Now then, do you want to know what used to happen in Winchester in the days before all of us were thought of?"

"Is it in the coaching days?"

"It might be. It's difficult to keep away from the thing hanging over us, isn't it?"

"It is a bit. Have I got to try?"

"I think it would be best."

"All right. Dad used to tell me about the coaching days, that was why I said that. But I think he used to make some of it up."

"The best historians have the same failing."

"Do you think the 'copter will catch him today?"

"Now you're doing it again."

"I'm sorry. Just tell me and I won't ever ask again."

"I'll tell you anyhow. I'm afraid it will help to catch him very soon. It's really the best thing, you know."

"I know really, but I don't want it to happen."

"Neither do I. And now, look at that building there."

Firmly history. And the boy soon lost to the world around him. A morning of history.

History for lunch. History in spite of every remark made at the table. History for Kristen Kett, back in the blouse and skirt she had worn at breakfast, silent again, without colour, eating nothing. History for everybody.

And all afternoon walking through the ancient streets of the town more history. Peter listened. A trance.

But not for ever. Teatime.

"And that must be all for today," Smithers said to Peter. "I don't suppose everybody else has your insatiable thirst for knowledge."

"It was wizard, sir," said Peter.

He sat in a dream still. Eyes withdrawn. Elsewhere.

Small talk. The weather. Daisy on the pleasures of tea drinking. Placidly chatting, with anxiety under the eyes.

And Major Mortenson. Not drinking tea. "Waste of time. Vita brevis." But there, listening.

Wemyss. Past caring whether nervousness showed. Darting looks at anyone who spoke. Anyone but Schlemberger.

Schlemberger not looking at Wemyss. And talking, talking, talking.

Whaa, whaa, whaa. The remorseless voice. Whaa, whaa. Hectoring, didactic. Whaa, whaa, whaa. The unending lecture. Whaa, whaa. Never at a loss for a subject. Whaa, whaa, whaa. A piledriver meandering.

"You're perfectly right, Miss Miller, tea is a mighty refreshing beverage. But on the other hand, major, you're entirely correct: it's a hell of a waste of time."

Whaa, whaa.

"That's the secret of the American success story. Basically, we don't waste time."

Whaa, whaa.

"What the old world fails to understand is that business is a philosophy, a way of life. You divide your days here into business and pleasure. We act business right through."

Whaa, whaa.

"Look at it marriage-wise. My exs act in a thoroughly businesslike way. A contract exists between us. Each side must endeavour to see that the other honours it, and at the same time must obtain maximum advantage from its provisions. It's a radically different approach."

Whaa, whaa.

"That's what made it so hard for me to get this murder affair straight at first. It was, after all, a European murder. I approached it from the wrong way, as if it had no special particularities, as an American murder in fact. So as soon as I saw it had nothing whatsoever to do with the States, I realised just who must have done it."

"And which of the people you said it was was it?" asked Daisy.

Schlemberger turned towards her. The rimless glasses at an angle of polite incomprehension.

"Pardon me," he said, "I think you must have failed to understand me. I have never hitherto accused anybody of committing this murder. I may have speculated about it aloud, as a deliberate attempt to open up the case, but that's a very different thing. A very different thing."

"I see," said Daisy. "And now you're going to tell us who really killed George."

Schlemberger looked slowly round the group. Listening in spite of themselves.

"You should never underestimate a woman's instinctive thought processes," he said. "Miss Kett was right when she said that Major Mortenson's confession was not intended to shield anyone. But she drew the wrong conclusion. Major, you had no difficulty in denying you were an accomplice of Miss Miller's. Can you deny that the only person you hoped to protect by your confession was yourself?"

Eyes turn.

The major looks straight at Schlemberger.

"I have offered an explanation," he said.

Bright blue eyes suddenly leaving Schlemberger to flick round the room.

"Something about convincing us anyone might have committed the crime," Schlemberger said. "European stuff."

"Go on," said the major.

Gaze once more steady on Schlemberger.

"All right, I'll go on. I'll go on to deal with another aspect of the case about which, in spite of a great deal of discussion, I have heard nothing at all."

"Tell me," said the major, "why aren't you going to the police with all this?"

"I prefer to run it my own way," said Schlemberger. "The police can come in afterwards."

"I see."

The major glanced round the room again.

"Go on," he said.

"Perhaps none of you remembers a curious incident that took place only a few minutes before the killing," Schlemberger said.

"Oh, the sovereigns," Daisy said. "I thought of them the other day. I meant to ask if they really were the proper thing or not. Then as usual it passed right out of my head. Were they real, major?"

"I've no idea," the major said. "I never opened the purse I was given either before Hamyadis was shot or after. I think the police took them away. I never saw them again."

"Neither did I open mine," Wemyss said. "You know I'm not sorry Hamyadis was killed. I wouldn't necessarily give away his murderer, even if I knew him."

"You seem to forget you have a duty," Smithers said.

"Duty," said Wemyss. "I recognise one to myself, certainly. But I don't think one need go beyond that. Not outside the public school, anyhow."

"Now I would put it just the other way round," Smithers said, "within the confines of a public school little harm results from any neglect of one's duty to society. In the outside world things are different. More than one person may believe he owes no duty but to himself, and one of those people may be a murderer."

Wemyss said nothing. His eyes were fixed intently on Schlemberger.

"But we interrupted you, Schlemberger," Smithers said.

"So you're not coming clean, major?" Schlemberger said. "I hardly expected it. We'll just have to go through the whole case till you see that you're fixed once and for all. We'll have to hammer in the points. That Hamyadis had caught you stealing money right at the start of the journey, that you knew he was waiting his time to hand you over to the cops, that the game with the sovereigns was just another bit of his cat and mouse tactics, that you made up your mind to shoot him before he spoke."

"Couldn't those purses be found so that we would know one way or the other?" asked the major. "I don't like being called a thief."

"I guess they were taken out of the coach and got rid of," Schlemberger said. "That would have been the reason for the second raid on it that night."

He smiled slightly.

"And all this talk about the States being the key to the problem. What hooey. A European crime. Ridiculously complex, bound up with the poverty of a decaying middle class. Literary. And just as soon as it came up against solidly applied business methods bound to fail."

"Please," said Peter, "the purses didn't have real money in them; I looked."

The major leant back in his chair. Slowly. Muscle by muscle. Then he laughed.

"It doesn't alter the case," shouted Schlemberger.

The major went on laughing.

"You're sure of that, Peter?" asked Smithers.

"Yes, I'm really sure."

"Real money or false," Schlemberger said, "what counts is that Hamyadis was threatening the major by calling him a thief in that way. Can't you see that? Who agrees with me?"

No one spoke.

Schlemberger walked towards the door.

"I see something in your logic," said Smithers.

"Thanks," Schlemberger said.

The slam of the door.

"Perhaps I shouldn't have gone on at him," Daisy said. "I feel sorry for him now."

"The fellow is beginning to get a nuisance," the major said. "You were quite right to try and take him down a peg."

"Anyhow, I don't think he noticed," Daisy said. "Which is a comfort, I think."

"I wish all the same he hadn't felt it necessary to do that," Fremitt said. "It's upsetting. It leads one to hope too much and to fear it."

"I can't stand it," Kristen said.

Her first words.

"Waiting, waiting, waiting," she went on. "Why can't something happen?"

"Come," Fremitt said. "You never know, at any moment the police may come to a decision. All we have to do is to attend to our own affairs and to wait."

"The police," Kristen said, "what are they doing? Nothing."

"Oh, no, that's not really true," Fremitt said. "They've been out all day with the helicopter for instance. They're still out with it now. I've noticed the distant sound of its engine every now and again all afternoon. Listen, you can hear it now."

They all listened.

Faintly above the noise of passing cars in the street and the chatter of passers-by the steady hum of the helicopter's engine.

No one spoke. The hum gained slightly in volume, then receded.

"You see," Fremitt said, "at work."

"Where are they now?" Kristen asked.

"Not far from the town, I should think," Fremitt said.

"Could we go and see it?" Kristen said. "Anything would be better than not knowing what's happening."

"I think there is no point in hampering the police," Smithers said.

"Please, sir," said Peter, "what Miss Kett said is true: it's awful just waiting."

"You want to go?" Smithers asked him.

"I do, sir. I really do."

"You know what you may see?"

"I'd rather see Dad caught, sir, than not know whether he has been or not."

"All right, then. If they're still working to the plan they were this morning we ought to be able to follow the whole thing simply by walking to the top of the hill outside. The helicopter should be working on the valley below. We'll probably be as high as it is."

"Let's all go," said Daisy. "We shall at least get to know something."

They got up to go. Fremitt darted at the hat rack in the hall and snatched his cap.

"There's a nasty chill in the wind towards evening," he said.

The others waited for him on the steps of the inn. Schlemberger appeared from a dark little used room labelled 'Smoking'.

"We're all going to watch the helicopter," Daisy called. "Are you coming?"

"Do they think they're going to get Dagg?" Schlemberger said.

"That can only be a matter of time," said Smithers.

"Guess a lot of problems will be solved when the police have a talk with him," Schlemberger said.

"Is it Dagg again, then?" Daisy asked.

"Now, now," said Schlemberger.

He grinned.

"I guess I've learnt my lesson," he said. "From now on I'm suspecting no one."

They walked quickly up the hill. The houses ended abruptly. A fence dividing country and town. After four minutes' more brisk walk they came to the top of the hill. There was a view right across the shallow downland valley broken up here and there by clumps of trees and occasional fields surrounded by hedges.

No one had spoken on the way up. Now Smithers said:

"I think this would be the place."

Silence.

The helicopter was easily visible working its way systematically over the ground in front of them. Three police cars could also be seen moving from point to point immediately below the plane. Every now and again one of them would stop and two or three blue uniformed figures could be seen running towards a patch of thick undergrowth. After a quick search one of the men would wave an all clear to the helicopter and the force would move on to the next point.

The evening was calm. Torpid. There was no wind to stir the trees or dispel the heat of day. A cloudless sky, pale blue, exhausted after the sun's attack. Faint haze on the horizon, but good visibility. A bird sang briefly, drowsily. The effort of the day over. Only the helicopter buzzed like the last bee.

They sat down along a low tussocky bank. A grandstand.

The major lit a pipe.

In front of them the search for Joe Dagg went on. Methodical, slow, regular. The working of some gigantic and complicated clock. A parade of figures at each quarter, and the steady whirr of the machinery.

Once the rhythm was broken. Someone leant out of the helicopter and signalled violently to the nearest car. Two policemen ran fast to a group of three stunted trees at the corner of a field. From the distance nothing could be heard. Only the two blue figures could be seen steadily moving to their aim. Ants.

But it was a false alarm. The first of the policemen to arrive picked up a sack from under the trees and waved it for the helicopter party to see. The plane promptly rose another twenty feet and moved off to its next section. The two policemen went back to their car, slower now.

The major tapped his pipe against his heel. The noise was startling.

"It's still wonderfully warm," said Daisy.

"And it's light too," Schlemberger said.

Wemyss stretched himself and lay back.

The clockwork search. To their right the sun imperceptibly moving nearer to the horizon.

The scutter of a match striking as the major lit another pipe.

When the smell of the tobacco smoke had lost its freshness there was another burst of activity from the searchers. The helicopter settled even lower than usual. The pilot roared its engine in two or three quick bursts apparently to attract the attention of the cars. They in their turn speeded up. One stopped and turned in a gateway, with the screech of brakes faintly audible. The three cars began to converge.

The point over which the helicopter hovered was a clump of fir trees crowning a small knoll. From the distance it looked as if the bare ground between the few trees could not have given any cover, but it was obvious that the helicopter party believed they had seen something worth investigating.

There was a considerable gap of open downland between the knoll and the nearest road. Two of the police cars arrived almost simultaneously at a gate at this point. Five men leapt from the first and four from the second. All set off at once at a steady run in the direction of the trees. A faint shout came from them to the watchers on the hill. The runners spread slowly into a wide line. A sixth man from the first car unexpectedly set out after his companions.

The helicopter still hung over the little clump of trees. A vulture.

When the searchers were within fifty yards of the knoll and beginning to bunch together again Schlemberger called out:

"Something moving in there. I saw something move."

A man appeared on the edge of the trees as if he had been thrown up by the pine-needle covered earth. He began to run in the opposite direction from the police. As he did so he seemed to shed a cloud of dust.

"It's Dad," said Peter very quietly.

"You're sure?" asked Smithers.

"I know the way he runs."

"He seems to be outdistancing them," Smithers said. "He goes very fast for a man of his age."

"He always did begin too fast," said Peter. "He'll have to stop soon. That's how I beat him in races."

The whole party on the hilltop was standing now.

"Did you say you beat him?" asked Wemyss. "Then I'll think better of offering a price."

"He seems to be making for that bit of woodland there," said Fremitt.

"It looks pretty extensive. If he gets there he might succeed in hiding again."

"I hope he gets there," said Daisy. "All that many against one."

"Yet one ought to hope for his own sake that he doesn't," Smithers said.

"He's gaining on them," said the major.

"I think the ground slopes gently in his favour," Fremitt said. "The pol—the others will begin to get the benefit of it in a moment."

They watched in silence.

"You're right about the slope," Wemyss said after a while. "Look, the police are gaining on him fast now."

"Dad's beginning to get his stitch," Peter said to Smithers.

"Do you want to go back to the hotel?" Smithers said.

"No. I couldn't. Oh!"

A cry of despair. Joe Dagg had stopped in his tracks.

He turned and faced his pursuers. They had spread out into a ragged line, some ahead, others behind, two or three bunched together in the centre and others well away from them.

Suddenly Joe Dagg began running again. Hard. And straight towards the line.

"Look, look," shouted Peter. "There's a gap. He's making for it. Good old Dad."

The police began to close in. Sprinting. Arms working.

For less than two minutes the result was doubtful. Then Peter said:

"Good old Dad. Good old Dad."

His father had gained a good lead by the manœuvre.

"Wait a bit," said Schlemberger.

They had reckoned without the policeman who left the cars after his companions. He was now running down the slope straight at Dagg.

Both men kept straight on.

Ten yards, five. No swerve. Four, three, two, one.

A collision. Arms, legs, a flurry.

Joe Dagg staggered up and ran on. Reached his first hiding place. The policeman stood up, felt at his stomach, gradually straightened up. The others joined him. They stood for two minutes talking. One of them pointed in the direction of the cars. The third vehicle had just drawn up. Six men got out. There was a great deal of waving. Some shouts could be heard. Then all the men spread out making a wide circle.

From the knoll no sign. Joe had disappeared again almost as soon as he entered the trees.

"He should have got to hell out of it while he had the chance," said Schlemberger.

No one said any more.

Gradually the circle of policemen closed in. Overhead the helicopter watched.

At last the searchers came to the edge of the little wood.

"There were moments when I regretted those bets," said Wemyss.

The policemen became half hidden by the few trees.

One of them suddenly ran clear of the knoll and began waving to the plane. It looked as if he was shouting.

"They won't hear him if that machine is half as noisy as it was when I met it this morning," said Smithers.

Several of the other policemen came out of the wood. There was no sign of activity in it, or of any prisoner.

"What do you think's happened, sir?" asked Peter.

"Something unexpected by the looks of it," Smithers said. "But I wouldn't try to guess what."

"But it might be anything, sir."

"It might. We'll just have to wait. Look, there's one of the policemen broken into a pantomime for the benefit of the inspector in the plane, if he's still there."

They watched the man. He had run a few paces from the others and was acting something out with enormous gestures. Soon it was plain what he was trying to say: No one in the wood.

The helicopter moved away.

"It looks as if they're going to land in that open space there for consultations," said Fremitt.

Suddenly the plane shot up in the air. An express lift.

Then it dived at an angle towards the next field. It seemed to have a definite aim.

A moment later from the hedge close by the spinney Joe Dagg broke cover again.

"He must have had a tunnel or something," said the major. "Damned ingenious fellow."

"He'll do it yet," said Wemyss. "He's yards ahead of them this time and going away from their cars. They're foxed."

But they were not foxed. With a louder roar of engines, distinctly heard on the hilltop, the helicopter swept over Joe's head. A figure dropped from it, arms spread out.

"Nosey," whispered Peter.

The inspector and his quarry fell to the ground together. A moment later the inspector stood up.

"Dad," said Peter, "he's——"

But already his father was struggling to his feet. The inspector leaned over him. Joe got up with his arms behind his back.

"Handcuffed," said Wemyss. "I would have lost my money after all."

"I wouldn't have minded losing, not a bit," said Daisy.

"I suppose this is the end," Fremitt said. "It seems unlikely. But when you think of it, it's only sensible."

Smithers put a hand on Peter's shoulder.

The whole party set off down the hill. They walked slowly. Not looking at each other.

When they got into the town Kristen said:

"I'm not going back to that bloody inn. I'd stifle."

"Don't go off on your own, dear," said Daisy.

"Why not? I won't get murdered now, I suppose. But what a muck up."

"No, it's not that," Daisy said. "It's that I've got something important I want to tell you all."

"Did you know all along, then?" asked Schlemberger. "You thought you'd let him have a run for his money. It was wrong, I guess."

"No, it's not that either," Daisy said. "I mean it is really, I suppose. Now I've got myself in a tangle and at a time I really ought to be clear. I'll tell you what it is: it's just that I know who the murderer is, and it isn't Joe Dagg."

SEVENTEEN

They stood in a knot round her in the street.

"If you knew all this time," said Wemyss, "why didn't you accuse whoever it was?"

"That was quick, Richie, dear," said Kristen.

"Quick?"

"Getting in that little claim to being innocent."

"What do you mean?"

Wemyss raised his voice.

"This is no place to discuss a matter of this sort," said Smithers. "I suggest we all go back to the hotel without another word."

Put on silence.

They walked a few yards to the hotel, went in in a troop and found the smoking room deserted. They crowded in.

A small room too dark to be used often. Little altered from the earliest days of the inn. A low ceiling crossed by a single misshapen beam. A deep fireplace designed for a heap of red embers now incongruously decorated with a sheet of orange coloured paper folded to a fan shape.

A flimsy veneer of Orientalism: a circus poster on an oak tree. The sofa covered in a gaudy Indian cloth, an elephant's foot waste paper basket, three peacock's feathers in a small Benares brass pot on the high mantelpiece. An enormous lopsided leather covered pouf. A single Japanese print hanging on the wall, slightly crooked.

When they had all crowded in Smithers tried the door handle. The door was firmly shut. He then turned and faced the others. Holding himself unusually erect.

"Oh dear," said Daisy. "Oh, do sit down everybody, please."

One by one they all sat down, awkwardly. Only Daisy and Smithers remained on their feet. Smithers still by the door. Daisy in front of the deep chimneypiece.

"You know," she said, "I'm not going to stand in front of you all and say a name."

"Not going to say a name, what do you mean?" asked the major.

"Only just that," Daisy said. "I know who killed George, but I'm not going to do anything like accusing them to their face here and now."

"But why not? Surely we've a right to know," the major said.

"I don't think we have," said Smithers.

He walked across and sat down on the pouf, the only vacant place left.

"If Miss Miller has evidence which she has been foolish enough up to now to conceal from the police, all we have a right to expect," he said, "is that she shall tell them as soon as possible."

"I do deserve a lecture, I know," she said. "I'm lucky to get such a nice one, and I suppose now I must go and see the inspector, but before I go I've got one thing I must tell you all. I feel I mustn't dodge a bit of pain when someone else is going to have to go through a hell of a lot."

She stopped and looked round at them.

"It's just to clear up my little contribution to the muddle," she said. "It was foolish of me from the start really. I should never have got into the habit of pretending I had never been to America just because it had such awful memories for me."

"There's still no need to revive them," Smithers said.

"Perhaps I'm best to in any case," said Daisy. "You see it was on that visit to Broadway that I told you about that it happened. First of all I lied about how long I was there. But I told you that. The show ran and ran. I suppose it had the effect of making Willy, that's my husband, you know, my only one ever, bored. He took to going to lousy night clubs—that's what I meant about George, he ran ones like them only not in New York— and then someone started him, Willy, I mean, off on drugs. He's in a home over there now. He won't ever come out. My call was to ask about him. It costs an awful lot but it bucks me up to hear he's happy when things get me down."

"He is happy, then?" asked Smithers.

"Oh, yes, he's almost always quite happy. It's just that it wouldn't be safe for him to be out. And now I think I must go along to the police station."

"Why didn't you go before, if I may ask?" said Fremitt.

Daisy looked at him for two seconds before she spoke.

"Because the person I shall be talking about is someone I very much respect," she said. "And I went on hoping the police would give up. I'm sure the person only killed George because he deserved to die."

"And now," said Smithers, "I'm going to escort you to the police station, and I think that at least one other person should come with me."

"You sound very solemn," said Daisy.

"If you really have information which you alone know and which would expose the murderer, it's a solemn business," Smithers said.

"Who's going with her?" said Wemyss.

"You must," Daisy said.

"Very well, I will."

"Quick again," Kristen said.

"It's only common courtesy," Wemyss said. "What right have you to go putting a meaning on it like that?"

"Only that common courtesy is something I've yet to find in you, Richie Wemyss. And you needn't think you're going to get away with this. I'm coming down with Daisy too."

"Well, you've made a point that that's a guarantee of innocence," Wemyss said.

"I think that anyone who wants to had better come," said Smithers. "Staying behind now would look like an admission of guilt."

"Then alibi or no alibi, I shall join you," said the major.

They all walked out to the street in a body and began to march along to the police station. When they were less than fifty yards away a police car drew up outside it.

Two uniformed constables got out and stood blocking the narrow pavement.

"Peter," said Smithers, "it may be your father."

"Will I be allowed to see him later?" Peter said.

"I should think so, almost certainly. I'll mention the matter to the inspector tomorrow morning."

As he was speaking Inspector Parker and Joe Dagg bundled together from the car and ran up the four steps into the station.

The others stood waiting.

"Handcuffed still, I see," said the major.

"Had I better wait a little?" Daisy said.

"No," said Smithers, "the sooner you're inside the station the happier all of us will be."

"All but one," said Wemyss.

"Can't you shut up, Richie?" Kristen said. "We've all got the idea: you're innocent whoever else is guilty."

Richard Wemyss compressed his lips and glared at Kristen.

"We used to be such friends," he said.

The imitation was adequate.

"I thought we were once," Kristen said. "But you've behaved so bloody callously over this business that I can see I was making a great mistake."

Before Wemyss had time to reply Smithers said:

"Once again I think we should find somewhere better than the public street to air our differences."

"I'll go in then," said Daisy.

They walked the last few yards. On the steps of the station Daisy turned.

"I'm going to ask one of you to do something," she said. "You know which one I mean."

Glances exchanged.

"Come and tell the inspector yourself as soon as you get the chance," Daisy said. "It's the best way."

She turned, hurried up the final three steps and in at the open door. They saw her say something to the constable at the inquiry desk. He took her into an inner room and shut the door.

Outside the party walked back in silence.

As they re-entered the inn Schlemberger said:

"That's a very remarkable woman."

"Either that or one with a very shrewd eye for publicity," said Wemyss. He looked hard at Kristen. She said nothing.

"I don't venture to doubt her," the major said.

"The curious thing is," said Smithers, "that she could be perfectly right or wildly wrong. She combines what I'm sure is genuine vagueness with a demonstrable shrewdness."

"Do you know," Fremitt said, "I think that is the first judgement I have heard you pass on one of the company. It's something I had observed. We have all, necessarily, been discussing each others' characters recently. But this is the first time you have committed yourself."

"I begin to be sure of my ground here and there," said Smithers.

"Well," Kristen said, "I don't care if anybody thinks I'm slipping off to the police station or not, I'm going up to my room."

"One moment," the major said.

He went and stood between Kristen and the stairhead.

"Before you go I think you have something to say."

"Oh, lord, what's this now?" Kristen said.

"Simply that you have accused a lady of committing a murder. I don't suppose anyone of us believed you, but now we've been privileged to hear that lady's explanation I think you owe us a few words of apology."

"Don't be silly," Kristen said. "I was all wrought up. If you only knew how bloody I feel. I mentioned it to Daisy afterwards; she didn't mind. And now, if you'll excuse me."

She pushed past the major and slowly climbed the stairs. Her face between the two thick swags of ash blonde hair, white. The deep slash of red lipstick more than usually prominent.

Before she was out of hearing the major said:

"You know what I'd do with a girl like that? I'd horsewhip her. She's behaved abominably: she's obviously quite unrepentant. She needs to have things brought home to her."

Going into Peter's room after dinner Smithers found him just scrambling into bed. The high hotel bed: the kicking pyjama legs.

"You all right?" he said.

"Yes, thank you, sir."

"No worries about this evening. I'm afraid you hear more than you ought to."

"I don't understand everything, but it's nicest to know what's going on."

"Perhaps it is. It doesn't worry you?"

"No. Dad will be all right, won't he, sir?"

"You needn't worry. Do you trust me when I tell you that?"

"Yes I do, sir."

"Good boy. Well, good night then. I don't want to be away from the others too long. That fish, you know, he may snap at any moment."

"Keep your eye on the float, sir. That's what Dad always tells me."

"Very good advice."

"Except he always forgets to do it himself."

"We're all human. Good night."

"Good night, sir."

"Oh, by the way, one little thing I've been meaning to ask you all evening."

"Yes?"

A yawn.

"Have you ever seen a sovereign?"

"You mean the money, sir?"

"Yes, a golden sovereign."

"Golden? Does that mean they are made of gold?"

"Yes, they are."

"Oh sir, and I thought there wasn't any money that colour."

"I thought you might have done. Poor Mr Schlemberger."

"Does that mean he was right?"

"The major didn't seem to think so, did he?"

"No, he didn't. Was what happened that I proved him wrong for the wrong reason?"

"That's about it."

"And that doesn't make him right."

"Nine out of ten for logic. Good night."

"Good night, sir. Poor old Schlemmie."

Smithers was followed back into the public room by Schlemberger, whom he had seen at the telephone on his way down stairs.

"Hell," Schlemberger said, "I knew this conference would be a flop right from the start."

"The inspector doesn't want you to go up to London?" said Fremitt. "I had hoped it might be convenient for me to go soon myself. There's a lot of business accumulating."

"So the case isn't over," said Wemyss. "Odd."

He took a long drink from his second brandy.

"I guess it isn't," said Schlemberger.

"Did he say anything, Nosey Parker? Anything about Joe Dagg or Daisy?" asked Kristen.

"Not a thing," said Schlemberger. "Just that he would like me to wait. He said I could go up soon. In the near future. I suppose that means soon."

"I think if someone were to leave this room now you might find yourself in London tomorrow morning," said the major.

"But don't kid yourself anyone's going to do that," Wemyss said.

They sat looking at each other. No more was said. Wemyss got up once, crossed to the bell, rang it and ordered another brandy. The quarters striking on the stable yard clock could be easily heard. It was still very warm.

At 10.30 the major said:

"Someone has got to make the first move. I'm going up to bed."

The others began to leave. Smithers got up and prepared to follow them.

"Has anyone seen my book?" he asked. "Volume 8 of *The Decline and Fall*. I'm sure I left it here."

"I read that once," said Kristen.

"Really," Smithers said. "Did you enjoy it?"

"It was very funny in bits," Kristen said.

"A possible view."

"But I don't remember it being all that long."

"A tribute to Gibbon, indeed."

"Was that who wrote it? I can never remember."

"Yes, that's who it was. Edward Gibbon. I wouldn't have thought one who 'sighed as a lover and obeyed as a son' would have been altogether sympathetic to you."

"He said that, did he? Doesn't sound much my line. Still I liked the book all right. Have you got to the bit yet where the hero is in prison and they smuggle caviare to him and one of the other convicts gets it and nearly upsets everything by wanting to complain about the quality of the marge?"

"I'm afraid we were talking about different books," Smithers said. "A pity. Yours is by Evelyn Waugh. But they do have nearly the same title."

"I thought it was a bit strange," said Kristen. "Have you read my one too?"

"I have," said Smithers. "And I enjoyed it."

"We must have a nice chat about it one day," said Kristen. "Or perhaps not really. Good night."

"Good night," said Smithers.

All the others had left.

At the door Kristen poked her head back in again and said:

"I would have liked to have watched to see if anybody went out of the front door instead of going up to bed, but I suppose they were all in a bunch."

"I confess to the same curiosity," said Smithers.

"Are you getting more human? Or am I just suddenly feeling a little better?"

Without waiting for an answer Kristen left.

During the conversation Smithers had been looking round the room for his book without success. Now he began a thorough search. It took him six minutes to find the volume tucked under the cushion of a small chair in the far corner of the room.

"Now why . . . ?" he said aloud as he went to collect the key of his bedroom from the hall board.

He reached for the now familiar hook. Nothing hung from it.

For four seconds he stared at the empty hook as if in a dream. Then he dropped his Gibbon, ran at a loping pace along a corridor and out by the back way into the yard. He turned sharply and increasing his pace followed the wall until he came to a small disused stable where a few oddments of garden tools were kept. By the fading daylight Smithers was able to see a short ladder propped in a corner. It had a rung missing about half way along, but looked otherwise sound.

Smithers seized it and ran back along the length of the hotel. The ladder over his shoulder swayed crazily.

About half-way between the tool store and the back door of the inn

Smithers stopped. He took a deep breath and then set his ladder up against the wall. He climbed it carefully. It creaked heavily at the top rung but two. But it served Smithers's purpose. With a heave but no serious danger he was able to get himself on to the gently sloping tiles running immediately under his own and some other rooms.

He stood for a moment leaning slightly forward to counterbalance the slope and trying to get his bearings. Then he set out on tiptoe.

His own window was wide open as he had left it earlier in the day. Cautiously he approached and stood beside it. He peered in.

And quickly drew back.

For as long as it takes to count ten he waited and then peered round the corner again. This time he acted quickly.

He put a foot across the sill and into the room, ducked down and swung the rest of his body in. Then he side-stepped smartly and stood upright with his back solidly against the bedroom wall.

"Well, Wemyss," he said, "I thought I might find you here."

EIGHTEEN

Wemyss was kneeling with his back to the window rummaging through the chest of drawers. The room was in disorder. Every drawer had been wrenched open and the contents flung out. The wardrobe had had all the coats and suits taken out and they were lying in a pile with the pockets protruding. The other seven volumes of *The Decline and Fall* were in a heap on the floor lying open and face down.

When Smithers spoke Wemyss wheeled round, lost his balance and went sprawling against the wall behind him.

"It's not here in any case," Smithers said. "I've already lost one valuable piece of evidence from my room. You don't think I'd make the same mistake twice, do you?"

"It isn't valuable evidence," Wemyss said.

"Well, not positive evidence I grant you," said Smithers. "But that packet has caused enough trouble during this business to have acquired the right to special protection."

Wemyss got to his feet. Suddenly like a gymnast.

"Where is it?" he said.

"Safely locked away," said Smithers.

"You've sent it away," Wemyss said.

An accusation.

"Well, why shouldn't I?" said Smithers. "After all it wasn't addressed to you. You seem to be taking the business much more to heart than I would have thought likely. Relations between yourself and Miss Kett in the last few days seemed to preclude this unusual devotion to her interests, if I may say so. Or was the whole quarrel this evening an elaborate deceit? You know, people must have been thinking as much. Before Hamyadis died there was such open courtship and since there has been such obvious quarrelling."

"There wasn't any deceit," Wemyss said.

He pouted.

"Then why all this?"

Smithers pointed at the pile of Gibbon.

Wemyss looked at him, calculating.

"What proof have you got that you ever took the packet?" he said.

"Proof? None at all. Why should I have? I'd have been much happier if no one had ever known that I'd got it."

"I suppose so. And you did look put out when the boy blew the gaff in that way."

"Did I? I must be careful to show less of my feelings."

Wemyss stood looking at Smithers. Smithers looked back.

At last Wemyss said:

"Look, you've read those letters. What are you going to do about them?"

"Do about them?"

"Yes, do about me? You know. What use do you mean to make of your knowledge?"

"Ah, I see. Forgive me for being so slow. The ingenious Miss Kett told you there was something in those letters in the packet to your disadvantage, did she? No wonder you were so active on her behalf."

"You mean there isn't anything about me in them?"

"My dear chap, as you well know, the packet was addressed to Miss Kett. I didn't think she could be trusted with it so I kept it. But I haven't opened it."

"You haven't. . . . You bloody fool."

"Our standards, as I have so often suspected, differ."

"Listen," said Wemyss.

He took three paces across the room till he was near Smithers.

"Listen. That packet contains information that is of vital interest to me. I want it. I want to get hold of it and destroy it. Are you going to let me have it?"

"Of course not," said Smithers.

He made no move.

Wemyss came two steps nearer. He was now only an arm's length away.

"You will send for that packet at once," he said, "or else . . ."

"Or else what?" said Smithers. "Don't be silly, my good man. You don't imagine physical violence will serve your ends, do you?"

"It might," said Wemyss.

"Listen to me," said Smithers. "At present the police know nothing about those letters. I didn't think they concerned them, and in the circumstances I decided to keep them until it proved necessary to hand them over. But if you were to assault me I would have no alternative but to mention the whole matter to Inspector Parker."

Wemyss unclenched his fist.

"I wouldn't have struck an older man," he said. "What makes you think that?"

"Observation of the behaviour of schoolboys has given me certain general concepts about human nature," Smithers said.

Wemyss sat on the end of the bed.

"Look," he said. "I think you've got several wrong ideas. Let's talk them over, shall we?"

Smithers stayed where he was and said nothing.

"You think I hate you, don't you?" Wemyss said. "You don't trust me, I can see that."

"I don't trust you, no, but if you go beyond that, you flatter yourself."

"All right. Never mind that. You have your ideas; I have mine. But that's not the point. What we've got to discuss is something quite different."

"Indeed?"

"Yes."

Wemyss looked at Smithers speculatively.

"Look," he said, "you haven't read those letters. You say so, and I'm quite prepared to believe you. Well, without reading them you can't know what's in them, can you? As it happens I do know, or at least I've a pretty shrewd idea. Hamyadis was not a nice man you know, I don't suppose you've any idea, shut up there in your neat public school world, of the sort of things a man like that can do. They would never even occur to you."

"I hope they wouldn't," Smithers said.

"No, exactly. You know really you were very wise not to open that packet."

"Thank you."

"It might have upset your faith in human nature."

"You told me you were at Harrow, I think," Smithers said.

"I was, but that has got precious little to do with what we're talking about now. This is the real world. It's a nasty place, Mr Smithers."

Smithers smiled.

"I suppose you think that the masters at Harrow had no idea of the sort of thoughts that you had while you were there," he said. "And of the sort of things you did, if you thought you could get away with them."

"What do you know about me?" said Wemyss.

A glint of fear.

"Don't worry, I haven't been having a confidential exchange of information with your housemaster or anything," Smithers said. "I was simply applying general principles. Not without success, it appears."

Wemyss jumped up again.

"Listen," he said, "don't try to be too clever."

"Now," said Smithers, "stop that. For various reasons I'm prepared to listen to what you've got to say. But any bluster of that sort, and I'll have no mercy."

"You keep on getting me wrong," Wemyss said, sitting down again. "There's no question of threats. I'm just trying to explain the essence of the situation to you. You haven't read the letters; you don't know what it's all about."

"Now there," said Smithers, "you're wrong. I have a very good idea what's in that packet. You have only to make a few observations to see. Take certain obvious facts about Miss Kett, add Hamyadis's somewhat transparent character, and it isn't difficult to decide what he would put in a packet and hide from her."

"If you're so clever," Wemyss said, "tell me what he did put in it then?"

"I'm clever enough not to fall for that. No, if you can't put two and two together for yourself I shall do nothing to spread a secret that one of the parties is very anxious, naturally, to keep."

"Kristen gave me a different idea of the packet when she asked me to find it for her," Wemyss said.

He looked up at Smithers interrogatively.

Smithers said nothing.

"She told me," Wemyss went on, "that she had said a lot to him about me. That she had used me to——"

He paused.

Words, one by one on the table.

Smithers stayed silent.

"She used me in a certain context," Wemyss said, "to try and regain her influence over that man, Hamyadis. You realise, of course, that she was on her way out with him."

"I know what you mean," Smithers said, "though I regret the lack of sensibility the phrase reveals. I think you are probably more or less right too. Except that the situation was rather more complicated, if I'm not mistaken."

"Oh," said Wemyss, "so you notice things like that, do you?"

"They were very obvious."

"Well, all right. That makes it easier to tell you in a way. Kristen told me that he had hidden the letters she had written to him on the coach somewhere. It was his form of humour. He said she could have them back if she could find them."

"Exactly. That wasn't difficult to guess."

Wemyss shifted his feet, moved the position of his hands on the bed.

"As I told you," he said, "she had put things in the letters about me. They weren't true. That was why Hamyadis took it so badly when he heard I wasn't Kris's brother. So you can see why I want to get hold of those letters and destroy them. The bitch."

A sudden tautening of the muscles, a convulsive gesture.

"It's a pity," Smithers said, "that your opinion of her, unfortunately expressed though it is, cannot be more generally known. If you and she are not exactly friends, you would appear to have had no motive for killing Hamyadis. As it is, your display of attentive gallantry in those first days has been assumed to be sincere, as you intended it to appear. And you have suffered accordingly."

"You seem to know a good bit about me," said Wemyss. "It's rather unfair. Either I am supposed to be a murderer, or I have to confess that I'm not interested in all this sex business. And some people think that that's worse than murder."

"I don't think so," said Smithers.

"Well, anyhow," Wemyss said, "I owe nothing to that precious Kristen. All I was doing was getting her letters. And I was damned unlucky not to succeed. In any case, now you see the position she's put me in, you'll let me have them, won't you?"

"They can stay where they are."

"But you said . . ."

"I said nothing of the sort. Those letters may yet play a necessary part in this business of Hamyadis's death, and they are staying where I put them."

"But . . ."

"I don't think you need worry too much about them though. It was shrewd of Miss Kett to tell you she had mentioned you in them. But you know Hamyadis registered a very genuine blank when your name was first mentioned to him."

"I didn't notice that."

"I would have been surprised if you had allowed yourself to," said Smithers. "But accept the word of a disinterested observer. Until the start of our coach trip Hamyadis had never heard of you."

"You're sure of that?" said Wemyss.

He pushed his legs out in front of him. Relaxed.

"Quite sure."

"It's odd. But I suppose it's quite possible. He was never really in the theatre, you know. A sort of hanger-on. Mostly night club entertaining, with the odd nude show tour. And Kris thought she'd try and kid me those letters were full of stuff about me."

He smiled again.

"She's all sorts of a bitch, isn't she?" he said. "Trying to trick me into doing her dirty work for her. I suppose she thought she was going to get away with it too. You wouldn't believe the sheer duplicity you come across in people like that."

"People like that?"

"Yes, you know, accent breaking down a bit when she gets excited. Heaven knows what her background is."

"I don't think duplicity is exactly confined to people with the wrong accent."

"Oh, I grant you the occasional black sheep. But Kristen's type almost always end up on the windy side of the law somewhere."

"A spot of blackmail or something like that?" said Smithers.

"Yes, that sort of thing."

"A practice which you yourself would find quite impossible?"

"Well, I don't claim to be a paragon of virtue or anything, but I don't see myself as a blackmailer since you ask."

"I see. You're not the sort of person, for instance, to take advantage of any information you may have come across in regard to this business of Hamyadis to make some money?"

As he spoke Smithers saw Wemyss's fingers, spread wide on the bed, go rigid.

Wemyss made no reply.

"Haven't I said enough?" Smithers asked.

"What do you mean?"

"Come, don't be stupid. You know perfectly well that I must be aware of your unsavoury dealings with Mr Schlemberger. Don't try to pretend that you don't understand me."

"But that—— That isn't blackmail," said Wemyss.

He slewed round on the bed to face Smithers.

"Isn't it?"

"But the man's keeping information from the police, I'm simply letting him off lightly."

"And if he is withholding information what right have you to do that? And fill your own pockets at the same time?"

"It isn't a question of my own pockets. I decided that it wasn't fair to go to the police, but I didn't want him to get away with it scot free."

"I suppose it didn't occur to you that someone who might have committed one murder would quite possibly not stop there."

"I can take care of myself, thanks."

"I've no doubt you do take care of yourself, but what about other people? Have you given as much as a thought to them? Of course you haven't."

"It's all very well to go on at me like that," Wemyss said. "But it isn't as if I've done anything very serious. What about that man Schlemberger? He probably shot Hamyadis after all. No doubt he was completely in his power and we all knew Schlemberger couldn't afford a scandal."

"What you have found out about Mr Schlemberger is a matter for the police," Smithers said. "And so is what I have found out about you. Only up till now I've thought it might not have to go as far as that."

"The police?"

"Blackmail is considered a very serious offence, and quite rightly so."

"But if I've caught a murderer?"

"If you've caught a murderer: you haven't up to now seemed particularly anxious to pass on your information to Inspector Parker."

"You seem pretty keen to see Schlemberger hung."

"I'm anxious to see justice done. It's the best society can manage to tidy up the messes it produces."

"Oh well, I don't know about that sort of stuff. But, look here, you can't go to Inspector Parker and tell him I'm a blackmailer."

"I quite easily could. It's the truth, after all. And I'm not sure that I shouldn't."

"Can't we come to some arrangement?"

"Perhaps. That depends on you."

"On me?"

"Yes. Tell Schlemberger that there's no question of you accepting money, and then tell him that he ought to let the police know everything about his connection with Hamyadis. You can add that there would scarcely be any question of proceedings against him now."

"But what if he tries to have a go at me? If he is the murderer," Wemyss said.

"I think you claimed you could take care of yourself."

"Couldn't you see him?"

"No."

"He'll be asleep now."

"You can wake him up."

"If anything happens to me I hope it's never off your conscience," Wemyss said.

"I'll worry about that. Now go and see Schlemberger."

"All right. And you'll forget about it all yourself?"

"I shall remember it," Smithers said. "But I won't make any use of it unless you give me cause. And now good night."

"Good night. I say, I'm sorry I made such a mess in here."

"That's all right. It was the least of your errors."

"I suppose so. You still don't think I ought to tell the inspector about Schlemberger myself?"

"No, I think you can leave it."

"Right, if you say so. Good night."

The door closed. Smithers carefully tidied the room. Then he went and fetched his book. He read in bed for an hour.

On the way down to breakfast next morning Peter said quietly to Smithers:

"Sir, has the fish tried a bite yet?"

"Not yet. But the bait is still there and I've got my eye firmly on the float."

"Will you let me know when the bite comes, sir?"

"I make no promises."

They went into the dining-room. Although they were no later than they had been the morning before they were not the first down. Already Daisy, Kristen, Wemyss and Fremitt were there. Only Schlemberger and the major were missing.

"Good morning, Mr Smithers," said Daisy.

A note of invitation.

"Good morning. You were at the police station till very late last night. I didn't see you before I went to bed."

"I was hoping somebody would say something about it," Daisy said. "No one else has managed a word. I was beginning to feel as if I'd caught halitosis from the night air—if halitosis is what I think it is."

"You want to talk about your conversation with the inspector, then?" Smithers said.

"Of course I do. It's not often I'm the first to know something. I want everybody to be hanging on my words."

"The first to know something?" said Wemyss.

He glanced at Smithers.

"That's better," said Daisy. "Some interest at last. Yes, I think there has been quite a development."

"You were able to help them then?" asked Fremitt.

"To tell you the truth," Daisy said, "I don't know. I told the inspector all I had to, and he twitched his great big nose over it the way he does. But I had the impression he knew it all along, and it didn't somehow seem quite as important after that."

"Did that surprise you?" said Smithers. "The inspector is a very intelligent man."

"I suppose he could have found out everything I thought I knew," Daisy said. "But, as nothing had happened about it, I had got the impression he couldn't have done. Now I'm beginning to wonder if I've made a mistake."

"Then the lateness of our two absentees may not be significant," Wemyss said.

"Oh good lord, did you think they were confessing?" said Daisy. "It never occurred to me."

"That lets two of us out," said Kristen.

"Now," Smithers said, "I don't think this is a time for parlour games."

"Yes, it could get down to rather few people if I'm not careful," Daisy said. "Perhaps I ought to tell you straight away and put an end to my doubts."

"I think not," said Smithers. "You have put the matter into Inspector Parker's hands. If he decides against you an apology in private would end the matter. We've had too many accusations."

"How nice to have all one's problems settled so easily," Daisy said.

"All the same," said Wemyss, "I wonder what has happened to Schlemberger?"

"And Major Mortenson," said Fremitt. "He's usually fairly punctual."

"Never mind them," said Kristen. "Daisy has got something to tell us."

"I was beginning to feel a bit out of the limelight again," Daisy said. "Thank you, dear. Because, you know, I really think I have got something to tell you."

The door opened and the old head waiter came in.

"Mr Schlemberger just telephoned," he said. "He asked you not to expect him for breakfast."

"Where did he telephone from?" asked Wemyss.

"I'm sure I couldn't say, sir."

"Was it a long distance call?"

"No sir, I don't think so. I wasn't asked to hold the line."

"Was it from a call box? Did you hear him press button A?"

"No, I don't think I did, sir. It seemed quite an ordinary call such as we often get from private houses in the neighbourhood."

"Thank you," said Wemyss, "that'll be all."

"Yes, sir. Was there any other lady or gentleman requiring anything?"

Lingeringly the old man left them.

Wemyss jumped up and closed the door.

"What do you think has happened to Schlemberger?" he said.

"I don't see why anything should have done," said Fremitt. "After all the major is every bit as late."

"He may have overslept," Wemyss said. "But Schlemberger is up and about. We know that. The question is, where is he? And what is he doing in someone's house?"

"They may have marked him down as an American tourist and offered him hospitality," said Smithers. "There may be a thousand and one explanations."

Wemyss looked at him.

"You're happy about his absence?" he said.

"Perfectly."

"But that doesn't account for the major not being here," Fremitt said. "He may have been attacked."

"Or he may have run away," Kristen said. "Or anything. But I want to know what Daisy has found out."

"I'm sorry," Fremitt said. "I too am anxious to hear, naturally. But for some reason I find myself unquiet—I think it's not too strong a word—about Major Mortenson. After all he has an alibi. That is, of course, if we assume that whoever attacked Peter killed Hamyadis, and I really think we can. So may I make one small inquiry?"

"I think we perhaps ought to," said Smithers. "The major has always been about early up to now."

Fremitt walked hurriedly across the room and rang for the waiter. There was not a long pause before he came back.

"Was there something wanted?" he asked.

"Yes," said Fremitt, "have you seen Major Mortenson this morning?"

"I haven't seen him myself, sir," said the waiter. "But I understand he has left his room. There was some talk about it in the kitchens."

"Left his room?" said Fremitt. "With his cases? Or what?"

"Oh, no sir, not with any cases. I meant simply that one of the housemaids was able to get an early start on the room. Is the major expected to be leaving then?"

Avid curiosity.

"No," said Smithers. "Major Mortenson isn't expected to go. It was simply that your turn of phrase misled Mr Fremitt."

"I understand, sir. I'm sorry, sir."

Two short bows. Bland disbelief.

"That will be all," Smithers said.

The old man hobbled out.

"Well," Kristen said, "are you going to raise the hue and cry and make fools of yourselves, or are we going to hear what Daisy has to tell us?"

"I don't think we need do more about the major than to wait for perhaps two minutes," Smithers said.

"Why not?" Fremitt said. "He may have left. Shouldn't we at least let Inspector Parker know?"

"There will be no need," said Smithers. "I caught a glimpse of Major Mortenson through the window just as Miss Kett was speaking. I think he will be joining us almost immediately."

The door opened and the major came in.

"Morning all," he said. "Just been down seeing that the horses were in good order. Wonderful morning."

"You're not the only one to think that," Wemyss said.

Quickly. In first.

"Schlemberger apparently is in full agreement with you," he went on. "He's out somewhere. Just telephoned to say he wouldn't be in to breakfast."

"He did, did he?" said the major.

He glanced at Daisy.

"No," she said. "I've already let half the cat out of the bag, if that's a thing you can do. I've told everybody I didn't mean Mr Schlemberger."

"Or me?" said the major.

He laughed.

"Had you broken my perfect alibi, eh?"

"No," Daisy said. "I put the two of you together."

"Glad to hear it," the major said. "You know me. Sancta simplicitas. But what did the inspector make of your revelations last night? Are you being made Chief Constable tomorrow, or what?"

"Well, I was telling the others," Daisy said.

Kristen sighed.

"I was saying that I'm a bit afraid I didn't tell the inspector anything he hadn't worked out for himself, but there was one odd thing. You know, if he already knew what I was going to tell him there was no reason why he shouldn't be quite happy. After all that silly game with his autogyro had been successful yesterday. But he wasn't happy at all."

"He may not like making an arrest. He may have doubts," Smithers said.

"Dad may have told him he didn't do it," said Peter.

"That wouldn't——" Wemyss began.

And then stopped.

"I think you're quite right, Peter," Daisy said. "I think that's exactly what your father did tell him. And what's more I think the inspector did believe him."

"But why on earth?" said Major Mortenson.

"Because after I'd told him my story," Daisy said, "and it didn't take all that long, then he really started putting me through the hoop again. He might have only just begun. And if you ask me he had. He was back at the beginning again."

NINETEEN

"Back at the beginning," Fremitt said. "No, I'm afraid you're mistaken. You must have got the wrong impression. The police don't go to all that trouble to find someone one day and then think they're back at the beginning the next."

"Is that all you've got to tell us, Daisy?" said Kristen.

"It may not sound much," Daisy said. "But I'm convinced it means a lot. The inspector's making a fresh start."

"Oh, come," said Wemyss, "you put us all into a great state yesterday with your intuitions, you can't go on expecting us to believe them."

"None of them were intuitions," Daisy said. "I've not much use for those. I know what they're like. I went to the police yesterday because I'd reasoned something out and I would never have rested till it was proved one way or the other while someone was perhaps suffering unjustly. Well, I might have been wrong over that. I'm not Aristophanes, or whoever it is about logic. But I'm not wrong about what happened to me at the police station. I know what people are getting at when they talk to me. And Nosey Parker was nosing away from the beginning again."

"Nonsense," said Wemyss.

He caught Smithers's eye.

"At least," he said, "I mean I can't really believe you, though I've no doubt you mean what you say."

"And I must reluctantly say the same," Fremitt added. "I've no doubt whatsoever that Inspector Parker intends to bring Joe Dagg to trial."

"Caught you that time, captain, he never damn well did."

The door open. Standing there grinning broadly: Joe Dagg.

"Dad," said Peter.

An arrow across the floor. Broad legs hugged.

"Dad, you didn't mind, did you?"

"I'd have taken the hide off you if I'd caught you the first day," said Joe. "But as you turned out to be right and me wrong, I think it's me that should be asking you if you minded. You know what it is, don't you? I'm a bloody fool."

"Oh, no, Dad, you're not. It was only because of the 'copter that they caught you."

"You're right there, lad. I had 'em cold till then. I knew I had. Come to that, I could see that great peering flying bug coming for long enough. I nearly beat that too. I built a tunnel, did you know?"

"We saw you get away, Dad. We were watching from the big hill just outside the town."

"Were you really, lad? I wish I'd known that. I'd have put on more of a show. What I ought to have done was to go round those coppers flattening them like a row of pancakes. They were asking for it you know. When I turned round and saw them strung out like so many bits of washing on a line I could have split meself. Did you see the way I tackled the bloke that was late for parade? He won't be late again."

"Well, Joe," said Smithers, "we're glad to have you back with us again, even though you don't seem to be as repentant as you ought to be."

"Thank you very much, brigadier," said Joe. "But you're wrong you know. I told the boy: I've been a bloody fool. I'll tell anyone who wants to hear. If you want a specimen of a gormless pin-headed rapid loading nitwit, look at Joe Dagg. Go on, I'll say, take a good look, note the partics, it's a classical case."

"They have let you out, haven't they?" said Kristen. "How can we tell you haven't slipped away?"

"What do you think I am?" said Joe. "Houdini's brother? Did you see the way they bundled me about? Handcuffs, strait jacket, ball and chain, and cut off me trouser buttons. I couldn't have got out of that lot no more than I can say no to a pint of wallop."

"I think we can take his word for it, Miss Kett, don't you?" said Smithers.

"I suppose so," Kristen said. "But if he has been let out——"

"Let out. Let out," said Joe. "That's the second time you've used the words. Makes me sound like what they call a mental detective."

He put his thumbs in his ears and wiggled his fingers in the air.

"If he has been let out," said Wemyss, "we've been let in."

"I'm going to say I told you so," Daisy said. "It may be mean natured, but when I'm right and everybody else is wrong I like to savour it to the full. Joe, I was the first to believe you were the inspector's best friend."

"Thank you for that," Joe said. "Not true, of course. You should have heard the talking-to I got. After we'd sorted ourselves out, that was. It wasn't so much what he said as the number of times he said it and the different ways of doing it that sprung naturally to his mind. Have you ever seen a chicken going around without feathers? Well if you have, that's me."

He caught hold of Peter, swung him wildly in the air and settled him neatly on one of his bull-like shoulders. A bench.

"And were you out of doors all that time?" Fremitt asked. "Do I gather that you didn't have any house where you could hide or anything?"

"That's right, major. Out of doors from dawn till closing time. Free as air. That was Joe. The great nature lover."

"And you've suffered no ill effects?"

"Never felt better in me life, except for heavy sinkings in the region of the stomach at the sight of old Nosey bearing down on me."

"Did you fret about the horses, Joe?" said Major Mortenson. "I kept an eye on them. You saw we had them out once? Inspector's idea, not mine."

"Cor, yes. I said to young Peter here at the time, it's their idea of the spider and the fly, I said. Only old Joe's a bit too fly to be caught by that sort of spider."

"Joe," said Smithers, "I'm not sure that you don't owe us an explanation as well as Inspector Parker. What made you do it in the first place?"

Joe scratched the back of his neck with a massive hand.

"Plain unvarnished stupidity," he said. "And, now Peter, me boy, what about bringing your old Dad his favourite pipe? Haven't tasted tobacco since I took to the great open spaces. You fetch me that, and run round the corner and buy me an ounce of dried hogwash, and then you'll be treated to the pleasant spectacle of your poor old Dad going green in the gills."

He heaved the boy off his shoulder, twirled him round in mid-air, set him down, and gave him some money and aimed a mock kick at his trousers as he ran out of the door.

Then quietly he closed the door and turned to face Smithers:

"That's why, of course," he said.

"I thought as much. But you know it was ridiculously unnecessary."

"Don't you start," said Joe. "I know just how unnecessary it was. Word of a police officer. But there was a bit more to it than you might think. The nipper's not mine, you know."

"Not yours?" said Smithers.

"He's a bit of a stray kitten," Joe said. "Left outside the pub one night. I found him, and I thought, 'Poor little bleeder, life in an orphanage' so I kept my mouth shut. Put out a bit of a story about my sister dying suddenly and got a woman in from the village for a bit. Not that I ever had a sister. I knew what orphanage meant. It's a rude word whatever way you spell it. But, of course, I knew all the time that I wasn't what the law calls right. I suppose really I'd pinched the boy. Still, it worked out okay for years. I did well by him. Sent him to a posh school, you know."

Simple pride. The mother hen.

"And then, right out of the blue, all this business. And all your past being gone over. I couldn't stand it. I know it was silly, but I saw them taking the boy away. And the more I heard about the cops the less I liked about them. So I said to meself, if they can't get at you they can't find nothing out about you, and off I went."

"Tell me," said Smithers, " 'the dago who ran away with your wife' was that what you might call protective colouring?"

"I don't know what you might call it, general, but I called it force of circumwhatsits. Somebody asks you something and you get a bit worried and make up some story. Then you start doing it when you don't have to. It leads you on, as the clergyman said when he followed his nose into the dressing-rooms of the Folies Bergère."

"And all this has come out now," Fremitt said.

"Come out. It's been dragged out, dragged open and dragged through. But that big great nose of his has got some uses besides poking into and prying out of. It can get in the way of seeing things it doesn't want seen all right. I've no complaints."

Peter came in with the pipe and a packet of tobacco.

"Saw Mr Schlemberger coming up the road," he said.

"Schlemberger," said Wemyss. "Was he alone? Which way was he going? Why didn't you tell somebody sooner?"

"I told you straight away," Peter said. "And anyhow if you want to know anything about him he's just come into the hall."

Wemyss leapt up knocking down his chair and ran across to the door.

"The boy's right," he called from the hall. "Schlemberger, I say, Schlemberger."

"Yeah?"

Schlemberger's distant voice.

"Er, can you spare a moment?"

"Sure, if you must. Only I've got to get my grip packed."

"Packed?"

"Yeah, that guy Parker said I could go at last. I've hired an automobile and I'm off in a few minutes."

"Oh, I see, he's let you go up for the day, has he?"

"No, he's through with me, I guess. He did a lot of apologising and Anglo-American friendship stuff and said I was in the clear."

"You mean he doesn't suspect you any longer?"

"Guess not."

Schlemberger's voice still from half-way up the stairs. In the dining-room ears strained to catch every word.

"Is he going to make an arrest, then?"

"I asked him about that, but he didn't give. Still I saw the major going in to see him just as I left, he may have made him change his mind."

In the dining-room eyes turn to the major.

"So you did——" Daisy began.

"Ssh," said Major Mortenson, "I want to hear what Schlemberger's saying."

"But the major's been here for some time," Wemyss said.

"Yeah, I've been fixing my car and everything," Schlemberger called back. "I'm off as soon as they've filled up with gas."

"Oh."

"So if you'll pardon me I've got to get all set."

"Yes, of course. Will I see you before you go?"

"Sure, sure. I was going to pop my head around the door of the dining-room and bid the folks au revoir."

"I'll be seeing you then."

"Yeah."

Wemyss came back into the room. Disconsolate.

"You heard all that I expect," he said.

"We did," said Daisy. "I was just taking the major to task for not telling us he'd been peaching to Nosey Parker."

"Merely a matter of business I had to discuss with him," the major said. "I didn't know Joe here was practically a free man and I wanted to ask the inspector to pass on a message about the horses. Felt responsible, that's all."

"And you didn't like to mention it, I suppose," Kristen said.

"To tell you the truth, I did not," the major said. "After Daisy's air of mystery and sub rosa hints I preferred not to mention the matter."

"But didn't Inspector Parker tell you he wasn't holding Joe?" said Fremitt.

"As a matter of fact in the end I simply left a message," the major said. "I was asked to wait and I hate kicking my heels in police stations and places like that. So I just told them I'd like a word with the inspector when he had a moment. That was why I didn't bother to mention my visit."

"It looks as if the inspector's got your message, colonel," said Joe. "Here he comes. Mind if I faint."

But Schlemberger came into the room instead.

A slightly shamefaced air.

"Well," he said, "I suppose you've heard the good news. You're done with Foster P. I'm here to say goodbye and good luck to you all. It's been difficult times, but I've made some very fine friendships, very fine."

"I'm only sorry you became involved with us in such an unsavoury business," Smithers said.

He crossed the room and shook hands. Schlemberger leant towards him and said quietly:

"That inspector said they wouldn't be 'taking further steps'."

"I hoped as much," Smithers said.

Schlemberger went on round the group. An earnest handshake for each person.

When he came to Joe he said:

"The inspector told me I'd find you here, Joe. I certainly am pleased it turned out this way."

"I'm glad it wasn't you that turned out to be the one," Joe said. "I don't know that I'd be pleased whoever it turned out to be. But I'm glad it wasn't you all the same."

"Guess so," said Schlemberger.

A modest glance at the ground. The curate facing the facts of life.

"Well," he added, "I think I hear my cab. Guess it's goodbye. The conference will be over pretty soon. I'll be on my way back to the States. Well, goodbye."

He smiled, looked round the room once, and went out.

Kristen and Joe crossed to the window and stood looking out.

"He's gone," said Kristen.

They heard the sound of the car's engine die away.

"Of course, the fellow was never really, as you might put it, in the running," said the major.

"You know," Kristen said, "he might be still. Give him enough rope. I wouldn't put that past the inspector."

"I can't see that there would be a great deal to gain by such a manœuvre," said Smithers. "Frankly I'm glad to see at least one person's innocence established."

"Oh yes," said Kristen. "You're right really. Good luck to him."

"Only it makes the circle that much tighter," Wemyss said.

"I'll tell you what I was thinking," Joe said, "that all that about enough rope might be more made for me than for him. Where's Nosey poked himself into now? I thought he was coming in to have a cosy little chat. Like afternoon tea with a boa constrictor."

"You didn't lose your voice in all those nights in the open then, Joe," said the inspector.

The door briskly opened.

"Speaking out of turn again," said Joe. "I think I'll have to go and be one of those monks."

Inspector Parker laughed.

"I was in charge of a petty thieving case in a monastery once," he said. "It was the gardener, as a matter of fact. But let me tell you that sort of life wouldn't suit you at all. Pretty long hours they do. And some pretty strict rules. Some very interesting things I learnt over that little job."

The nose wriggled. Satisfaction.

"I came up early," he went on, "because I wanted to catch you all before you went out. I've more questions to ask I'm afraid. I shall want to see you all in turn, with the exception of you, major, and you, Joe, of course. Mr Smithers, if you're not busy I think I might as well see you first."

"Certainly," said Smithers.

"I've laid on that little office again," Inspector Parker said as they left the room. "I don't know what work they do here, there never seems to be anyone using it."

"It certainly looked a little neglected last time I was in there," Smithers said.

"And when was that?"

The inspector was walking half a pace ahead of Smithers. He did not turn to ask the question. Smithers looked at him hard before answering.

An inscrutable neck.

"I had occasion to put something in the hotel safe the other day," Smithers said.

Inspector Parker opened the door of the little room. A constable sitting in the corner stood up.

"What was that you were hiding away?" the inspector asked.

Smithers did not reply.

"Oh, I forgot," said the inspector. "No questions outside the strict limits of the inquiry. Idle curiosity not encouraged. Never mind, I've plenty to ask within my duties. Shall we sit down?"

He motioned Smithers to the swivel chair on the far side of the table. Smithers sat down. The chair, which was padded with rubbed leather red in the highlights, black from age elsewhere, creaked ominously. Smithers

put out a hand and steadied himself against the table. He found dust cling-
ing to his fingers.

"Terribly stuffy in here," the inspector said.

He pushed at the window. It did not budge.

"Jenkins, see if you can open this damned thing," he said. "We can't
three of us sit in here without a breath of air."

The constable put down his notebook and pencil and went across to the
window. He tugged and heaved at it without success. Sweat glinted on the
back of his neck.

The inspector walked up and down a strip of carpet without talking. At
the end of each turn he glanced at Constable Jenkins.

"If the heat doesn't inconvenience you," Smithers said, "I'm quite prepared to put up with it. I've forced enough frowsty filthformers to endure
a little fresh air in my time, I deserve to feel the boot on the other foot."

"No, it's not good enough," said the inspector. "I may be stuck in this
place all morning. I'll fall asleep if nothing's done about the atmosphere.
It's a terribly hot morning."

Constable Jenkins grunted as he heaved at the hooks of the bottom
frame of the window.

"It certainly looks as if it will get sultry," Smithers said.

The inspector took two more turns.

"Go and get some help, Jenkins," he said.

"I think I shifted it a little then, sir," said Jenkins.

He heaved and grunted again.

Suddenly the window shot up.

"That's a bit better," Inspector Parker said. "Don't bother about the
top. Let's get started."

The constable wiped his grimy hands on his trouser legs and returned
to his corner chair. The inspector stood with his back to the window looking down at Smithers. He held his hands in an attitude of prayer in front
of his face and flapped them apart from the wrists just catching the tip of
his nose each time the fingers came together.

"Let me put to you a question I asked almost at the beginning of this
inquiry," he said. "One which you singularly failed to answer."

"I did my best according to my lights," said Smithers.

"Hm."

The inspector looked gloomily down at Smithers. A big fly buzzed past
him into the room and circled slowly round the dusty lampshade. When
it had completed the second circuit, he said:

"Are you prepared to tell me what you have observed about some of your companions?"

"I won't answer 'No' to that," Smithers said. "I have seen a good deal more of them since we first met. There are some things I think I could say about some of them without feeling I was romancing in an important matter."

"Ah, now we're getting somewhere."

The inspector took a pace forward, grasped one of the three relegated dining chairs, swung it round and sat on it back to front.

"You know," he said, "some of the people I have to deal with in this case are tricky customers. Of course, I've dealt with tricky ones before, but these need a lot of pinning down. It's like direction finding for a plane. I was in R.A.F. Intelligence in the war, you know, had to deal with a bit of bother at a direction finding station once. I learnt a thing or two about it. You have one listening post at say Point A. It gets a signal from a plane. But it can only tell you that it's somewhere along a beam from the post to the plane. You have to get another listening post fairly far away to get the signal as well and plot its beam before you can do a spot of calculating and tell the pilot where he is."

Smithers shifted in his chair. The leather was sticking to his clothes in the heat. The bluebottle left the lampshade and began flying round the inspector's head.

"It's like that with this business," he went on, "except that there's only one listening post, my own, that I can trust completely. So I have to get as many fixes as I can to hope to know what one or two of the people I'm looking into are playing at."

"You've had plenty of reports, I should imagine," said Smithers.

"Yes, but they generally give answers pretty far removed from my own suppositions. Take Miss Miller, for instance. Here's a question about her I want answering. I've been supplied with a good deal of information on it directly and indirectly. Most of it flatly contradictory."

Smithers undid the button of his coat.

"Yes?" he said.

"It's this: how intelligent is she? Just that. But you should hear the answers I've had."

"That doesn't surprise me. Miss Miller contrives I think to be both exceptionally acute and unusually vague. It depends how things are presented to her. If it is to do with anything she apprehends through her senses you can rely on her to hit the nail on the head every time. On the other hand she doesn't manage reasoning."

"I see," said the inspector.

He sat silent as if trying out a hypothesis.

"More or less my impression," he said. "Though you put it very strikingly."

There was a low growl of thunder.

Inspector Parker got up and looked out of the window.

"It's clouded over," he said. "There isn't a breath of fresh air."

He wheeled round.

"Wemyss has quarrelled with the Kett, hasn't he?" he said.

"The Kett?"

"Miss Kett, the film girl. It's what the publicity people call her. A gimmick. I've been into her background. But I asked you a question."

"I expect most of your listening posts report the same thing. Relations have been publicly strained."

"Why?"

"I can't tell you."

"Come."

The inspector swiped at the big fly which swerved slowly and avoided the blow.

"Come, don't let's start that again. You've had several confidential talks with the Kett."

"Miss Kett told me she was interested in the history of Winchester."

"No more to say?"

"Nothing."

"I suppose you know that you're the trickiest of the lot?"

"I act on perfectly consistent principles."

"Exactly. I can deal with the human, but . . . You ought to hear what some of them have said about you."

"I'm glad I haven't."

The bluebottle buzzed towards a tattered flypaper. And swerved away.

Constable Jenkins took out a handkerchief and dabbed at his forehead.

"What was the relationship between Hamyadis, the Kett and young Wemyss?" said the inspector.

"From what I have gathered recently she was encouraging Wemyss in order to reinstate herself with Hamyadis."

"That's better. She's quite bright actually, isn't she?"

"More so than you'd think at first."

"This moaning about illness, that's an act, of course."

"There I cannot help you."

"Can't you? I'm surprised. Is the major really interested in those horses?"

"I think he goes to see that they're being looked after almost every day. I suppose he won't need to any longer. But I don't think he shares Joe Dagg's passion for them."

"Would you say of him that he is more head than heart?"

"Allowing for the over-simplification, I would."

"Juries like simplicity."

"Yes, you and I have different ends in view. I have to weigh characters before I mould them. You look for something black and white you can put before a court during a morning's hearing."

"You put me in a bad light. Would Fremitt climb out of his bedroom window dressed only in his pyjamas?"

"No."

"You've been interfering in this business, haven't you?"

"You put me in a bad light. If I have heard or seen anything relevant to your investigation, I have told you about it."

"You'd be prepared to swear to those impressions of the scents you smelt in the coach house in a court of law?"

"I would."

The fly landed on the flypaper, and flew off.

"Would you be good enough to spend the morning in the inn or nearby? I may want to see you again."

"Certainly."

"Thank you. And would you ask Miss Kett to see me?"

Smithers got up. His clothes hung from him limply. There was another long growl of thunder.

As he reached the door Inspector Parker said:

"Look, if you tell me that scent business was so much nonsense, I promise I'll do nothing about it."

Smithers turned.

"But it wasn't nonsense in the least," he said. "After all young Peter noticed it as well."

"There could be various explanations of that," the inspector said.

He was prowling up and down the room again. Quickly. The movement of his body stirred the thick air. But the heavy breeze brought no coolness.

"There's suggestibility, I suppose," Smithers said. "But it's a little far fetched."

The inspector stopped dead.

"There comes a time when perhaps you have to rely on the far fetched," he said.

He wriggled the tip of his nose. Prying.

"Besides," he added, "that isn't the only explanation I had in mind."

"I can think of nothing else," said Smithers.

"No? Sit down again a minute, would you?"

He pointed to the sticky chair Smithers had left.

Smithers took it again.

The bluebottle left the window pane where it had been silent since Smithers had begun to leave and flew round the room once more. It went so slowly that it seemed scarcely to have enough momentum to keep in flight. Its buzz was louder.

"Let me suggest something really far fetched," said the inspector.

He came and rested his hands on the edge of the table near the place where the dusty black leather had rolled back from the corner. He leant over towards Smithers.

Smithers took out his handkerchief and wiped the palms of his hands.

"If someone wanted to establish the presence of a woman in a dark room at night," the inspector said, "it wouldn't be difficult to get hold of some of her scent, to soak a handkerchief in it . . ."

Smithers stuffed his handkerchief back into his pocket.

A bead of sweat ran suddenly down the side of the inspector's immense nose and dropped on to the table.

". . . and to pull it out in the dark at the appropriate moment."

"What nonsense."

The improbable classroom lie put in its place.

The inspector went back to the window.

"Yes," he said, "nonsense after all. It must be the heat in here. Thank you very much. And you will send Miss Kett to me?"

Smithers got up.

"I will," he said.

The door knob slipped in his sweaty hand.

It turned. He went out. The inspector was standing by the window, rolling up an out-of-date newspaper and eyeing the bluebottle.

Smithers found the rest of the party sitting in the lounge. All the windows were wide open, but it was still very hot. Everybody looked listless.

"You were with him long enough, brigadier," Joe said. "I thought he'd popped you inside."

"Yes," Smithers said, "I suppose it was quite a time."

"You don't look too well," Daisy said. "Are you all right? You're awfully pale."

"Yes, I'm all right thank you. It's very airless in that little office,

I'm afraid. Miss Kett, the inspector would like a word with you there. You look coolly dressed but . . ."

"But it wouldn't do to shock old Nosey Parker by changing into a bikini," said Kristen. "I only hope he doesn't keep me too long then. I can't stand this heat."

"It looks as if it may really come to a storm soon," Fremitt said. "That will at least reduce the temperature to some extent. I really would almost welcome a good rainy spell."

Kristen looked apprehensive.

"I hate thunder," she said. "I really hate it. Oh well, I suppose I shall have to go and get this over with."

When she had gone Daisy said:

"I'm a little worried about her. This heat is really getting at her, poor kid. And I know what it's like not being able to cope with thunder. I believe it sometimes brings it on too, only I don't think she's really at that stage yet."

Nobody said anything until Fremitt asked:

"At that stage? Do I understand . . . ? But perhaps . . . ?"

"You mean you didn't know?" Daisy said. "I thought she'd almost certainly told you, even if it wasn't so obvious."

"Obvious," Wemyss said. "Are you saying she's going to have a baby?"

"But I thought everyone knew all the time," Daisy said. "You did, didn't you, Mr Smithers?"

"Yes," he said.

"And I can see you did, major. Well, I hope she isn't in that little poky office too long, not if it's as hot as you say it was."

"I suppose it was Hamyadis," said the major.

"That's what the trouble between them was," Daisy said. "You wouldn't expect him to do anything to help, would you? As soon as he saw she was going to be a nuisance he showed his nasty side, and there was plenty to show, poor old George."

"In that case——" said the major.

But he decided to keep this thought to himself.

For a long time no more was said.

And Kristen was away in the office even longer. One hour six minutes later they heard the door burst open and the sound of high heels tapping rapidly on the bare floor of the hall.

As Kristen started running upstairs the sound of sobbing was easily audible.

"I've half a mind to tell Nosey Parker what I think of him," said Daisy.

"He's a policeman: it would do no good at all," the major said.

Daisy got up and went out into the hall.

"You don't think she's going to remonstrate with the inspector, do you?" said Fremitt. "I can't help feeling it would be inadvisable."

The sound of voices came into the room. Daisy's and a deeper one which Smithers recognised as Constable Jenkins's.

"I'm sorry, ma'am," the constable was heard saying.

Daisy's words were less clear.

Then the constable said:

"The inspector's making a very important phone call. You can't go in."

Daisy came back to the lounge.

"I suppose I was silly really," she said. "I'm glad he gave a good enough excuse for me to give it up and save my face."

They sat on in silence.

Peter, who had been playing with some ants which were coming into the room through a crack in the floorboards, got up and came across to Smithers.

He stretched up and whispered:

"Please sir, any sign of a bite? I've been thinking about it."

"A nibble, Peter," said Smithers quietly. "I think I can say there's a nibble."

"Right, Jenkins."

The inspector's voice. Loud, decisive.

"Up we go."

The sound of steps on the stairs. Heavy, in time, military.

"Do you think something's happening?" asked Wemyss.

"Probably going to lunch," said the major. "These people eat extraordinarily early."

Then confused steps on the stairs again. Coming down. Not in step. Mingled with the clop of high heels.

And Kristen's voice:

"I'll have to see my lawyer."

The inspector's:

"All right, all right. We'll see to all that at the station. Now for your own sake come along without fuss."

TWENTY

Sitting in silence in the lounge they heard the distant slam of a car door.

Then the inspector's voice shouting above the noise of the engine starting up:

"Just wait one moment. There's something I want to get hold of straight away if I can."

A moment later he came into the lounge. He looked hurried, set-faced, businesslike.

"Mr Smithers," he said, "a word with you, if you please."

An order.

Smithers followed him out.

The inspector carefully shut the door of the lounge and said in a low voice:

"I've been hearing a good deal from Miss Kett. Was it the packet addressed to her that you put in the hotel safe the other day?"

Smithers looked at him for an instant.

"Yes, it was as a matter of fact," he said.

"I shall have to have it, of course," said the inspector.

He strode across to the reception desk and pressed the bell. Until the clerk came running along the corridor he kept his finger on the button.

When the girl appeared the inspector nodded briefly at Smithers.

"I want to get that packet I deposited in the safe the other day," Smithers said. "I want to give it to Inspector Parker here and he's in rather a hurry."

"Certainly, sir," said the clerk.

They went into the little office. It was still airless and very hot in the room. The girl knelt in front of the safe—bright steel heel protectors—and fitted the key in. A click. The door swung open. She took the big buff envelope from a compartment and handed it to Smithers.

Smithers slit it open and took out the packet addressed to Kristen in Hamyadis's sprawling hand.

"Can I give you a receipt for this at the station whenever you care to come down?" said the inspector.

"Certainly," Smithers said.

"You can trust me not to use them unless I have to," the inspector said. Smithers looked at him.

"I suppose I ought to have acted on that principle from the start. But I have always been sure they were not relevant."

"Perhaps they aren't," said the inspector. "I'm sorry to have to take them like this. You did very well to get hold of them."

"I'm sorry I acted as I did," Smithers said.

The inspector hesitated a moment and then said:

"Look, I must go. I can't afford a slip-up now."

He hurried from the room, ran across the hall and down the hotel steps. Smithers heard the roar of the car engine fade away.

He went back to the others.

"I know I shouldn't ask," said Daisy, "but what did he want?"

"You shouldn't ask," Smithers said.

He sat down.

"They have arrested her, haven't they?" said Wemyss.

"No," Smithers said, "I don't think there's been a formal arrest. But from the inspector's tone I don't think it will be long delayed. I have the impression they prefer, when they can, to do these things in a police station."

"Please sir," said Peter, "did you think this was going to happen?"

"I had no idea it would all be so unpleasant," Smithers said.

"That's just it," said Daisy. "I don't care whether she did it or not. It's foul."

"Will she be properly represented?" said Fremitt. "Ought one of us to do something?"

"John," Daisy said, "I can't go on any longer without knowing about this one way or the other. It turns out to be much more horrid than I'd ever thought possible. John, is she guilty?"

Fremitt: a pink of pleasure at the unexpected christian name. Then indecision.

"I don't know," he said. "I really don't know. The police must be right, I suppose."

"It isn't a good enough answer," Daisy said.

Sadness. Weariness.

"John, I shall have to ask straight out. Did you kill George?"

Round the corner and into the full force of a bucket of water. The utterly blank face.

Daisy smiled.

"You don't have to answer that one now," she said. "I suppose I've made a fool of myself again. But tell me just one thing. Didn't you know about the postman? Didn't you know that that postman is so incurably chatty that he's always late? Didn't you know that the last collection from that box is always at least a quarter of an hour after the right time, and that you hadn't got any sort of alibi for the attack on Peter?"

"But it said on the box: 7.30 p.m.," Fremitt said.

A new order of things to be slowly mastered.

"I can see now that you would never think it didn't go just then," Daisy said. "But you always seemed to dislike poor George so much. And then you had been to America, hadn't you?"

"Yes, yes, I had been to America."

Fremitt got up and began to walk out.

"You can't know how sorry I am," Daisy said.

"But you don't need to be," he said. "In the circumstances you couldn't have thought anything else. It was just that I had no idea."

He saw a chair and sat down again.

"So I suppose it really is Kristen, after all," said Joe. "Poor kid. And this is the end of it all."

"Nonsense," the major said. "It's nowhere near the end. It's unpleasant enough I grant you for the girl, but she's by no means a wilting flower. She hasn't hesitated in the past to accuse other people of murder. The boot's on the other foot now. It won't do her any harm. After all, they can't hope to secure a conviction."

"Can't they?" said Smithers. "Why should you think that?"

"They don't stand a chance," the major said.

He got up and leant against the empty fireplace.

"You've only got to think over the events of the past few days and put yourself in the place of a clever defending counsel," he said. "The girl herself would supply him with his first argument. We know that the case she made out against Daisy was trumped up, but it sounded nastily convincing. Think of what an unscrupulous Q.C. could make of it."

"How would this happen?" Daisy said. "Would there be a big court scene with me in the box? I played one once. I kept thinking then how nice it would be. Only I suppose real life would be different as usual."

"You wouldn't be the only one to be accused, though," the major said. "Look at you, Joe."

"Not in that way," Joe said. "I had enough of that to last a lifetime before I took to the fresh air cure."

"The police apparently are satisfied that you had nothing to do with the murder," the major said. "But nothing's happened to alter the facts. The case against you is as good as ever. Better, in fact. We all know the sort of man Hamyadis was. He was perfectly capable of using the information Joe gave us the other day to play cat and mouse with him."

"You don't have to pretend about that any more," Peter said. "I made Dad tell me. Mr Smithers says it's always best to face things."

"You'll face a thing or two if you don't hold your tongue, my lad," Joe said. "And if we are going to have this sort of talk I think you'd better run out and play. I'd forgotten you were here."

The boy looked crestfallen for a moment. Then he said:

"Okay, Dad."

When he had run from the room the major said:

"Well, isn't what I've told you true? Hamyadis would have been pretty unpleasant about the boy, wouldn't he?"

"Only he didn't know about him," Joe said. "Nobody did till I told old Nosey."

"No, he didn't know. But what proof of that is there?"

"Look here," said Joe. "Am I being got at? Because if I am, captain, there might be murder done yet."

"All right, all right," the major said. "I wasn't making out it was true. But that attitude wouldn't look too good in court. Still let's concentrate on someone not present and avoid unpleasantness. What about our American friend? There again, he's been officially cleared. But, you know, he behaved pretty suspiciously at times. That business of rushing up to London was never satisfactorily explained."

"Come," said Fremitt. "He must have offered some explanation to the police. He was not bound to repeat it to us."

"Perhaps you're right," Major Mortenson said. "But remember he was the only one of our party with firm links with the United States and it's pretty generally known Hamyadis behaved in a very shady way over there. Defending counsel could make quite a bit out of that."

"A bit thin," said Wemyss.

Deliberate words.

"All right," the major said turning to face him. "Let's see how you'd fare in the box, my boy. What would you answer when you were asked about your relations with the Kett girl?"

"That's got nothing to do with the case," Wemyss said.

A flush. A glint of anger in the eyes.

"Look at that," the major said. "A cross-examiner wouldn't ask for better. The very picture of someone hit in a vital spot."

"Now listen," Wemyss said. "Your thesis is interesting enough, but there's no need to go muck raking in that way. Stop it, that's all."

"I say no more. My point is proved twice over. A plain case that would appeal to a jury as something they could understand."

"Oh, come, a lot of poppycock when all's said and done."

Wemyss sat gripping his chair arm. Betrayed by the too studied tone.

"We'll go no further," the major said. "Let's hark back to absent friends. But first let me make it clear that what I am about to say is pure fantasy. But nevertheless, something that might raise doubts in a jury's mind. Let's think about young Peter."

He glanced at Joe.

"All right," Joe said. "I won't eat you this time."

"Good. Well then, consider the possibility that two guns were not fired simultaneously when Hamyadis was killed after all. You know on the face of it it is very unlikely. You'd need steady nerves and a keen eye to do it."

"I think this is a bit I'm not going to understand," Daisy said.

"It does depend on looking at the whole business vice versa," Major Mortenson said. "But all it means is this: that it might have been possible to fire a bullet belonging to an automatic out of the Durs Egg pistol. Young Peter could be the killer."

"Could I really?"

The boy's head appeared over the sill of one of the open windows. Jack-in-the-box.

"Peter," said Joe, "I thought you took it a bit calmly when I buzzed you off."

"You certainly heard no good of yourself," Smithers said. "But you don't exactly look a picture of guilt."

"I'm sorry," said the major. "I had no idea the boy was there. I'd never have suggested all that if I'd known."

"It was jolly exciting," Peter said.

"And now," said Smithers, "it's time you really did leave us. I want you to go down to the big stationers where we went the other day and ask them if the issue of *Edward Gibbon Studies* I ordered has arrived yet. It might be here and I'd like to see it as soon as possible."

Reproachful eyes.

"You wouldn't like it if you did stay," Smithers said.

He smiled.

"Okay, if you say so," said Peter.

The head bobbed down.

Joe went across to the window and leant out.

"He's gone this time," he said.

"I'm making my point plain, I hope," said the major.

"You mean that any one of us could have done the murder," Daisy said. A statement.

"Exactly, even I myself. After all I confessed to it once just to make that point. The case against me could be made out to be pretty nasty."

"And what about Mr Smithers?" Daisy said. "Or has my counting gone wrong again?"

"I'll complete the round if you like," said the major. "There is in point of fact a case of sorts to be made out against every one of us. Now just listen to the Kett girl's counsel asking Smithers here why he came on this trip at all. It was plain from the start he didn't like it. Yet he came, and he stayed. It's odd, you know. And since the murder he's taken a pretty active hand in things. It looks suspiciously like confusing the trail. Suspiciously. Add to that the fact that he's studied the history of coach travel in all its aspects. The technical knowledge required would come very easily to him. Well, Smithers?"

"I plead not guilty," Smithers said.

No one laughed. A challenge had been issued. Ambiguous but impelling.

Wemyss, who had been lounging back with studied amusement since the major had made out a case against him, sat forward. Daisy let her embroidery fall to the ground and made no move to pick it up.

"You know, major," Smithers went on, "what you have just been saying reveals a remarkable state of affairs. Here are nine people caught up in the deliberate killing of a man whom some of them hardly knew. And yet each of them seems to have been in a position to have been the killer."

"My point," said the major.

"Joe," Smithers said, "I want to ask you something."

"As long as it isn't whether I killed Hamyadis or the date of the battle of 1066 I'll do my best, brigadier."

"Joe, I know you were getting restless before you and Peter left us, but, tell me, did you get a word of warning or anything that finally sent you off?"

Joe looked puzzled.

"You know," he said, "there was. But I'm damned if I can remember it now. I know it was something I couldn't understand at the time."

"Something about being an accessory before the fact?"

"That was it, brigadier. I thought I could take it all till the major there happened to say about that. I didn't understand what it meant, of course. But as soon as I knew I was up against the law as well as the police I quit."

"Now Fremitt," said Smithers.

An incisive turn of the head.

"The theory of the transferred bullet just now, it wasn't new to either of us, was it?"

"No," Fremitt said, "I had had that idea and felt it my duty to tell you so. Or at least——"

Feeling his way.

"Yes?"

"To be strictly accurate the idea didn't occur to me spontaneously. I was led to it in conversation. I think it must have been with you, major, because we seem to have gone on to arrive at the same point."

"I don't remember it," said the major.

"Fremitt," Smithers said. "When you were telling me about the idea, you used a couple of Latin phrases. Not something you usually do, I think?"

"I suppose not," Fremitt said. "Latin tags are more in your line of country, major, if I may mention it."

Smithers turned and looked at Wemyss.

"Now, I am about to reveal, in part, a confidence, but I shall refer to nothing that will embarrass anybody."

The major tapped the iron fender noisily with the heel of his pipe.

"Ssh," Daisy said.

"One of us," Smithers said, "suggested to Schlemberger in a private talk not so long ago that he was the person who killed Hamyadis. I came to learn of this conversation. The person making this accusation used two words quite uncharacteristic of their way of speech. They said they had taken a tip 'verb sap'. I think it's not difficult to see where the tip came from."

The major took a pace into the centre of the room. He looked down at Smithers.

"You're implying that I have been responsible for the atmosphere of suspicion we have lived in," he said.

"I am saying that you persuaded one of our number to suspect Schlemberger, and that you sowed the seeds of a particularly nasty idea in Fremitt's mind. I happened to detect your hand in this because of some uncharacteristic uses of Latin tags. In the case of Schlemberger, I believe your plan succeeded better than you hoped and something was unearthed which might have meant that Hamyadis was blackmailing him. However, evidently the police have decided that he had no more than a possible motive. As for Peter, you concocted an extravagant idea which if it came to the point could have been simply enough disposed of by those ballistic experts you despise so much. I find that hard to forgive."

"The man who stood aside from all the tittle-tattle," said the major.

"I am saying that you played on Joe's fear of the police and filled him up with a lot of nonsense about being an accessory before the fact, which he clearly never was, so that he made off and drew suspicion on his own head," Smithers went on.

The indictment.

"I am saying that it was you who made the mock attack on Peter, partly to confuse the situation further, and partly to provide yourself with an alibi. Did you think no one would see that it was perfectly easy for you to have ridden one of the horses back here and cut the time for the journey by half or more? Did you think that you had only to stir up enough mud—even mud against yourself in that staged confession—and no one would ever see through it? Did you think you were clever enough to get away with murder?"

A glove at last thrown.

The major's bright blue eyes left Smithers's face for an instant.

In the room silence.

Then the major said:

"The elephant has laboured and brought forth a mouse. Well done, sir, you've concocted a fine omnium gatherum. I won't stay and listen to such rubbish."

He strode to the door.

"Major," Smithers said.

The major stopped, his hand on the door knob.

"I took certain steps to confirm this accusation."

Major Mortenson turned to face Smithers again.

"Go on," he said.

The others sat watching, at the bullring.

"You told me once that I was an interfering old maid for letting Miss Kett accuse Miss Miller of the murder," Smithers said. "You were quite right, I did that. I wanted to see what a wanton attack on someone you obviously liked would produce."

"And what did it produce? I simply told you what I thought of you. I'll repeat it if you like."

"What did you tell Inspector Parker when you saw him before breakfast this morning?" said Smithers.

"I left him a message about the horses. I didn't see him."

"And on the strength of a message about the horses he was going to omit you from his interviews today? I suggest that you did see him. And that you made your last and most serious accusation. To punish Miss Kett for her attack on Miss Miller you tried to secure her arrest by telling Inspector Parker that she was going to have a baby by Hamyadis."

"So that's the best you can do, is it?" said the major. "Then I think I can match it."

He took two paces towards Smithers.

"We're not half-way there yet," said Smithers.

"Perhaps because we're travelling in precisely the wrong direction," said the major. "I can see I've been too magnanimous in not making it plain how Hamyadis really met his death. Only one person could in point of fact have committed that murder: only the man with the technical knowledge. I've read your travel history, Smithers. You had that knowledge."

"What possible reason could I have for killing Hamyadis?"

"And what possible reason could I have? You'll have to do better than that."

"Very well," said Smithers. "You have said that I had the necessary knowledge to kill Hamyadis in that way. So I may have done. But if I did, how much more did you. You had more than the general knowledge needed, you had the particular information. You were the person who played on Hamyadis's vanity to make him leave the weapon in the coach the night before the murder. It depended on you alone that everybody learnt how to melt the lead out. You were the person who charged the Durs Egg pistol with plenty of powder so that its noise was sure to mask the silenced gun."

The tense watchers move. Glances exchanged.

"All very clever," the major said. "But you have most carefully avoided the key question. I repeat: what possible reason could I have to murder George Hamyadis?"

Smithers looked steadily at him.

"Because he was not George Hamyadis but George Brown," he said.

"Brown. You——"

The major jumped back. His hand fumbled in his jacket pocket. The hard blue eyes looking at Smithers with mounting passion. Then suddenly the hand jerked out of the pocket and a pistol was held pointing unwaveringly at Smithers's stomach.

A Durs Egg pistol.

"The second of my pair," said the major. "And make no mistake. This one is loaded to kill."

"Put it down," said Smithers. "It's over now. You've nothing to gain."

"Don't be too sure of that. I fought you all every bit of the way. I'll fight you to the end. You thought I was beaten when you found Brown's gun in the coach, didn't you? But I heard you boast to the boy where you would hide it. I turned the tables then, I'll turn them now."

"Brown?" said Daisy. "Who is Brown?"

"You've heard all about George Brown, my dear," said the major.

His eyes never left Smithers. Intense, probing.

"I had to tell the story of how he betrayed Anamapur to make sure that the man I knew as Hamyadis was Brown. He looked almost the same without the beard, but he'd grown fat—fat on his pickings. But after all the years I caught him. I thought I'd lost him for ever when I recovered after my wounds there. Especially when I found that, thanks to the official mind, he'd been welcomed as nearly the saviour of the town and then had left India for good. But a big beard and a spell in America: they weren't enough to protect him after all."

"I see," said Daisy.

The major still looked at Smithers.

"But how you got to know," he said, "is beyond me. I'll admit that. I laid the trail so well. All the talk of America. Never a word about India."

"One word about India," said Smithers. "Pani: your little trick to see if the Armenian Hamyadis knew it was Hindustani for water. You couldn't conceal how tense you were as you played it, and it stuck in my mind. Now give me that pistol."

"One step," said the major, "and I shoot."

"My dear fellow," Smithers said. "I am not going to let you go."

"Except that I hold the final argument," the major said. "One shot from this"—the pistol in his hand jerked a little—"what you might call the argumentum ad baculum."

A twisted smile.

"Now," he said, "I'm going to leave you. You will all be so good as to turn your backs."

Nobody moved.

"Daisy, please," said the major.

"Oh, well," Daisy said, "I suppose it's cowardly, but I shall be able to think of some good excuses later on."

She turned.

"Fremitt, Wemyss, Joe."

Slowly they turned round.

"Smithers."

"No," said Smithers, "give me the gun."

Glances met. Steady, questioning, hard.

"Take one single step," the major said, "and I'll blow your brains out."

"You're aiming too low, major," said Smithers.

And stepped forward with a hand out to take the gun.

The others heard the soft footfall on the worn carpet of the lounge. There was no other sound to mask it.

They half turned.

Smithers was advancing. A second step.

The major fired.

In the tense silence shattering noise.

And a whirl of movement. The major turning and leaping for the door almost the instant of the shot. Smithers falling. The door flung back in the major's face. Inspector Parker. A grapple. A heavy chair sent flying. Smithers groaning. Daisy running towards him.

And as suddenly as the noise, silence again.

The major limp underneath the kneeling inspector. Smithers still and white. Daisy without a word tearing at his clothes feeling for the heart. The others dumb.

Then Inspector Parker, Nosey Parker, spoke.

"I'd give a great deal to know just exactly what's been going on," he said.

"He's breathing," said Daisy.

"Of course he is," Nosey Parker said. "Didn't you see the wound in his thigh?"

Smithers opened his eyes.

"Hallo, inspector," he said. "You came very opportunely."

"I'd just heard from the forensic people," the inspector said. "Horse dung on the pillow used for that bit of trickery over Peter. It came from the farm where the coach horses were kept."

"So science did the trick in the end," said Smithers.

"Perhaps," Nosey Parker said. "But I thought our troubles were far from over. Thank you for taking a hand."

"Never again," said Smithers. "I prefer not to have to deal with anything more dangerous than a catapult."

He fainted.